# Idi & the Sirocco Witch
Book three of the 'Born to Be' series

Book one 'Idi & the ~~~~~~~~~ t'
Boo ~~~~~~~~~~~~~~~~~~~~~~~ ia'

This book ~~~~~~~~~~~ to my Father in Heaven;
Whose love sustains me.

**Contact Tracy**: www.facebook.com/tracytraynor
borntobetracytraynor.wordpress.com
www.tntraynor.co.uk

"Idi & the Sirocco Witch" Copyright © 2017 Tracy Traynor
– All rights reserved

*To Julie
One of my biggest fans :)
a supportive friend.
Really hope you enjoy the end of Idi's story. love T Traynor xx
First signed copy!
02-11-2017 xx*

## The World of Talia

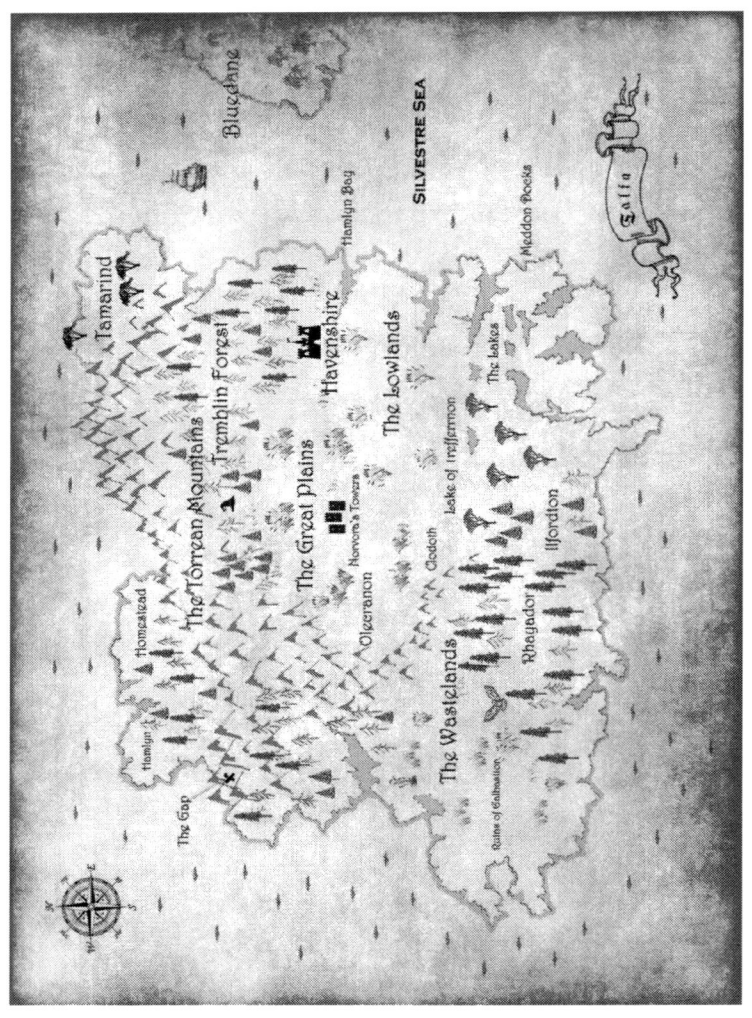

## List of Chapters

1. The Sirocco Witch
2. No Show
3. Power Potions
4. Choices
5. New Friends
6. The Hunter
7. Bluedane Shores
8. The Binding Spell
9. Rodanti
10. Hide-and-Seek
11. Oops-a-Daisy
12. The Way In
13. Reputation
14. No Thanks
15. Nowhere to Hide
16. The Brothers
17. Crannog's Gang
18. Knowledge is Power
19. Family
20. Group Hug
21. Seven Years of Peace
22. Coming of Age
23. The Gate
24. Destroyer of Souls
25. Name Day
26. Leona
27. Homecoming
28. Stratagem
29. A Meal Shared
30. Annihilation Hill
31. A Quest Complete
32. Lost & Found

## Chapter 1 – The Sirocco Witch

Concentrating on every pain-filled limp, they stumbled with their heads bent across the splintered crevices of the dry-baked Wastelands, not noticing the gradual emerging of budding shoots that promised life. Returning across the scorpion-infested desert was out of the question as they were too exhausted. Instead, they were chancing their luck by continuing northwards, hoping against hope to find a safe, albeit long, route home.

Sebastian would raise his head, check the land in front of them, and then lower his eyes again to concentrate on avoiding the large cracks. They had twisted their ankles several times already and they were sore and swollen. He took another swift look around before returning to glowering at the red earth. He took a few more steps and then stopped and looked up again.

As Sheryl came alongside him he reached out and grabbed her arm, pulling her to a halt. She raised her chin to the right and looked at him sideways, her mouth too dry to speak. He nodded and pointed, and Sheryl turned her head slowly to see what he was looking at.

Something was flying towards them. Sheryl squinted and raised her hand to cover her eyes as she concentrated. Her lips were cracked and raw and she had to swallow to try to moisten her throat before she could speak.

"What is it?" she asked, her voice wispy and hoarse.

"I don't know," Sebastian croaked. "Whatever it is, I hope it's friendly because it's coming straight towards us." There was nothing except dry earth in every direction around them, so with nowhere to hide, they no choice but to wait. They dropped their bags and stood watching the approaching blob.

"I think it's a bird," said Sheryl.

"Yes, but what kind of bird is that big?"

The heat-haze made it hard to concentrate on the shape that came ever closer, which was obviously flying straight towards them. As it came closer, the shaky, pulsating image became more solid and, as it came into focus, they could see it was a giant lammergeyer. Its soft white breast, stark against the blackest of wingspans, was striking, but its black, mask-like markings, on its otherwise white face, clearly showed off his vulture characteristics.

Sheryl took a step closer to Sebastian as she realised it was nose-diving towards them. Sebastian pulled his sword out of his scabbard with his right hand, while wrapping his left arm around Sheryl's shoulder. At first he held the sword up as a warning, but he didn't have the strength to keep it there, and the sword did a slow nosedive until the point rested on the ground.

"There's something on its back," Sheryl mumbled. The closer the bird came to them, the clearer they could see its passenger. A woman sat on its back, her legs to one side, her ankles crossed and pressed in against the bird's body. Her left hand held on to the bird's patagium, while her right hand was raised high in the air, and to all intents and purposes seemed to be on fire. The woman wore a deep-blue dress, from which an emerald sparkled from the scooped neckline. Her hair, like her hand, was so intensely red that it looked like flames as the long curls billowed around her.

The breeze from the lammergeyer's wings was actually a much-appreciated cooling touch, but more welcoming was the fact that the giant bird came to rest on the sand a short distance away, with no evident intention of killing them.

The woman slid down the side of the bird and gracefully walked towards them, the burning light from her hand now gone. The azure-blue of her dress shimmered, like sun-kissed waves, and seemed to change shades as she moved. Sheryl and Sebastian were too shocked to speak and the stranger smiled softly at them.

"I've come to take you home," she said.

They looked at her in silence, not able to take in what she was saying. Sheryl actually thought they were looking at a mirage and wondered why on earth she hadn't conjured up a nice cool lake to swim in or a dinner table shamefully overladen with food.

"Oh! How silly of me. Here." The vision offered them a leather flagon. "Drink," she told them.

Sebastian accepted the offering, too close to death to worry it might be poisoned. He unscrewed the top, smelt inside and then tipped his head back to let the cool, refreshing water slide down his throat. He paused a moment to make sure he wasn't stricken down and then passed the flagon to Sheryl. She drank greedily and Sebastian pulled it gently off her.

"Slowly," he warned, "otherwise you'll be throwing up over me again." They stared at each other for a few seconds then turned back to the woman.

"Who are you?" asked Sheryl.

"What do you want?" asked Sebastian.

"I am Moriya, and I only want to help."

"I don't understand. How did you find us and why do you want to help?" said Sheryl, puzzled.

"I know all things, and I yearn to help in all things."

"That's really not an answer," said Sebastian, tightening his grip on his sword.

"It is all the answer I am going to give." Silence followed for a moment as they regarded one another.

"And how do you plan to help us?" asked Sheryl eventually.

"By asking Lammi to fly you home." They both looked at the giant lammergeyer dubiously. "He's strong and he'll carry you back to Havenshire swiftly." Both Sebastian and Sheryl snapped their attention back to Moriya.

"How do you know where we live?" Sebastian quizzed. Moriya tilted her head and looked at Sebastian with a 'really?' expression on her face.

"How do you know?" Sheryl repeated softly.

"Life is always about choices. Do you want to accept my offer of help or do you want to continue wandering aimlessly in the desert?"

Sebastian and Sheryl threw each other a quick, questioning look and then Sebastian turned back to the redhead.

"We accept your offer," he said, and Moriya smiled.

"Good. Then go quickly, for the people of Havenshire are dying in their hundreds and you need to take the Soc to Idi as quickly as possible."

"Why are they dying?" asked Sheryl.

"And what is a Soc?" asked Sebastian.

"Saussurea Obrallata Clandestine, the flower in Sheryl's pocket. The battle with the demons might be over, yet their poisonous bites and scratches are still killing people. You don't have time to delay. Come, you must be gone before it is too late."

"Too late for what?" asked Sheryl, as they moved towards the gigantic bird.

"Now try not to be afraid, and hold on here," said Moriya, pointing to a fold in the bird's neck.

Sebastian got on first and offered his hand to help pull Sheryl up behind him. She snuggled into his back and wrapped her arms tight around his waist.

"How will you get home without the lammergeyer?" Sheryl asked.

"I have my own ways of travelling. I don't need Lammi. I brought him along for the pair of you."

"Oh," Sheryl answered softly. She was too tired, and secretly far too grateful to be leaving the desert and the scorpions behind, to really analyse this strange situation and woman too much. The bird spread its huge black wings and rocked back and forth a moment before suddenly springing into the air.

"Thank you," Sebastian called out, as they were lifted high into the sky. *I think*, he thought to himself as the bird dipped to the left and swung around to head south.

"Go with blessings," the Sirocco witch said.

## Chapter 2 – No Show

Twitching his head nervously, Norvora's huge horse drifted a few steps to the left. The wizard pulled the reins slightly and the stallion stood still. Irritation was sweeping through Norvora's painfully thin body, and the twitch in his neck revealed his anger.

Where *is* that rotten witch and her brood?" he asked, to no one in particular. His soldiers, trained beyond thinking, remained statue-still, waiting for his instructions. Norvora's bony, claw-like fingers began tapping against the reins as he scowled at the mist-soaked lands in front of him. They had nearly won the previous night – would have won, in fact, if those pesky Brothers hadn't turned up with the fairies. Tonight, though, would see the end of Havenshire and all who lived there.

Norvora was flanked on both sides by his own Asidion army, and beyond these mindless submissives, four hundred and ten platoons of goblins mustered, waiting for the chance to inflict their overdue revenge on their enemy. He wanted Shona by his side for, although she was loathsome, she was more trustworthy than the goblins. Then, when the demons arrived, it would be chaos, destruction and victory!

The minutes slipped by with the weight of hours and his anger boiled inside like a furnace. *Where was that witch? Where were the demons?* The Grey-moon was long gone and the

Silver-moon of night was shining bright, so the demons should have been here by now. To make things worse, the Three-witches in his head had gone silent and offered no advice.

There was movement to his left and he turned his head slightly to see Bevan approaching. He didn't dismount, instead making the stout goblin crane his neck backwards to address him.

"We won't succeed without the demons," said Bevan. "I am taking my men away." He looked at the black holes that were Norvora's eyes, and the snake-like scales that seemed to fade in and out on his cheeks, and gritted his teeth to stop himself shivering. "I would rather live to fight another day than be slaughtered here tonight," he added.

Norvora's silence wasn't intended to be threatening, but Bevan suddenly felt the urge to plead his point. "My men are superstitious, and without the presence of the witches here for a second night, they believe we will lose this battle with the humans, especially without the force of the demons. Not that they wouldn't charge, of course, if I ordered." Bevan felt fear for the first time in his life as he watched Norvora's face take on the appearance of a snake, and it took all his willpower not to take a step backwards.

Norvora's body started stretching upwards, swaying and slivering, slowly transforming into something vile. His men didn't move a muscle as their leader hissed and spat out a long-forked tongue. From his height, Norvora could see for miles in all directions. There were no signs of either witches or demons; he slowly slunk back into his human form.

"Go," he spat at Bevan. "I will call for you when you are needed."

Bevan bowed deeply to the 'Protector of the First-Witches'. "We will camp underground. I will have someone watch your towers; if you raise the flag of the snake I will come straight to you."

Norvora nodded his acceptance of the goblin's statement, and then Bevan returned to his army to usher them to safety before the humans decided to attack. Within minutes, the goblin army had faded into the evening mist.

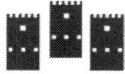

Norvora waited just a moment longer and then turned his horse around to head back to his towers. Once his army were returned home he would go and seek out that conniving witch and find out why she hadn't answered his summons. He would take the orb containing the witches with him; maybe they would teach Shona some respect.

\*\*\*\*\*\*\*\*\*\*

Idi and Marcus stood together on the primary turret and watched, amazed, as the armies surrounding the castle began to leave.

"What do you think has happened?" Idi asked.

"I don't know, son, but whatever it is, I am grateful beyond belief. We would not have survived this night if they had attacked again."

"Aye, that's the truth," said Myles, who, with hands on the wall, was peering into the ever-darkening land around them. "Shall I tell everyone to stand down, do you think?" Myles asked, turning around to look at Marcus.

"Yes, I think so. The demons haven't turned up this evening. We can only praise the Elements about that, for who knows what happened to them. I think we have a reprieve for a short time. Let's rest up while we can."

Myles nodded at Marcus, who had confirmed his own thoughts, then went to start the chain of commands needed to organise everyone.

Marcus looked at Idi. "You look exhausted. Go and get some sleep while you can."

"I can't, I need to attend to the sick. I'm not positive, but I think anyone who was either bitten or scratched by a demon is dying. I have tried to heal people but all I seem to be able to do is ease their pain. I'm afraid, Marcus, that many will die this night even without a battle."

"If you don't get some sleep you won't be able to heal anyone. Go. Find Katrina, and then take some rest. I'll go and sit with the king until you wake."

"I can't rest while people are dying," said Idi.

Marcus reached out and put his hand on Idi's shoulder. "You must Idi. You need to replenish your magic when you can. Who knows what the morning will bring?" He sent a sleeping spell from his palm into Idi. Idi looked at him, slightly cross, but before he could say anything, he was crumbling.

"Here. Help me!" Marcus cried out to some nearby soldiers. With their help, Marcus had Idi carried to his room. After the soldiers had gone and Idi was lying on the bed, Marcus placed his hand on Idi's forehead and sent the very last remnants of his magic flowing into the lad's exhausted body. He wobbled slightly as the magic left him, feeling weaker than he had ever felt in his life before. His magic, which had carried him to the age of seventy-seven with almost as much energy as a twenty-year-old, was now fading. For the first time in his life, he felt like an old man and his body was a mass of aches and pains. *You've done me well, my old friend, magic, but don't desert me yet for there is still much to do.* He didn't know what good he would be to the king except for his knowledge of healing plants, but he had promised Idi he would go. At the door he paused and took a last look at the young man who had become like a son to him.

Idi's dreams were filled with fear. He ran and ran, but those who chased him came ever closer. His heart beat wildly and his body was drenched in sweat. *I'm no good, I'm useless. I can't save them. I need to save them.* He flung his head from side to side and his arms flailed in the air. *The quest, I must complete the quest. The Oracle is relying on me. Katie. Katie, I must save Katie.* He was crying in his sleep. Tears poured from him. Something cool was placed on his forehead, nice and soothing.

"Hush."

Calm descended and replaced his nightmare. He felt someone stroking his hand and it calmly brought him out of his dreams. He opened his eyes and saw the top of Katrina's head as she bent over his hand. She must have sensed he was awake because she suddenly looked up at him, her crystal-clear, light-blue eyes full of worry. She flung her arms around his neck and buried her head in his shoulder. He reached up and slowly stroked her hair.

"It's alright, Katie, love. I'm alright, honest." Eventually she sat back up, her little, pointy chin wobbling as she fought back the tears.

"Gallagher's not alright. He's dying." She could no longer hold back the tears and started sobbing.

Idi sat up immediately. *Of course… the Black Death. How have I been able to sleep?* Then the memory of Marcus's touch on his shoulder returned. He swung his legs around and stood up. Immediately feeling woozy, he sat back down.

"Here," said Katrina. "Marcus said you should drink this to speed up the return of your strength and magic."

Idi took the glass she offered and knocked back the drink in one go. Immediately, the strength the honey-elixir gave flooded through his body like a wave of heat.

"Where is he?"

"He's in the king's chambers; apparently he promised you he wouldn't leave his side until you woke," replied Katrina.

Idi smiled softly. "Not Marcus. Gallagher."

"Oh," said Katrina, with sudden hope in her eyes. "He's in the squire's quarters. I'll show you."

She put her hand in Idi's and clasped it tight. He gave her a gentle squeeze in return, and then she was leading him through a maze of corridors until eventually she opened a door, slowly and cautiously looking inside. Idi sensed her dread that they might be too late, her friend already dead.

"Stay here," he said, kissing her on the head. For once, she didn't argue but sank back against the wall as fear for Gallagher filled her.

The smell of death rose to assault Idi's senses and he hastily put the back of his hand in front of his nose. The room was a huge dormitory with two rows of simple beds. About a third of the beds had young boys lying in them. That some were already dead was obvious as the families around them howled their grief. He looked at each bed quickly, searching for the young lad who had practised sword fighting with Katrina. He found him in the last bed by the window. A young woman was clasping his hand and rocking back and forth in her chair slightly. The lad was ashen, his cheeks hollow, his breathing short, sharp rasps that were painful to listen to. Idi closed his eyes for the briefest moment, thanking the Elements that Gallagher was still alive.

"You're the magician!" cried the woman, jumping out of her chair, hysterical hope in her voice. Everyone in the room went silent and turned to look at Idi. After the briefest of moments, they started bombarding him with requests to heal their loved ones. He backed against the wall in shock as they rushed to touch him and plead with him. Overwhelmed, Idi cried out to them to stop. They went quiet for a moment and into that silence Katrina came charging, her face angry, her lips clenched tight.

"Move back, move back," she called. At first, they were hesitant. "He can't bring anyone back from the dead. He doesn't know how to cure this illness either, but he can help with the pain if you just allow him some space." The people were crestfallen; with disappointed faces they returned to the beds. But the room was quieter now, calmer and accepting.

Idi went to Gallagher's bed and sat on the edge of it. Picking up the young lad's cold hand, he started sending healing down his arm. As Idi's hand grew hot with the healing-magic, a tiny bit of colour came back into Gallagher's cheeks and his rasping eased slightly.

"Was he bitten?" Idi asked the woman when he had finished. She moved forward and lifted her son's top. Three long scratch marks glowed bright-red across his chest. Each of them was gaping and oozing black pus.

"Get hot water and cloths and keep it as clean as you can," said Idi.

"Can you do no more?" the woman asked sorrowfully.

Idi looked at her. *I'm a failure.* He shook his head and moved to the next bed. Although he couldn't cure any of the lads, everyone in the room was grateful for the pain relief and easing of agony. Katrina helped the family members by showing them the way to the kitchens to fetch hot water. She went back and forth tirelessly, but each time she entered the room she averted her eyes from Gallagher.

When they'd done all they could, Katrina took Idi by the hand and led him away. There was a small chamber off the main kitchen where all the heads of the king's servants had their meals. It was this room to which she pulled her papa, the numb magician. She'd brought food in already and set it on the table, under the cover of a cloth to keep off the plethora of flies that had invaded the castle since the illness began. She pulled back the cloth and offered Idi bread, ham and cheese. He didn't accept it and dropped his chin to his chest.

"You have to eat," she told him firmly. She put her hands on her hips and glared at him until he gave in and picked up the food she'd prepared. It was hard to swallow as he didn't want to eat, but so as not to worry Katrina he finished what was on his plate. She brought him a big tumbler of milk and he smiled. *Honey-mead would go down better.* Katrina pulled her chair as close to him as she could and he put his arm around her.

"Papa?"

"Yes."

"Is the burden of prophecy heavy?"

"What? That's a deep question. Why do you ask?"

"I just want you to know, if it is too heavy for you, I will help you carry it."

*Oh, my little love, you shouldn't be worrying about your papa at your age.* Idi took a slow, deep breath and let Katrina's love wash through his downtrodden spirit.

"And what might you know of prophecy?"

"I know that a child has been born who will rise up to unite all the people of Talia, and that he was born to be our king. I know he's lost somewhere, without his mother and friends. And I know you've been given the task of saving him, and therefore saving us all."

"You seem to *know* an awful lot."

"I might not have magic but I do have good ears."

"Do you now?" Idi said, ruffling her ears under her hair.

"You think you'll never complete your quest and it hurts your heart."

Idi dropped his head and laid his cheek on the top of Katrina's head. He didn't answer; he was too choked up.

"Both Marcus and I know you will complete your quest, Papa. We believe in you."

"So, if the demons and Norvora come back again tomorrow and finish this war by slaying us all, will I still be able to complete it?"

Katrina knocked Idi off her head and stood up. Looking at him crossly, her hands once more on her hips, she huffed.

"I thought you were dead and the Pica Pica brought you back to me. I know now, that nothing may be as it seems or feels. We don't know why the demons didn't come in the night. Maybe they're dead."

"That would be a blessing."

"Yes, it would. So each morning there is new hope, is there not?"

Idi looked at her and nodded slowly.

"We will fight until we win and we will search for Absalom until he's found."

*You're my precious girl*, Idi thought with pride. "Well, stop trying to stuff me up then," he said. "Let's get going. I think it's time to release Marcus from his promise."

Katrina grinned. "I love you, Papa."

"I love you too, my little philosopher." Katrina wasn't too sure what that meant, but it sounded good, so she took it as a compliment. The two of them went striding back down the corridors, side by side, and headed towards the king's chambers.

## Chapter 3 – Powerful Potions

The lammergeyer flew seamlessly, rising and dipping on the air currents, as it carried them across the lands of Talia. The great cities of Rhayador and Ilfordton seemed like tiny scars on the vast and beautiful stretch of land that led to Havenshire. Sheryl clung to Sebastian's back and marvelled at the speed at which they travelled. The wind was too strong for them to hear each other and so Sebastian simply pointed as they passed the Lowlands of the Earth-clan domain. *We're nearly home, Amber*, thought Sheryl, so happy at the thought of returning home to the clan. *Will they be able to heal me?*

The huge bird landed gracefully in a field a short distance away from the castle walls. They slid down the his side and wobbled a bit as they got their land-legs back.

"Thank you, Lammi," said Sheryl. The bird cawed coarsely, then took a few quick steps and sprung into the air once more. They watched him for a moment and then looked at each other.

"Are you alright?" Sebastian asked.

Sheryl knew he wasn't referring to exhaustion or dehydration, but to the fact that she was technically no longer a witch.

"Yes and no. I hope Amber will be able to help me, but first we need to find Idi and give him the flower."

Sebastian offered her his hand and they jogged, as quickly as they could, across the fields to the drawbridge. Sebastian scanned the castle walls and the surrounding fields and felt dread build inside him as he absorbed the wreckage of battle. Sheryl stumbled when she realised that a wooden cart, standing ominously on its own, was piled high with dead bodies. She gagged as the stench of death engulfed her and Sebastian grabbed her and pulled her into his chest.

"Don't look," he said, steering them across the littered pathway to the drawbridge, holding her head against his chest. The guards had seen them approaching and six foot soldiers and two knights came across the bridge, swords in hand to meet them.

"Stop, strangers, and declare your intent," demanded one of the knights. Sebastian looked at them in surprise.

"It's me, Torra," said Sebastian. The knights looked at him, puzzled. "It's *me*, Sebastian." The knights continued to look at him for a moment and then slowly recognition dawned.

"Sebastian?" cried Torra. "Well, bless us all, we thought you were dead."

"Sorry to disappoint, but I'm still living," Sebastian said, smiling.

"Well, you've thinned out a bit, my boy," said Martin, laughing. "Wait till the others hear you've returned. Cheer them up no end and, Elements bless us, we could certainly do with some good cheer right now."

"We need to find Idi," said Sheryl, disengaging herself from Sebastian's arm.

"He's back at the castle," said Torra. "Come, we'll all go." They practically ran through the cobbled streets until Sheryl stumbled again.

"Here," said Torra, and in one elegant movement lifted Sheryl and carried her in his arms. She had no strength to argue and simply lay her head against the knight's golden breastplate. They ran in silence through the debris of the bombarded city, weaving among the people who were clearing up the streets and removing the dead. Sebastian wanted to ask so many questions but it was taking all his strength to keep up. Eventually they arrived at the inner castle walls and Sebastian was relieved to find it still stood intact. They went straight to the kitchens where Torra put Sheryl down in a chair by the open fire and fetched her a cup of warm cinnamon tea, from the pot that was never empty on the huge wooden table.

"Stay here and rest a moment," he said. "We'll go and find Idi for you." Sebastian nodded. He was out of energy and collapsed on the floor, leaning back against Sheryl's chair. In what seemed like no time at all, a commotion was heard in the corridor, followed by a group of people filing into the kitchen.

"You wanted to see me?" asked Idi, while Marcus, Katrina and several knights gathered around the fireplace.

Sheryl put down her cup and reached inside her pocket. "We were told you would be able to use this to heal people," she said, passing a velvet bag to Idi. He accepted the bag, looking puzzled.

"What is it?"

"It's a Saussurea Obrallata Clandestine," answered Sheryl.

"What?" asked several people at the same time.

"It's a flower with very magical powers," said a voice from the doorway.

"Amber," said Sheryl, and tears of relief fell down her cheeks. Amber came across the room, taking off her gloves and cape and dropping them on a chair.

"May I?" she asked, holding out her hand for the bag. Idi didn't hesitate and passed it to her. Very gently, she pulled on the bag strings and opened it up. She carefully folded the velvet backwards, making sure she didn't touch the flower itself. A beautiful aroma instantly filled the kitchen and several people whispered 'Ooh' when they saw the vibrant colours of the flower. Amber handed it back to Idi.

"Do you know what it's for?" Marcus asked.

"You need to put it in a vat of honey and send your magic to merge with the ancient magic within the flower. If it accepts you, it will flood the honey with healing power. The old books of Shyne say that, apart from death, there's no limit to its healing powers."

"Maybe you should have it," said Idi, offering the flower to Amber.

She shook her head. "Oleanna was very clear – you're to have it."

Idi turned to look at the head cook. "How much honey do you have?" he asked.

She hurried to the larder and came back carrying a large earthenware tub. "I'm afraid it's nearly empty," she said, passing it to Marcus.

Marcus placed it on the table and peered inside. "It's not enough," he said flatly.

"Where can we get more?" Idi asked the cook, who shrugged her shoulders.

"Things have been mighty hard for all of us for a long time now, and I've not been able to buy honey for ages."

"We have some back at the farmhouse," said Amber, but not enough to fill the pot, I don't think. I'll go back for it now. Sheryl, are you coming with me?" Sheryl looked up at Amber, her face reflecting her pain. "You wish to stay here?" Amber asked in surprise.

Sheryl shook her head a little bit. "I've lost my magic, Amber. I can't fly any more."

Sebastian put his hand on Sheryl's shoulder to offer her comfort. Amber looked at them both for a moment then nodded.

"Right, I'll go now. We'll talk about everything when I return." She turned to look at Marcus. "It still won't be enough. You'll need to send out a call to everyone to bring every tiny bit of honey they have to us." With that statement, she turned and headed out of the kitchen. As soon as she passed through the door, she took to the air and was gone.

"Okay, everyone, go spread the plea as quickly as you can. Anyone who has honey needs to bring it to us immediately; explain what it's for so no one holds back."

Within moments, all the kitchen staff and knights had gone, leaving them in the quiet. Sebastian sank back down on the floor beside Sheryl's chair.

"You two need to go and find somewhere to rest," said Marcus. "Katie, take them to rooms near ours, will you?"

"Yes, of course," said Katie. "Follow me," she said, looking at Sheryl and Sebastian. They were too exhausted to argue and got slowly to their feet.

"You'll come and get me if you need me?" said Sebastian.

"We will," answered Marcus.

Alone in the kitchen, Marcus and Idi sat at the huge wooden table and looked at each other.

"Do you think it'll work?" asked Idi.

"I think if Oleanna sent them to find it, then the flower must be powerful indeed, so yes, I think it'll work," replied Marcus.

Idi slowly opened the velvet bag on the table. The beautiful aroma instantly rose to greet them and they inhaled deeply.

"It's beautiful," Idi whispered. "How do you think the Oracle knew we'd need it?"

"I don't know how it all works, Idi, but I believe that, sometimes, they see glimpses of the future."

"Like me, saving the One?"

"Yes."

"We haven't even found him yet."

"No, but we will in good time."

"What if I can't do it? I couldn't prevent all those people dying in battle."

"You're not an Element, Idi. Of course you couldn't save everyone. However, you did all you could, and that is what's important. None of us can do more than that." Marcus paused and reached across the table to put his hand over Idi's. "The Elements look to our hearts, Idi, not to our actions. They search our intentions and motivations, for these things reveal our true soul. A man can do many good things to appear righteous, but if he does them to boost his own appearance, then, as far as the Elements are concerned, he might as well not have bothered."

"Katrina has such faith in me, Marcus."

"I know, as do I, son. One day you will believe in yourself as well." There was a swooshing sound outside the door and then Amber came striding into the kitchen, closely followed by three other Earth-clan witches.

"That was quick," said Idi, looking up in surprise.

Amber came and placed a large jar of honey on the table. "This is all we have left, unfortunately. I've sent someone to the Water-clan, so hopefully they'll arrive with some more shortly." She took off her gloves and cape and dropped them on a chair near the fire, and then came to join them at the table.

"Do you know how I reach the flower?" Idi asked.

"I'll show you. Lean forward."

Idi leant across the table and Amber reached up and placed her hands around his face.

"Let me in," she whispered.

Idi instantly relaxed and closed his eyes, and suddenly Amber was inside his head. She threw colour spectrums around in his mind, building a web of spells. At one point it was so vibrant he couldn't look at it, as she created a whirlwind and spun the colours into a cone, and then it was gone. She withdrew from his mind.

"Once you have the cone, you offer it to the flower. If the flower accepts it, she will dissolve and flood the honey with magic."

"How do you know how to do that?" Idi asked.

"I've studied the ancient books for most of my life. I always longed to find a Soc but never knew where to look. You are blessed, Idi, for Oleanna to believe in you so much."

Idi felt humbled as he stared at the flower.

"Right, let's pour our honey into your pot," said Amber, nodding at Lowen. Lowen untied the string, lifted off the checked cloth and carefully poured the honey into the large pot. Before she had finished, two of the kitchen maids came rushing in carrying small containers.

"We've found some!" said Rose, excited. "Also, lots of people from town are making their way up the hill, so we think more is on the way."

They were right. As soon as they had scraped the small amount of honey out of Rose's jar, people started arriving in the kitchen with their tiny offerings. One by one, the villagers, farmers, builders, gatekeepers, and even lords and ladies came offering their tiny vessels of honey. Each one held only a small amount, but as they emptied them into the large container, it began to fill. Hope filled the atmosphere with each added portion. Instead of returning home, the people stayed in the courtyard of the castle, standing huddled in small groups, their eyes anxious and waiting for the magic that might heal their loved ones.

Idi felt their hope and expectation but it didn't make him nervous, as the people had previously done in the sickroom. He knew this wasn't about him; it was about the magic of the flower and Oleanna's belief that he could reach it. With the last drop of honey not quite filling the pot, Idi sent a silent prayer that what they had would be enough. He carefully picked up the flower and placed it on top of the honey. The flower instantly curled up into a tight ball. Idi looked at Amber anxiously, fearing it was dying.

"Carry on," she told him softly.

Idi closed his eyes and began pulling on his magic. He created the magic web Amber had shown him, spun it into a cone, then put his hand very gently on the flower and offered it his magic. At first, the flower didn't respond and Idi had a flicker of fear he was failing. Then he felt the flower move under his fingers and opened his eyes to look. The flower slowly uncurled itself and started trembling. As it moved, gold dust began to pour from its anthers, dropping into the honey. Then, suddenly, the flower disintegrated and sank. Idi looked at Amber questioningly.

"How do we know it's ready?" he asked.

"It's ready now," she said, smiling back at him.

"Should we pour it into individual pots, so people can take it back home?" Marcus asked.

"No," said Amber. "It must stay in the pot or it will lose its power, and only Idi may ladle it out. Sorry, Idi, this does mean you have a lot of people to attend to."

"That's fine," Idi answered. "We need to see the king first."

"I will carry the container for you, Idi," said Myles, stepping forward. Idi nodded. A small troop of people followed Myles along the castle corridors that led to the king's private chambers.

Two knights stood to attention outside the king's room; one of them tapped gently on the door and then opened it to allow Myles and the others to enter.

Cassandra, who had been holding her father's hand, jumped up when she saw them. "You have something?" she asked with sudden hope.

"We do," answered Idi. He came up to the side of the bed with Myles beside him. He dipped a tiny silver spoon into the honey and took out a minute amount, then carefully brought the spoon to Hamish's lips. The king's breathing was laboured and sounded painful, his cheeks were hollow and white, and to all those present he looked like he was at death's dark door. Idi tipped the honey slowly between the king's lips.

"Try to swallow it, your grace," he said. Everyone crowded round the bed, waiting for the miracle cure to make the king open his eyes and declare he was as good as new. Nothing happened. Idi stood poised with the spoon still in the air and looked at Amber, worried. She shook her head slightly.

"The books didn't say how quickly it worked, or how much honey to give someone. I suggest we wait a short while and, if nothing happens, give him a bit more."

Idi turned around to look into the pot. *Oh, Elements, there isn't much in there, not enough for everyone as it is. Please make one teaspoon be enough.* The ticking of a huge clock on the mantel over the fire sounded as loud as a huge bass drum, as they stood staring at their king.

Cassandra picked up Hamish's hand and brought it to her cheeks. "Please wake up, Father. I've only just got you back in my life, please come back to me." As she finished speaking, the king's eyes flickered slightly and Cassandra sucked in her breath. "It's working. Give him some more, quick." Idi turned to get a bit more honey but Marcus put his hand over the pot.

"Wait a moment longer, lad," he said. Idi turned back to the king and put his hand on his forehead. He sent waves of healing from his heart, down his arm and into the king. Suddenly the king coughed and his eyes flew open, full of fear.

"Don't let me die!" he yelled, before coughing violently.

"We won't, Father, we won't. Idi, please, give him some more honey."

But Idi had seen the black slime in the king's mouth and suddenly knew what to do. Filled with confidence, his power increased dramatically and he sent it flowing through his body once more into the king. The king's body was racked with coughing and two knights helped Cassandra sit him up. Suddenly, on one loud burst, the king spewed up a flood of black gunge. With the liquid out of his lungs, the coughing eased and they laid him back against the pillows. Slowly, a pale rose colour flooded his cheeks and the death-grey tinge of his lips disappeared. Hamish opened his eyes and Cassandra threw herself onto him, crying in relief. The king raised a hand to hold her head while his eyes sought Idi's attention.

"They were dragging me down to the pits of the Depths. I fought them as much as I could, but if you hadn't reached me when you did, they would have had my soul. I am indebted to you once again, magician."

"It wasn't me who found the flower; Sheryl and Sebastian need to take the credit for this."

"Teamwork did it then. I thank you all."

"We need to go," said Katrina, tugging at Idi's sleeve. Idi glanced at her, then back to Hamish.

"There are many needing us before it's too late. We had best go, your grace."

"Go," said Hamish, waving his hand at them. "I will talk with you later." Most of the people in the room bowed their heads, then hurried back into the corridor after Idi.

"Where first?" asked Myles, who was still holding the pot.

"The squire's room," declared Katrina. "Quickly, Papa." Idi nodded and the group hurried down the passageways after Katrina. The news of a possible miracle cure had reached there already and most of the relatives were standing anxiously in the hallway as the group rounded the corner.

There was a rush at Idi, everyone pleading for help, begging him to see to their relative first.

Amber stomped her foot heavily on the floor. "Order," she yelled. "The magician can only do one at a time. We'll start at one end of the room and work through."

The people reluctantly returned to the beds of their loved ones. Idi followed Katrina to Gallagher's bed. He looked dead. He wasn't moving and his mother had her head on the bed, sobbing with grief.

"Papa, please," said Katrina fretfully, grabbing Idi's arm. Amber put her arm around Katrina and pulled her away.

"Come along, child. He won't be able to do anything with you clinging to him," she said.

Katrina reluctantly let go of Idi and allowed Amber to comfort her. Myles held the honey up to Idi, who dipped in the spoon and took it straight to Gallagher's mouth. His lips were slightly parted and Idi poured the tiny amount of honey through them, then instantly started sending his healing to the young lad. They watched him for a while but there was no change. Marcus leant down and put his ear over Gallagher's mouth. He came up after a moment.

"He's still breathing," he said. "Carry on to the others, lad. I'll sit with Gallagher for a while longer."

"Can't you give him some more honey?" asked Katrina.

"Sorry, love. There isn't enough and we need to share it evenly between as many sick as we can," replied Idi.

Katrina pulled herself away from Amber, and knelt down by Gallagher's mum and started talking to Gallagher, encouraging him to wake up. Idi's heart contracted in pain but he had to leave them. As he moved on to the next bed, he sent up another silent prayer to the Elements that there would be enough for everyone who needed it.

The day was long and filled with mixed emotions. Most of the people he gave the honey to recovered fairly quickly, but for some it was too late. When he offered them the honey he never knew if they would recover or not, and the disappointed sorrow of the mourners filled him with sadness.

The troop stayed together the entire day. They took it in turns to carry the pot and help and support Idi as much as they could. The magic power of the flower amazed them all as the honey seemed to reduce in volume miraculously slowly. The last drop of honey was dispensed to the son of a farmer's wife, who had already lost her two eldest sons and her husband. She watched Idi without emotion as he ministered to her son, but when her son sat up and called for her, she collapsed with joy, sobbing on the floor.

As they walked out of her cottage, Marcus, who was carrying the honey pot, announced it was empty. Idi took two more steps and collapsed. There was a rush of people to help pick him up and carry him back to the castle. As the troop made their weary way back through the cobbled streets, they were met with an atmosphere of silent awe. People came out of their homes, stood in the doorways and lined the streets to pay their respects to the greatest magician Talia had ever had. Idi was unaware of what was happening, though, as he lay limp in the arms of the knights who carried him.

## Chapter 4 – Choices

Raymond was dreaming. He was aware he was sleeping, but this brought him no comfort as events and people raced towards him. At first, everything was happening at great speed, images and single words racing past him, as if flying in the wind. He stood braced against the tempest, legs and arms apart, tilting forward slightly to prevent himself from being blown over. Then, as the onslaught ran out of power and started to wane, everything began to slow.

Now he felt like he was the one flying… well, tumbling… through different pictures while everything else had come to a stop. With a jolt that made his body shake the bed he lay on, he came to an abrupt halt. He hovered over a huge island, which somewhat resembled a massive butterfly in flight. He dropped again, and moaned as his inners lurched, and then he was floating above a great city. He had never seen anything like it before. Most of the buildings had deep-red, spiral roofs. Contrasting with these rich cones were the pastel shades of the painted stone houses that sat beneath them. Raymond could see it was a wealthy city, even from this height. No beggars sat at the city entrance; no rubbish littered the dainty cobbled streets or floated in the clear harbour waters. He dropped a distance downwards and his stomach heaved as he fell.

Now he was close enough to smell the most tantalising aromas that drifted up to him from the market stalls, which neatly lined a huge square in the centre of the city. He could see people clearly now and marvelled at their strange attire and the dark tan of their skin. *Where is this place?*

As if in answer to his question, he was suddenly moving again, being thrown across the pointed rooftops towards the most impressive building he had ever seen. From the guards who patrolled the walls around the grounds, and from the size of the building, he knew this was the royal residence of whatever land it was he was imagining. He heard a boy laughing. *Absalom?* Now, he was determining where his body should fly, so he dived across the beautiful ornate gardens, and headed towards the sound. It came again, but this time the laughter was that of a boy and a girl. *Absalom, where are you?*

He wove through myriad marble statues and stopped suddenly in front of a breathtaking fountain. Three glass Oracles seemed to be flying over a large pool and pouring water from unicorn horns that cascaded down like delicate waterfalls. On the fountain steps sat Absalom, laughing with a beautiful girl. Raymond dropped his body again until he was standing in front of them.

"Absalom," Raymond said. They ignored him and carried on with their private chatter. Raymond reached out to touch Absalom and his hand went straight through him. Shocked, Raymond slowly brought his arm round in front of his face to examine it. *I'm astral flying, but how?*

"Absalom, where are we?" he shouted, knowing it didn't matter how loud he got; Absalom wouldn't be able to hear him. Absalom looked up, puzzled, and then returned his attention to his delicate friend. *Did he hear me?* Raymond cupped his hands around his mouth.

"Absalom," he boomed. "Where are we?"

Absalom jumped up and anxiously looked around.

"What is it?" the girl enquired.

"I thought I heard someone call my name," he answered.

"I didn't hear anything," the girl said.

Absalom shivered. "Sometimes Bluedane can be amazing, and other times it gives me the creeps."

Whoosh! With a sound similar to a sharp intake of breath, Raymond was sucked back through his maze of visions and came, with a none-too-pleasant plop, back into his body. He was instantly awake, yet instead of opening his eyes, he reached into the spirit realm in search of Marcus.

\*\*\*\*\*\*\*\*\*\*

Marcus raced down the corridors with the speed of a young man. So intent was he on finding Cassandra, he didn't have time to stop as he raced around a corner and crashed into Hamish.

"I beg your pardon, your grace," he said quickly, reaching out to steady the king. "Are you okay?"

"I'm fine," replied Hamish with a smile. "Where on earth are you rushing to with such haste?"

"I know where Absalom is, your grace. I need to find Cassandra. We should leave as soon as we're able."

Hamish felt the blood drain from his face. "How have you found him?" he asked flatly.

"Raymond found him. He's in Bluedane. I can't wait to tell Cassandra." Marcus bowed his head and made ready to leave.

"Wait," snapped Hamish, grabbing Marcus tightly by the arm. Marcus looked surprised. "I must talk to you first. Come with me." The king's voice brooked no argument and, although he was concerned, Marcus followed him down a passageway and into his private chambers.

"You can't tell her where Absalom is."

"You knew where he was all the time?" Marcus said, shocked.

The king went to a side table and poured wine into two glasses. He came back and handed Marcus one.

"Yes."

"But..." said Marcus, searching for the right words.

"Yes, it is a terrible thing to do," said Hamish, emptying his glass with one gulp.

"Then why did you do it?"

"To save the kingdom. Come, let us sit by the fire. I feel distinctly old, all of a sudden."

They sat in the high-backed, comfortable chairs placed on either side of the fireplace and regarded one another closely. It was three days since the great healing and most people were back to being completely healthy, the king being one of them. His cheeks were ruddy red and his skin had a healthy glow. No one would have guessed he had battled death so recently.

"She has a right to know, your grace."

"I have already lost her once, Marcus. It fills me with dread to think I might lose her again." Hamish watched Marcus as he gazed into his glass, swishing the drink around. "Are you not interested to know how I know where he is?" Hamish asked. Marcus looked up.

"I think you should tell me," he answered.

Hamish obliged, going into a lengthy account of his meeting with King Peidro. When he had finished he looked at Marcus, hopeful the magician would understand his reasons for not telling his daughter where her son was.

"Deeds may be done with good intent and purpose but that does not mean they are always acceptable. Cassandra has a right to know her son is well and cared for, if nothing else. If you don't tell her, I will."

Hamish felt a sudden panic strike at his inners; Cassandra was his joy. She had forgiven him once, but he doubted she would do it again. However, if she was going to find out, then he should be the one to tell her. "Then we'd best go and find her," he said.

They went straight away, walking swiftly through the long corridors of the castle, with two of the Hadrian knights in tow. They eventually found Cassandra in the kitchen gardens, helping with the rebuilding of the vegetable garden walls. Hamish tutted. She shouldn't be here, doing this, but since her return from Tamarind, he'd been unable to get her back to normal princess duties. She looked up and smiled when she saw them approaching.

Then Cassandra noticed the serious furrow on her father's forehead and the smile slid from her face. She put down her trowel, wiped her hands on her apron and went to find out what the bad news was.

She nodded at Marcus before looking at Hamish. "Shall we go to the rose alcove?" she asked.

Hamish nodded and they followed her as she led the way out of the vegetable patch. She went to her favourite stone bench, surrounded by satin-white roses, and sat down, preparing herself for the bad news.

Hamish knew no other way to present the information so he went straight into detail about his meeting with King Peidro and all that had happened. Different emotions flickered across her face as he told her what had happened, and Hamish had no idea how she was taking the news. When he finally finished he was extremely nervous. She remained silent for a moment, digesting the information. Breathing in deeply, she calmly folded her hands in her lap and then let the breath out slowly and nodded.

"I will leave in the morning," she finally said.

Marcus gave a slight nod. It was what he had expected, what he'd hoped she'd say.

"If you go to take him away from Peidro, he will probably kill you," said Hamish. He might even go to war with us again. We couldn't fight him, Cassandra. If you go, you may be signing the death sentence of us all."

"What will be, will be. It is not my responsibility to save all of Havenshire. I need to find my son, to bring him home and keep him safe." Cassandra observed the saddened look on her father's face, and knew he didn't intend to stop her. "Peidro has no idea what danger Absalom is in. I need to be with him."

"So be it. I'll see to your needs for the journey." Hamish paused and looked at Marcus. "You and Idi will go with her?"

"Yes. It is what the Oracle foretold we should do. We must find and protect him at all costs," replied Marcus.

"Then Elements bless and protect you all," said Hamish.

Cassandra stood up, taking her father's hand in hers and squeezing it tightly as they walked back to the castle. Once inside, they separated. Cassandra lifted her dress and ran to her rooms to pack, leaving Marcus and Hamish in the great hallway.

"I will protect her with my life," said Marcus.

"Thank you. Will you take the Brothers with you?"

"No, I am going to ask them to remain, to protect you."

The king gave a weary smile in response; if he didn't love his people as much as he did, he would be going with them.

"We will return. Everything will be okay, I'm sure of it," said Marcus.

Marcus found the Brothers in the library, all of them surrounded by half-open books as they sat crossed-legged on the floor and shared information they had just read. They looked up and greeted him as he entered and Marcus went and sat down in a comfortable chair near them.

"Is everything well?" asked Caldwin.

"I'm afraid I must leave you again," he replied.

"Where do you head now?" asked Thomas.

"Bluedane."

"What would take you there? I thought relations were strained between us," said Tanner.

"The One 'born to be king' is there. We must go and see if we can rescue him."

The Brothers all started closing and piling up their books.

"When do we leave?" asked Kailin, placing his books on a table.

"I need you all to stay here and protect the king." Marcus answered.

"Not doing that," said Caldwin. "He has his knights. No, we will be coming with you, Marcus."

"Norvora is still alive and no doubt planning his next move. The Fire-clan still side with him, and although the demons haven't come back yet, that doesn't mean they won't return. I really need you to protect the king and the people of Havenshire." Marcus looked at their set faces and knew they weren't convinced yet. "If you and the fairies hadn't turned up when you did, slicing through Norvora's back defences, we would all be dead now. This is what we were born to do, to protect others. It is a worthy and honourable thing that I request of you. Besides, I don't know how easy it will be to sneak even a few of us into Bluedane; it'll probably be impossible to disguise a whole group of us."

"I will stay," said Thomas. "Just come back to us quickly, Marcus." His love and concern for his teacher were reflected on his face.

"Me too," said Kailin.

"Aye, and me," said James.

"As you wish," said Caldwin.

"I'm going with you," said Tanner. "I know, in my bones, that I was born to be by your side. I let you leave without me once, and I won't do it again."

Marcus looked at him for a moment, trying to ascertain whether he would be able to change his mind.

"So be it," he finally answered. "You all have my thanks for being here."

They stood and formed a circle. Marcus lifted his right hand and placed it on Caldwin's left shoulder; the others did the same to the person to their left. When the circle was complete Marcus started chanting "Kreedalin, suewarin, harvicta". When he had repeated it three times, the Brothers joined in with him. Quietly, they repeated the words, over and over, and as they did a light appeared in the centre of the circle. It grew in size, almost filling the circle, and kept changing colours, and then the Brothers stopped their chant. The light merged its colours, becoming like a rainbow, and then exploded, drenching them all in its brilliance. For a moment, the Brothers wore the rainbow as it clung to them and then slowly paled.

"May the strength of love protect us," said Marcus.

"May the light always guide our way. May our hearts always be pure, and may we serve with honour," replied all the Brothers.

The young lad sent to find Idi and give him the news found the magician in his chambers. Once he'd passed on the information the lad gave a deep bow and hurried off to find Katrina.

Idi was feeling old and tired and standing was an effort. He walked slowly to the window and leant against the cold stone wall as he observed the people of Havenshire trying to restore their city. He would have liked a rest before beginning a new adventure; he yearned for a quiet period of doing normal things. He drew a deep breath and stretched, then shook his shoulders and arms, trying to shake off the sluggish feeling that was on him.

It wasn't long before Katrina burst into the room in a flurry.

"Won't take me long to get my things," she declared, reaching under the bed and pulling out her bag.

"I want you to stay here, Katie," said Idi.

She stopped what she was doing and turned to look at him. "We are a family," she declared. "Where you go, I go."

Idi looked at her stubborn chin and pondered on the best tactic to take with her. Just then, the door opened and Marcus came in.

"Ah, good," he said, "you're here. Do you know where Rubin is?"

"Right behind you," came a deep voice.

"So, you've heard the news then?" asked Marcus.

"Yes, he's in Bluedane. I'm packed and ready to go," answered Rubin.

"Me too," declared Katrina, pulling the strings closed on her bag.

"Good, then let's be going," said Marcus.

"We're taking her?" asked Idi in surprise.

"Of course," said Marcus. "Nowhere is safe these days, so she might as well be with us."

Katrina beamed. Idi bent down and picked up his bag, throwing his spare breeches in before pulling the strings tight.

"Let's get going then," he said.

The courtyard was full of people when they entered, including Gallagher, who carried a bag on his shoulder.

"You should stay here, Gallagher," said Idi. "We don't know how long we will be away."

"If you don't mind, I would very much like to accompany you," replied Gallagher.

"This is not a trip for children," said Hamish.

"Begging your pardon, your grace, but if Katrina can go, then so can I. I am a better swordsman by far."

"Oye!" said Katrina.

"Yes, but she's a dragon-slayer," said Rubin with a smile.

For some reason, Marcus felt it was right that Gallagher should go with them.

"Does your mother know?" Marcus asked.

"Yes, sir, she does," answered Gallagher. "She said I owe my life to Idi, and that it is right for me to serve him."

"You don't owe me your life," said Idi.

"Well, it seems we'll have another traveller with us then. My, but this is a big group." Marcus did a quick headcount. Idi, Katrina, Gallagher, Rubin, Cassandra, Tanner and himself. Not exactly a small number to try to sneak into another country, but so be it.

"Hello!" Everyone turned around to look at two small girls who were grinning at them.

"Hello," said Marcus with a smile.

One of the girls took hold of her dress and twisted on the spot. "We want to come with you," she said.

"I'm sorry, girls," said Marcus, "but I'm afraid we're going on a very dangerous mission. You can't come."

The girls giggled, and then, with a flick of the eye, they transformed into a human-size fairy and pixie.

"Valarie and Losia, what are you doing here?" asked Thomas.

"Heard you were going on a quest, so thought we'd tag along," said Losia, giving him a wink.

"We don't know if we'll be coming back. The Bluedanions might kill us as soon as they discover we're there," said Idi.

Losia instantly transformed into a little girl again and started crying. "I can't find my mummy," she wailed, then turned back into a pixie. "Once we know what they look and talk like, we'll change into children from Bluedane. You don't have to worry about us, we're far safer than you lot."

"We can go where you can't, Marcus. You need us," said Valarie.

Marcus nodded; he couldn't deny they would make great scouts and spies.

"Let's be gone then," he said.

After brief hugs and shoulder-pats and nods of farewell, the group of nine mounted horses and headed for the port.

Hamish had sent a guard ahead of them, to identify a trusted captain who would sail them to Bluedane, and hopefully drop them off at a small harbour where they wouldn't be noticed.

The guard introduced them to Jackson, the ship's captain, and then left to go back to Havenshire.

"I've been paid mighty 'ansome, to take you across the waters, but I'm letting you know now, if at any time my men and I are in trouble we'll be cut-and-running right quick," said Jackson.

"Of course," replied Marcus. "We wouldn't want you to go into danger. If you could drop us off on a quiet shore, that's all we'll ask of you."

Jackson looked them all up and down, assessing them, and then nodded. "Right-e-o then. The tide's high so let's not waste any time," he said, before turning round and heading up the gangplank.

"Have you been on a ship before?" Katrina asked Gallagher.

"No," he said, looking up the gangplank with a mix of awe and fear.

"Nor have I," said Tanner. "Come on, me laddo." Tanner ruffled Gallagher's hair as he walked past him and stepped onto the gangplank. Gallagher squared his shoulders and followed him, without looking down at the sea as he went.

Rubin put his hand out to help Cassandra. She didn't need it but she smiled and took his hand. She put her foot forward to step on the gangplank and found she couldn't put it down.

"What?" she said, trying her hardest to put her foot on the wooden walkway.

"What's wrong?" asked Marcus and Rubin at the same time.

"I don't know," replied Cassandra. "Every time I try and step on the gangplank, I can't put my foot down. It's like something invisible is stopping me."

The hairs went up on both Marcus and Idi's arms as they felt the magic spell at work.

"Idi, you see if you can go up," said Marcus.

Idi took a tentative step once Cassandra had moved out of the way. Nothing stopped him and he walked up with ease.

"What's wrong?" Tanner asked Idi.

"It seems some kind of magic is preventing Cassandra from coming aboard," replied Idi before going back down.

Tanner and Gallagher followed, and they stood in a group on the dockside, wondering what to do.

Valarie came up too close and blew some dust off her hand at Cassandra. Cassandra instantly sneezed.

"Oh, I see," said Valarie.

"What do you see?" said Cassandra, rubbing her eyes.

"Have you made a magic pact with someone?"

Cassandra went red; she didn't really want to tell anyone about her encounter with Shona.

"Have you?" asked Marcus.

There was nothing for it but to tell them. "I made a pact with Shona," she said.

"What?" said nearly everyone present.

"I thought she knew where Absalom was," said Cassandra defensively.

"What did you agree to?" asked Valarie softly.

"To let her teach me magic," answered Cassandra. She couldn't voice the fact that she had agreed to become a witch.

"She bound you?" asked Valarie.

"Yes."

Everyone looked at Cassandra, not knowing what to say. Valarie eventually went up and hugged her.

"I'm afraid you won't be able to come with us," she said softly.

"Why not?" asked Cassandra, tears beginning to flow and anger building inside her.

"You can only be a certain distance away from the person you are bound to. The only way you could go to Bluedane is if Shona goes with you," said Marcus.

Cassandra clenched her fists. *I'll kill that witch!*

"Do you want us to go ahead, or return with you?" asked Marcus.

Cassandra weighed things up for a moment. "Go! Protect my son if you can. I will find Shona and ask her to release me and join you as soon as I can."

"I'll stay with you," said Rubin. "You shouldn't travel back to Havenshire on your own."

Cassandra gave a quick nod of agreement, and then went to stand in front of Idi. "Please promise me you'll protect him," she said.

"With my life," replied Idi.

Cassandra searched his eyes for a moment and then hugged him. "Thank you," she said, standing back.

Uncomfortable 'goodbyes' were exchanged, and then the shrunken group of seven went aboard. Cassandra and Rubin stood on the dock until the ship had sailed out of sight.

## Chapter 5 – New Friends

The howling of the pack brought the group to a sudden halt. One after another the wolves howled into the night, sending shivers down their backs. The goblins huddled closely together and Thara clasped her hands over Timo's ears, trying to hide the sound from him, but he knocked her away. The Brothers drew their swords and, pulling on their magic, automatically moved in front of the group.

"It's okay," said Leona, "they just want to talk to me." Everyone turned to look at her.

"How do you know?" asked John.

"Because they called to me. I need to talk with them."

Just then, a huge, white wolf came from the trees into the clearing where they were. He moved with grace and confidence some distance before them and then stopped. Leona took a few steps forward but Raymond grabbed her arm to stop her.

"What you doing?" he hissed. "You don't know if it's friendly." The moment he stopped her, the pack of wolves came out of the trees and stood behind the alpha wolf. They didn't look so regal as they fidgeted on the spot and pulled back the skin over their teeth and quietly growled.

"He has no intention of hurting me," said Leona.

Raymond let go of her arm, and the wolves stopped their growling. Leona walked out to meet the great white. Everyone held their breath as she approached the wolf without fear. She stood by the wolf for a while and then bent down and wrapped her arms around his neck. When she stood up again he shook his head from side to side before turning and heading back into the forest. The pack slowly turned and followed their leader away, and Leona made her way back to the group.

"We have new friends," she declared.

"How come?" asked Damien.

"They call us the demon-killers, and have pledged to help us if we ever need them."

"How would we call them?" asked Matthew.

"I can call them inside my mind," said Leona, tapping the side of her head. "That's why they called to me, because they could hear my thoughts."

"I'm not sure I like them," said Timo.

"You don't like anything," said Obane.

"Now, you big oaf, you know that's not true. You know how much he likes snakes," said Thara.

"I hate snakes!" chirped Timo.

Obane and Thara laughed at their secret joke and Obane gave Timo a kick in the backside.

"What's that for?" yelped Timo, leaping out of the way.

"To toughen you up, dope!" laughed Obane.

"I didn't think you liked wolves either," said Timo, rubbing his behind.

Obane coughed then straightened himself up to his full height. "Well, you know, I've never really had a need to get to know them," he answered, and gave another cough.

Celestine put her sword back in the sheath on her back. "This is a good time for us to make our farewells," she declared, looking at Bert.

"Urrr, yes, of course, we should be heading off now. Very nice meeting you all," he said, nodding like mad at the humans.

"Why not come to Havenshire with us?" asked Anthony.

"Pwrrrr," growled Celestine.

"Oh no, we need to find a new life for ourselves. Once Bevan knows we helped you, well…" Bert lifted his hand and pretended to slice his throat.

"Well, you're welcome to stay with us," said Damien. "We make quite a good team, don't you think?"

"No, I don't think," declared Celestine. "What I think is that you humans have tried your hardest to wipe us from the face of Talia for hundreds of years, and I don't see that changing any time soon."

"Celestine," hissed Bert. "These people saved us in the forest."

For just a moment, a flicker of remorse shot across her face. Then: "But these are only a handful of humans, Bert. In their cities there are thousands of them. We wouldn't be safe."

"I know, and that's why we have to part ways. But these humans are our friends."

Celestine looked at Bert and knew he spoke the truth. "Be well on your journey, find shelter and food all your days," she said, nodding at them. The other goblins all muttered the same departing blessing.

"May the light always protect you," answered the Brothers.

For a moment, the sadness of the situation seemed to surround them all, then the goblins headed east across the clearing, in the opposite direction to the wolves.

"Why can't we be friends?" asked Leona.

"It's hard to explain," replied John. "Because of the past, we have inbuilt beliefs about each other that make it hard for us to see beyond that, to the personalities that now live in our old enemies. Maybe one day we will look at goblins and see them differently."

"I hope that day comes soon. They're my friends, especially Timo," answered Leona.

The Brothers headed south down the mountain slopes, hoping to find the right path that would lead them to

Havenshire. The skies had been a dark grey all day and they hadn't been walking for long when it started to snow.

"That's all we need," muttered Raymond. They carried on for a short while but the snow began to fall quicker and thicker. Huge snowflakes fell and covered everything, turning the mountain white.

Damien put his hand up and called them to a halt. "It doesn't look like it will stop soon," he said, scanning the skies. The others looked up at the darkening clouds.

"What shall we do?" asked Matthew. Just then, there was a loud, screeching hoot from the skies. They peered through the falling snow and saw a dark shadow flying above them.

"He wants us to follow him," said Leona.

The Brothers didn't question her or whether they should follow an owl. They knew now that a deeper magic than theirs was at work all around them.

Sometimes they lost sight of the owl, but then he would hoot, calling them forward, and so, slowly, they made their way down. John took a piece of thin rope and tied it around both his and Leona's wrists; the storm was worsening and he didn't want to lose her. They constantly stumbled and fell forward as they walked into rocks and bushes. John tried to keep counting heads to make sure they were staying together, but now his eyes could take the snow-battering no more, and he gave up and kept his head down, trying his hardest to prevent Leona from falling. No one had heard the owl hoot for a while and the Brothers were faltering, wondering how they would stay alive in the icy snow if they didn't find shelter soon.

Suddenly, into raging, whistling wind came the sound of the wolves howling. John felt shivers go down his back and wondered if they really were safe from the pack. He tried calling to the others. He brought his hands to his mouth and yelled, "Stop." He waited a moment for a response.

Someone else called out: "We're stopping."

Then someone bumped into John and he turned around.

"Raymond," he yelled against the horrendous noise, "we have to stop."

"We're here," yelled Raymond at the top of his lungs.

The snowfall was so thick, and the wind was whipping it around in swirls, so it was impossible to see more than an arm's length in front of them. John pulled Leona tight against his side and then reached out and grabbed Raymond's coat belt.

"Here," shouted Raymond, as loud as he could.

"Here," came a faint answer, and then Damien came into view.

"Come here," yelled John. "Come and stand on the other side of Leona."

Damien fought against the wind until he stood behind Leona, then he joined in with John and Raymond and started shouting.

A moment later, they heard Matthew and Anthony call back to them.

"Now what?" shouted Anthony.

"I think the only chance we have of staying alive is to shift the snow to the earth below us and see if we can dig a shallow. If we can all huddle together, our body warmth just might keep us alive."

Leona started crying.

"We'll be fine," said Raymond, trying to reassure her, but not really feeling fine himself. They shoved most of the snow away with their feet, but, to their dismay, the earth below them was really shallow and, once scraped back, revealed only rock.

"Should we try and find somewhere else?" shouted Anthony.

"No," John shouted back. "The storm must abate soon; hopefully it will go as quickly as it started. Let's sit with backs to each other and pull our blankets over us. When we're ready, we'll see what magic we can conjure."

They huddled into the tightest group possible, putting Leona in the middle.

John tried calling fire to his hands, but it was immediately blown out by the wind. Anthony and Damien exchanged a few whispers, their heads touching so they could hear each other, and then began chanting and waving their arms. Blue bits of lightning flew from their fingertips. *Whatever they're trying to do, it's not working,* thought John. Then the lightning seemed to form into a sphere and started rolling in the snow. Slowly, as they continued their incantation, the light-sphere began to build a wall of snow around the Brothers.

When Matthew and Raymond realised what they were doing, they raised their hands and joined in with the magic spell.

John smiled as he wrapped his arm around Leona's shoulder. "We'll be fine," he told her, although he felt like he was really reassuring himself.

Soon, a largish wall of snow surrounded them, and being sheltered from the wind made all the difference, as they could both see and hear each other now without screaming. With the snow shelter around them, the Brothers set about building a magic dome to shelter them from the snowfall. Snowflakes landed on the invisible dome and, within minutes, they were encased in a snow-covered ball that was rapidly lost under a blanket of white.

"It has to pass soon, right?" asked Raymond.

"Elements bless us, but I hope so," replied John. "I've never seen such a ferocious storm in all my days."

They remained silent after that, locked in their own thoughts and silent prayers. Despite the cold and their perilous position, they began falling asleep. John was the last one awake, praying earnestly to the Elements, asking them to intervene and cast the storm aside. Soon, even John could keep his eyes open no longer and he joined the others and fell asleep.

The wind crashed down the mountain, relentless and without mercy. It spun mini snow tornados and sent them crashing over the mountain. The snow wall the Brothers had built got bigger as snow brushed up against it. Before long, the gap over the Brothers heads began to grow small, and then, just before dawn, it disappeared completely.

At first John was disorientated. *Where am I?* Then, very slowly, the memory of sealing the demon Gap, parting ways with the goblins and, finally, the storm came back to him. He tried opening his eyes but found it really hard. He pulled his hand out of his glove and reached up to his eye; his lashes were frozen. He cupped his hand over his mouth and nose, and started blowing warm air up over his face.

A scratching sound came from somewhere close and John stopped, remembering it was that sound that had woken him up. He very gently rubbed his eyes, now thawing with the heat his body was generating. He gave Anthony, who was next to him, a gentle shove and whispered.

"Wake up."

Anthony was instantly awake. "The storm's gone," he said, noticing the quiet straight away. He pushed the hood back from his face, shook his body, and smiled at John. "We made it then."

"Aye, seems so. Can you hear that?"

"Hear what?" answered Anthony.

"Listen," said John. They listened and the scratching became very apparent in the quiet.

"What is it?" asked Anthony.

"I don't know. Time to wake the others. Tell them to be careful if they can't open their eyes. My eyelashes were frozen. In fact, wait a moment…" He gently clicked his fingers and a little flame appeared in the air. He waved his hand a little to move the flame along and then clicked his fingers again, creating another flame. He did this until there were ten little flames in the snow-cave with them. Very quickly, the air warmed up, but it did more than that; it began to eat the small amount of oxygen that was left in the snow-cave.

"Switch them off," hissed Anthony, as he created a blue light that would neither warm them nor use up their oxygen. The scratching seemed to intensify and suddenly a wolf howled.

The sound of the wolves woke the others.

"We have to get out," Leona announced and immediately fell upon the wall, pulling at it with her hands. The Brothers took only one second to take in what she was doing and then they were pulling at the snow above their heads, searching for the sky and some air. It felt like an eternity had passed, although really it was only a few minutes, when suddenly a hole appeared in the side of the wall where Leona was scraping. A wolf snout appeared and sniffed, before retreating and howling. The Brothers turned to the hole and started pulling at the snow with all their might, as the wolves pawed at it from outside. Soon, a hole big enough to crawl through had been made and the Brothers grabbed their blankets and bags and pushed and pulled each other out of the snow-cave, which had both saved their lives and almost killed them.

As they stumbled out into the crisp morning air, they found themselves surrounded by the wolves. The alpha came and sniffed at Leona, then raised its head and howled. The others joined in and the noise was deafening. When they finished they turned and, as one, ran across the snow and were gone.

"These new friends are beginning to grow on me," said Damien.

"Me too," said Matthew.

## Chapter 6 – The Hunter

A tiger stalks through the tall, golden grass of the Shimtarin plains. His deep-golden, black-lined fur glistens like gold under the Grey-moon of winter. His white whiskers twitch as his golden nose picks up the scent of his prey. He slows his breathing and sinks his body slowly down upon the dry-caked earth. Slowly, he creeps through the long grass, constantly pausing, checking he's not been detected.

The impala are twitchy. They step about nervously, their ears flicking back and forth, trying to detect where the danger will come from. The tiger stays still and watches for a long time until they begin to settle again and return to their grazing. Their beautiful tan fur makes them hard to see among the tall, dry grasses but the tiger has his eye firmly fixed on the one he knows instinctively is the weakest. Not the smallest, but something in his bandy, dipping ways reveals his victim's fault, a slightly malformed leg.

He starts inching closer, practically moving on his belly; then, when he knows he is as near as he can get unnoticed, he leaps into action. With agility and strength, he springs forward. The impalas cry out their warning to each other and take flight, racing and leaping in huge sprints across the plains and away from danger. He doesn't hesitate in his determined hunt and within moments he has the impala's neck in his mouth and uses his body weight to bring him down. Triumph!

Absalom awoke sweating, and sat up in bed. His head was spinning. There's a coppery taste in his mouth and he licks his lips. For a moment, he's disorientated, not understanding why he has hands instead of paws, and skin instead of fur. Then, the realisation that he's been dreaming again comes to him. *I'm the tiger? I was the tiger. I want it to be real. I was so strong. I was the king of the plains!* Absalom fell back against his big, fluffy pillows and closed his eyes. *Maybe if I go back to sleep I will be him once more?* The dreams had started straight after the welcoming party; they didn't come every night, but frequently. *I wish I knew his name. Maybe he's called Absalom, like me.*

As he lay there, willing himself to be the tiger again, a gentle tap came on the door, and he groaned. He picked up the pillow and placed it over his face. *Go away.*

"Your highness?" came a gentle voice.

Absalom groaned. "Go away," he said, in a muffled voice from under the pillow. "I don't want to get up yet."

"The king has asked you to join him on today's hunt. You should be dressed and in the main hall as quickly as possible," the head maid answered, pulling back the curtains.

Absalom threw the pillow and jumped onto his knees in a flash. "We're going hunting?" he asked excitedly.

"Yes, your highness. Would you prefer blue, black or green attire today?"

Absalom didn't hesitate. "Blue, please, and a short top. If I wear a dress-thingy today I won't be able to ride properly."

The maid walked into the clothes room and waved at two young servants in the doorway to hurry up. They rushed over to a table near the window and set it up with an array of breakfast food.

Absalom found he was hungry and his stomach growled as soon as he spotted the pink strips of beef on the meat platter. He ripped open a bread roll, still hot from the oven, and shoved as much of the beef as he could inside. After taking a massive bite, he started pulling off his nightshirt. The head maid was there instantly to help him. His days of arguing with the staff were long gone, and now he simply allowed her to both undress him and dress him again in his day clothes. When he was finally dressed, he took a large swig of freshly squeezed orange juice, grabbed a banana and started running down the hallway. The head maid smiled. She had been Rodanti's dresser and contentment washed through her as she realised that Absalom was finally more than happy to let her do her job.

"I'm here," announced Absalom, jumping over the last four stairs and landing in the hallway with a star jump. Piedro raised one eyebrow at him, showing he wasn't entirely impressed with his entrance. Absalom dropped his grin and walked, as straight and regal as he could, towards his grandfather. Piedro tried his hardest not to laugh, but he couldn't prevent the smile twitching at the corners of his lips.

"I hear you have been having horse-riding lessons," said Piedro, pulling on gloves.

Absalom nodded. Rubin had taught him to ride back in Tamarind, but only small ponies. The grooms and trainers of the royal stables had been teaching him to ride huge stallions.

"Do you feel confident enough to ride across the plains?" the king asked.

"Yes, sir," answered Absalom. Piedro looked at him.

"Please, stop calling me sir. Either grandfather or, if you can't bring yourself to call me that, Piedro will have to do."

"Yes, sir," said Absalom, instantly going red.

Piedro regarded him for a moment as if he were weighing him up. "Let's start," he said. There was a rush of movement, as both guests and servants went outside. As they approached the waiting horses and the servants helped the guests up onto the saddles, Absalom stood a little lost, not knowing where to go.

"This way, your highness," said a young groom, bowing low. Absalom sighed in relief and followed the lad to a moderately small horse. The groom cupped his hands and put them out for Absalom to stand on. Absalom ignored them, stuck a foot in the stirrups and jumped up on his own.

"Why haven't I got a stallion?" he whispered to the groom, bending low so no one else would hear.

"The king's orders, your highness," the lad answered. Absalom sat straight and let the reins lie loosely in his hands. *So, you don't think I'm good enough yet*, he thought, looking at his grandfather. *I'll show you.* The groom took the horse by the bit and led him over to the king's horse.

"Are you comfortable?" asked Piedro.

"Yes, thank you… grandfather." Piedro smiled.

"We will trot some distance, then once on the plains we will break into a gallop. If at any time you wish to stop, simply slow your horse and one of the grooms will accompany you back." Piedro looked at Absalom's set chin. "There is no shame in turning back. We all do it from time to time, and I, myself, returned many times before the end of the hunt when I was your age."

"I'll be fine," replied Absalom.

They set off slowly through the palace grounds and down the cobbled streets of the surrounding town. Once they exited the town, through the enormous, heavily ornate city gates, they turned right and headed towards the plains.

"What are we going to hunt?" Absalom asked.

"Tigers," replied the king.

Absalom felt a chill run through him. His heart started pounding and his hands became sweaty.

"Why tigers?" he asked quietly.

"They are kings of the wild beasts, and to us represent strength. Whoever kills one is said to absorb the animal's will and so become strong themselves."

"Have you ever killed one?" asked Absalom.

"Yes, I have killed three in my lifetime. It earns me great respect among the people."

Absalom went quiet. He didn't want to kill a tiger, and nor did he want anyone else to kill one. Just then, a horse and rider came racing across the plains towards them. Before long, a servant of the royal household pulled up next to the king, and bowed low in his saddle.

"Your grace, we have spotted several on the Shimtarin plains, towards the west. They have recently eaten and are sleeping." He bowed again and turned his horse around to join the back of the group.

Piedro waved at the weapon-bearer to come forward. Once the man was beside the king, he offered up the tall basket full of spears. Piedro inspected the tips of steel carefully and then pulled one out of the basket. The weapon-bearer then went to the other guests and offered them the basket.

"Today you will watch, another day you will be given a spear," said Piedro.

Absalom just nodded his acceptance. He would never want a spear to kill a tiger, and when he felt brave enough, he would tell his grandfather that. The king nodded towards the servant holding a bugle, who promptly lifted it to his mouth and blew a series of short-pitch blasts from it. The king was first off the mark, and went galloping across the plains towards the Shimtarin divide. The guests and servants were quick to respond, and Absalom found he needed to give his horse little encouragement before it went chasing after the stallions.

As expected, Absalom fell dramatically behind the group as his small horse couldn't keep up. He felt anger at being behind and ground his teeth as he rode. He had tried to ignore them completely but he had spotted Loreiei and her sisters among the guests assembled on the lawns to watch the hunt begin. She would think him even more of a fool now he was on this small horse and falling behind the others. His knuckles turned white as he held the reins tightly.

As the group went further away from them, Absalom's horse naturally slowed her pace. Absalom didn't push her; he was happy not to watch the tigers being hunted. He was aware that a servant rode a horse some distance behind him and figured the man's job was to watch over him.

Absalom began scanning the land around the plains. Short runs of trees and shrubs broke up the view now and again, but mostly it was just sandy grasslands as far as the eye could see.

The land undulated, and gave him the impression of waves on the sea. For some reason he felt drawn to the east and gently pulled on the reins to make his horse change direction. He could hear the servant following him. As the horse moved gracefully over the plains, Absalom closed his eyes. He felt like he was flying, and stretched out his arms, feeling the breeze whisk by.

He sniffed in deeply and caught the smell of a female. Instinctively, he squeezed his knees against the horse's thigh to make her run faster. He dropped his hands to the reins and willed the horse to race like the wind, never opening his eyes. He vaguely heard the servant call out to him but chose to ignore the warning. Her scent was getting stronger and he knew he was closing in. He tilted his head to one side, listening above the horse's hoof stomps to what lay beyond. He pulled back his lips and snarled, *why is she in my territory?*

Suddenly, his horse pulled to a stop, neighing in fright. Absalom went flying, landing harshly on the ground. He rolled for a moment, and then opened his eyes. He was okay, and got shakily to his feet. Then, in a split second, he took in the tigress standing in front of him and the servant chasing towards her with his spear in his hand.

"No!" screamed Absalom, running to stand between the tigress and the charging horse. The servant's horse reared high, its two front legs pedalling in the air; the servant held on for a moment and then slid to the ground, dropping his spear. The horse went charging off across the plains.

The tigress turned her attention to the servant still lying on the floor, and moved with intent towards him.

"No," shouted Absalom again, standing between the servant and the tigress. She shook her head and snarled at him. Absalom loosened his trousers and promptly began to pee all over the ground in front of the servant. When he'd finished he retied his trousers and glared at the tiger. He brought back his lip and snarled at her, *I'm the king of these plains*. She stopped flicking her tail across the ground and took a more humble stance.

"Go," Absalom told her. She had just turned to leave when, out of nowhere it seemed, the king and his men appeared.

"Noooo," Absalom pleaded. Too late. The spears were thrown, and three of them went into the tigress. "No!" screamed Absalom again, running towards her.

"Stay back, you fool," yelled the king, half jumping half sliding off his horse and grabbing hold of Absalom before he could reach the tigress's side. "She's not dead yet, she can still kill you." Absalom fought against Piedro, but the king wouldn't let him go.

Suddenly there was a pitiful whining and everyone turned to see a couple of servants pulling a baby tiger towards them with a rope. They brought it before the king.

Piedro looked at the red-faced Absalom. "Do you want your first kill?" he asked.

"No," spat Absalom. "Please don't kill it."

"It won't survive without its mother to protect and feed it," answered Piedro.

"Please don't kill it," said Absalom with pleading eyes. The king was puzzled.

"Would you look after it then, because it can't stay on the plains?"

"Yes," said Absalom with sudden hope. "Yes, I'll look after it. Please, please can I have it?"

"If you killed it you would have its strength," said Piedro, still puzzled.

"Your grace," said the servant who had followed Absalom.

"Speak," said Piedro.

"Your grace, his highness already has the strength of the tiger in him. He wouldn't let the tigress attack me, and she submitted to him and was backing away when you came. I have never seen anything so awesome in my life." Then, as he thought about what he had said, he hastened to add, "Except for when your grace killed the last tiger. *That* was magnificent."

The statement reminded Piedro that he had seen the tigress turning away and about to leave as they approached. If he hadn't seen it with his own eyes, he would never have believed it.

"How did you do that, Absalom?" he asked.

Suddenly, Absalom was a little afraid. How could he explain that he dreamt he was king of the plains?

"I don't really know," he answered, shrugging his shoulders.

"You must have done something?"

The servant made as if to say something, but Absalom cut him off.

"I just snarled and waved my arms at her. I think she knew I wasn't afraid of her."

Not only the king, but everyone else present, was looking at Absalom with a mixture of admiration and disbelief. Suddenly Piedro laughed.

"Well, now you have something to really impress Loreiei with. I think her opinion of you may change after this." The guests joined in with the laughing, and Absalom glared at his grandfather.

"I'm not marrying that girl," he declared. Piedro looked at him, amused.

"It seems taming a tiger has made you fierce," he said.

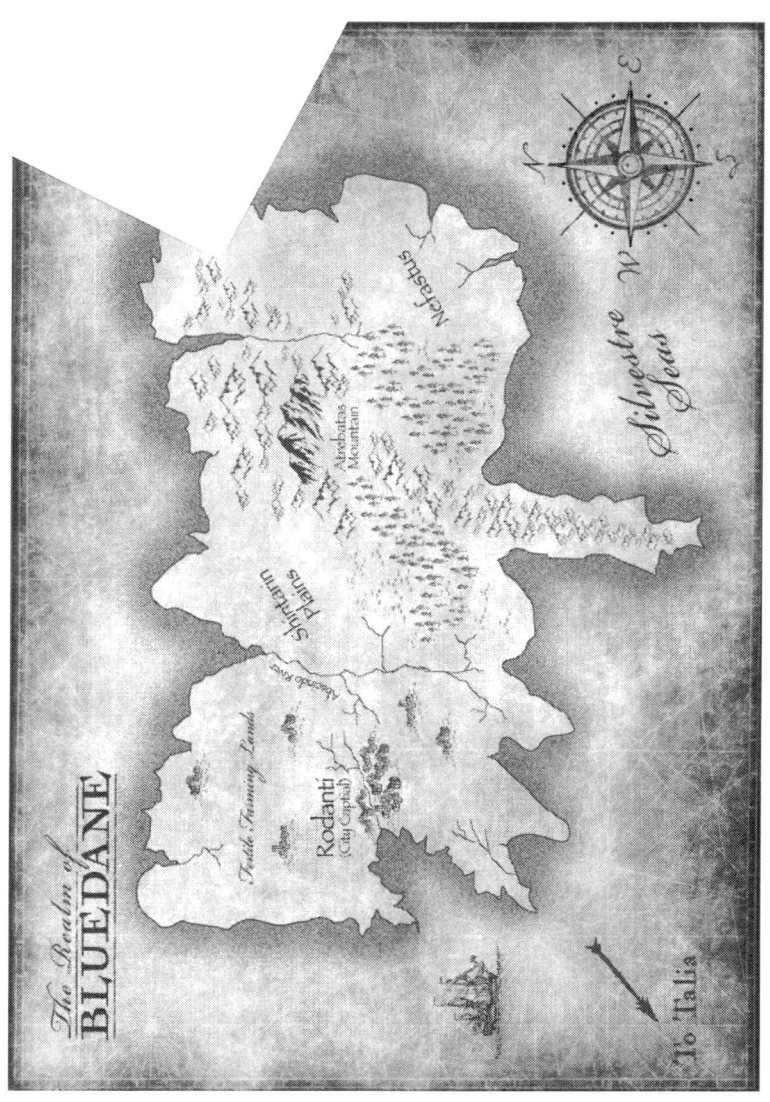

## Chapter 7 – Bluedane Shores

After three days of plain sailing without seeing another vessel, an excited atmosphere spread across the ship as land was spotted in the distance. Valarie and Losia were in their fairy form and sitting on top of the tallest mast.

"You sure about this?" asked Losia.

"U'uh," answered Valarie. "'The One' is here and he's being called by the dark-half, I can feel it."

"You had a chance to kill him when he was born. Why didn't you do it?"

"Because everyone deserves a chance to be able to choose between their dark and light selves. He might choose the light yet, and all will be well."

"And if he chooses the dark?" asked Losia.

Valarie turned to look at Losia with sadness on her face. "Then I will do what is necessary to save Talia," she answered. Movement caught their attention and, as they looked down, they could see Marcus and Tanner going onto the bridge.

"Come on, let's see what the captain has in mind about landing," said Valarie. The two of them flew like butterflies, down and around the mast, and then darted onto the bridge where they transformed into human-sized fairies. The captain was clearly uncomfortable with their sudden appearance. Losia sat daintily on a stool, crossing her stripy-tight-clad legs seductively in front of her and winked at the captain. He coughed, and hastily turned his attention back to Marcus and Tanner.

"We've come as far east of Rodanti as we can without going beyond the Atrebatas mountains. It seems the Elements have blessed us for we haven't come across any Bluedane ships, which is quite remarkable. We'll find a cove and drop you off as soon as we can. We need to be gone before we're spotted."

"We appreciate that. You have our thanks for risking the lives of your men," replied Marcus.

"So, is Rodanti the main city of Bluedane, or just a seaport?" asked Tanner.

"It's both," replied the captain. "It used to be called Karankas but the king renamed it after the death of his son. The city is huge and packed with people. You'll not find it anything like Havenshire, and I'm afraid you'll stick out like sore thumbs."

"We won't," declared Losia, promptly changing herself into the image of the captain.

The captain instantly made to cross his forehead with his finger. "Elements bless us," he gushed.

Losia laughed and changed back into a fairy. "And what about you two?" she asked. "Can you change your appearance?"

"Not like you, but we have ways of making ourselves blend in," said Tanner, throwing a chameleon-spell around himself. A sparkling light shimmered over his body, and when it had gone, Tanner was dressed in a similar way to the captain.

"Can Katrina and Gallagher do the same?" Losia asked.

"No. We'll have to borrow some children's clothes and hope no one notices their pale faces," said Marcus.

Just then a sailor came in. He touched his hand to his cap and then announced, "As close to shore as we can get, Captain."

"We'll row you ashore. Are you ready?" asked the captain.

"Yes, we'll just get our things," replied Marcus.

In no time at all they were climbing into the long rowing boat. The captain leant over the side and waved. "I wish you well," he called as the two sailors with them began rowing towards the cove. When they could row no more, the sailors jumped out and pulled the boat onto the beach. Everyone clambered out, and no sooner had they thanked the sailors than they were pushing the boat back out to sea. The group stood on the sand watching the boat as it returned to the ship. As soon as it bumped alongside, they began to move up the shore.

Idi saw a flicker of something in the distance, and put up his hand to shade his eyes as he looked out to sea.

"Marcus," he said.

Marcus turned round. "What is it, son?" he asked.

"I think a Bluedane ship might have spotted the schooner."

Marcus looked across the glistening water and realised Idi was right. The schooner had upped anchor and was making ready to run, but it would be no match for the Bluedane galleon.

"What shall we do?" asked Tanner.

Marcus thought things over for a moment. "If you each take an elbow, and channel your power through me, I will call up a storm. At least it won't be easy for the Bluedanions to find them then."

There was no need to ask twice. Both Tanner and Idi took hold of one of Marcus's elbows, while he began to call to the Elements.

"Ferrosnitavious. Caldimtarindon. Sorcrikoohektundia." Instantly the wind picked up speed and began whipping up the waves.

"Ferrosnitavious. Caldimtarindon. Sorcrikoohektundia." Thunder cracked in the distance and with its deafening roll came a mist.

"That should do it," said Marcus. "Now let's get out of here before anyone comes to investigate the strangeness of the storm."

They hurried across the beach and went up into the grass-filled dunes. The mounds and ridges seemed unending, and the slug of walking in sand made their race for cover long and tiresome. Katrina found herself falling behind but was too proud to call out for them to slow down. She was concentrating hard on making her legs work and didn't notice that Gallagher had slowed so she could catch him up.

"You doing okay, Katie?" he asked.

"Yep," she answered, not looking at him and pushing herself forward.

"You sure?" he asked.

"Yep," she snapped, through clenched teeth.

"You…" began Gallagher.

"If you ask me if I need help, I'm going knock your teeth out," Katrina hissed at him.

"You're a bad-tempered goat, do you know that?" said Gallagher, increasing his pace and the distance between them.

*I'm sorry*, Katrina thought, but she couldn't bring herself to say it out loud.

Eventually they made it out of the dunes and came to hard ground.

"Heading west?" Tanner asked.

"Yes, so long as we keep the sea to our left we will eventually reach Rodanti. Let's hope it's an uneventful journey."

"We're going to fly ahead and check out the land," said Valarie.

"Good idea," answered Tanner. "You can steer us away from any villages before we get there, keep the chance of being seen down to a minimum."

Valarie and Losia, transformed into their natural size, went darting through the air and were soon out of sight.

"Wish I could fly," said Gallagher.

"Me too," said Katrina.

"You should find flying easy," muttered Gallagher.

"Why's that?" replied Katrina.

"'Cos you're always flying off the handle, that's why," laughed Gallagher.

"You," yelled Katrina, throwing her bag to the ground and lurching at Gallagher. He laughed and sidestepped, and she lunged at him again.

"Got to do better than that," he laughed, dropping his bag, and sort of half dancing, half leaping out of her way. She chased him for a few minutes until she knew she'd never catch him and collapsed on the ground laughing.

He came and plonked himself down in front of her.

"When we get a chance, we need to increase the speed of your lunges. You'll never win against a better swordsman if you can't outmanoeuvre them."

"Come on, you two, time to get going. You can *play* later," said Idi, ruffling Katrina's hair. She knocked his hand away and huffed as she got up.

They had walked a great distance by the time Valarie and Losia eventually returned.

"Thought you'd left us for a moment there," said Idi lightheartedly. Valarie and Losia came down to the ground, instantly transforming into two strangely clad men. Their skin was dark-brown, their hair long, black and straight, and their clothes brightly coloured assemblages of wraps, shirts and very baggy trousers.

"Can you make yourself look like this?" Valarie asked.

Marcus and Tanner instantly wove their magic and changed their appearance. Although their skin was now dark-brown, their faces remained the same, unlike Valarie and Losia, who had completely changed their features and were complete strangers. It took Idi several attempts, but finally he called up the correct magic to change his appearance. Once the men had changed their looks, Valarie and Losia transformed themselves into Bluedanion women.

Their hair was long, black and straight like the men, but they wore tightly fitting trousers and loose-flowing tops. Their fingers were covered in rings and both of them had a golden ring through their nose, as well as large hoops in their ears.

"We haven't seen any children yet," said Valarie.

"Did you come across a village?" asked Marcus.

"No, just a group of travellers," answered Losia. "They were playing violins like I've never heard before and the women were dancing. It was beautiful and I wanted to stay and join in."

"Well, if there isn't a village around, I think we'll be safe to set up camp somewhere for the night without any worries of being discovered," said Marcus. "Thank you, ladies." Losia giggled at being called a lady and flounced her head to make her hair bounce on her shoulders.

A short time later, they came across a small clearing with a stream running to the left and thick forest to the right, and decided it was a good place to stop.

"Why don't you two see if you can catch us some fish for supper?" said Marcus to Katrina and Gallagher.

"Sure thing," answered Katrina, and started stripping off her trousers and boots.

"What you doing?" asked Gallagher.

"Going to catch supper," said Katrina, wading into the stream. She promptly bent double, and started searching the water for silvery movement.

"There's some trout here," she called, smiling up at Idi.

"My favourite!" answered Idi.

"She hasn't got a rod," said Gallagher to Idi, puzzled.

"She likes to catch them in her hand," answered Marcus.

"But that can take all day," replied Gallagher.

"Yep, keeps her out of mischief for hours. We love it!" laughed Idi.

Not to be outdone, Gallagher decided to join her, so he stripped off his outer trousers and boots and waded in. They glanced at each and, instantly, a silent challenge was exchanged. They turned their attention to the water and focused with determined intent. Katrina plunged in her hands, lightning quick, and pulled out a trout.

"A'ha," she cried in triumph. But then the trout wiggled and jumped from her hands. Gallagher barked a laugh and went back to studying the water. Not long after, he was diving his hands in and out of the water like a madman, but was unable to get a grip on any of the fish. As he got flustered and went red, Katrina got the giggles.

"Not so easy, is it?" she said.

He ignored her and carried on with his attempts at catching a fish. "If I had a rod I'd have loads by now," he muttered to himself.

"And if I didn't have you splashing around like a troll, I'd be cooking some by now," Katrina laughed.

The others set up camp and Tanner collected a pile of wood for a fire. Once he had dug a hole, he dropped the branches in and clicked his fingers. Flames instantly jumped up and began to burn the wood.

"We shouldn't use too much magic," said Marcus, "in case it attracts attention. To be honest, we don't know who else will be looking for Absalom, now he's taken the necklace off."

"Do you think Norvora will be here?" asked Valarie with a shiver.

"I don't know. But I think it's safe to assume if we know where he is, then so does Norvora, and that being so means he would have sent his men, or worse, demons, here by now."

"So what's the plan?" asked Tanner. "Once we've found him, are we abducting Absalom and taking him back to his mother?"

"That's more or less what I had been thinking," answered Marcus. "But I don't think it will be easy."

"You rotter," yelled Katrina. The group looked up to see a soaked Katrina and Gallagher trying to make a hasty retreat.

"If eating a varied diet is dependent on those two, I think we might be going vegetarian tonight," said Losia, who was sitting crossed-legged on the grass in front of the now0blazing fire, starting to pop potatoes into the ashes.

"I'm going to give them a helping hand," said Valarie, walking towards the stream's edge. She was human-size, but in her fairy form, and her wings fluttered on her back. She began waving her arms around as she quietly whispered a spell. Tiny lights started sparkling in the air all around her as she made her arms weave and dance with grace. Katrina and Gallagher stopped their messing around to watch her.

"She's so beautiful," whispered Katrina.

*Not as beautiful as you*, Gallagher thought.

The air surrounding them was filled with hundreds of tiny, sparkling lights. They fluttered about and, as Katrina and Gallagher put their hands out to touch them, they burst just like bubbles. Suddenly, a trout leapt out of the water to try and swallow a glitter-light. Then, as it was dropping back into the stream, another jumped up, and then another. Soon, myriad fish were leaping as high as they could.

"Be quick," said Valarie, "it won't last long."

In the beautiful, glittering haze that surrounded them, multiple little rainbows appeared in an explosion of amazing colours. Among the colours, Katrina and Gallagher started grabbing the trout and throwing them onto the land, where they flipped about until Tanner put them in a basket. It wasn't long before the colours and the flickering lights faded away, and the trout stopped jumping.

"That was amazing," said Katrina, as she waded back to the bank near Valarie. "Thank you."

"You're welcome, little one," answered Valarie.

"How many did we catch?" asked Gallagher, coming out of the water behind Katrina.

"There's twelve large ones, and eight little ones," said Tanner. Katrina knelt down by the basket and then started throwing the little ones back in the stream.

"What are you doing?" said Gallagher. "We can smoke them and have them tomorrow."

"They're too small, they haven't lived their life yet," answered Katrina.

"You're too weird," said Gallagher, pulling off his wet top and reaching into his bag for a dry one.

The rest of the evening was merry, as they sat around the fire eating and sharing tales. Once the Grey-moon had set, Valarie created a lantern and hung it from a branch, gently throwing a soft glow around them. It wasn't too long before they started bedding down for the night.

"I'm going to keep first watch," Tanner said.

"I'll do the midnight shift," said Marcus.

"I'll take the early hours then," said Idi.

After that, everything went quiet, except for the night creatures that scurried around the forest floor.

**********

The black snake watched as they fell asleep, assuming they were safe, and then he slid through the branches of the tree.

As he slithered to the ground, Norvora changed back into his human form. Painfully thin, his gaunt face looked like he was a hundred and twenty years old, as opposed to the thirty-seven he really was. The witches had stolen youth from him as well as his free will, and he cursed the day he'd found the doomed orb. Back then he'd thought he would be able to control the witches; they were trapped inside, after all. What a naïve fool he had been. Now he was bound to them, and even death wouldn't separate him, as they recalled his body over and over again for service. One thing gave him purpose and hope, and that was the whispered promise they'd given him. If he could manipulate Absalom into setting them free from the orb, they would release him and let his binding to them be broken by death.

As he strode through the woods, he was too tired to hold himself upright and, his black-clad body relaxed, hunched and twisted, he walked towards Rodanti with the demeanour of an old man.

\*\*\*\*\*\*\*\*\*\*

Idi was instantly awake when Marcus gently shook him.

"Been quiet," Marcus whispered. Idi tapped Marcus's arm, stood up, and stretched.

The first two turns of the hourglass were quiet and Idi, who had been sitting on the edge of the clearing, got up to stretch his legs. He started a circuit around the sleepers, trying to walk as quietly as possible.

"Idi," sang an eerie voice. The hairs on his arms stood up.

*Did I imagine that?*

"Idi," came the voice again.

*Nope, not imagined.* He looked at Marcus and wondered if he should wake him, then decided he would see who it was first. He didn't head straight to where the sound had come from; instead he darted into the thick of the trees and made a path that he hoped would take him around the caller. This way he would be able to see if the person was alone. If not, he would come back and wake the others.

The voice didn't call again, but Idi felt confident he was heading in the right direction. It wasn't long before he came out of the trees a little further downstream. Standing in the water was a beautiful woman. Her hair was flaming-red and cascaded down her back. Her dress was silver and sparkled like a thousand stars. Idi knew he should be wary and keep his distance, but some inner knowledge told him she was friendly.

"Hello, Idi," she said, her voice soft and flowing like honey.

"Hello," he answered. She moved, as if gliding, through the water and came to the bank. As she stepped onto the ground and walked towards him, Idi realised her dress wasn't wet.

"I have been looking forward to meeting you," she said. He should have asked her why that was, but somehow it felt unnecessary to speak. She reached out her hand and Idi took it without hesitating. He felt love and warmth flow from her into his heart. He felt his eyes well with water, as strong emotions raced through him.

"I want you to know that you were born to be, you. You will succeed in your quest and the world of Talia will owe you much. Do not doubt. Do not waver. Believe in yourself always, and then your power will increase without measure. Remember, timing is perfect and does not always run the way you want it to. And lastly, remember that words are containers of power, so use them wisely." She let go of his hand and started moving back into the water.

"Who are you?" Idi asked.

"I am Moriya, the Sirocco witch," she said with a smile before disappearing.

## Chapter 8 – The Binding Spell

Cassandra paced the room in complete frustration.

"Please sit down," said Rubin, for about the tenth time.

"Why will she not come?"

"Maybe, because she doesn't like being summoned?" surmised Rubin.

"It's been ten days!" snapped Cassandra, finally flopping down on the sofa. "She's made her point, she could come now."

"Maybe she's busy?"

"Oh, for goodness' sake, busy doing what? Casting spells and cooking frogs?"

"Gathering an army to destroy Havenshire?" replied Rubin.

Cassandra went quiet at that statement. It was true. Although Shona and the Fire-clan hadn't turned up to side with Norvora during the battle, she was in an alliance with the wizard.

"If she wants to kill us all then why would she bind me to her?"

"I don't profess to know the minds of normal women, let alone witches," said Rubin quietly. "What's more, I think you should tell your father what's going on."

"He's been through enough and I would spare him any more heartache. His guilt over handing Absalom to Piedro is great. Should I make it worse by telling him I can't go to my son?"

"Then let us go back to Tamarind. Shona won't be able to find you through the mountains."

"I'm sure the binding will let her know exactly where I am. But you should go home, Rubin."

"That's it? After all this waiting for you, you decide you don't want me around any more?"

"Oh, Rubin," said Cassandra, coming up and laying her hand on his arm. "I've never meant to hurt, ever. You have been a good and loyal friend to me since the first day we met. If things were different, if peace reigned in Talia, I would return to Tamarind with you."

He lifted her hand to his mouth and kissed it. "I will return home for I feel out of place here. Will you send for me if you ever need me?"

"Of course I will, without hesitation."

"Then once you have gone to be with Shona, I will return to Turtledoff and Martha. But what will you tell your father then?"

"I think I must lie to him and tell him I'm returning with you, that castle life is no longer for me."

"That will hurt."

"Yes, but not as much as telling him I'm going to be a witch!"

They went and sat on the sofa together, holding hands.

"Why do you think she wants me to be a witch?" Cassandra asked, staring into the fire while imagining herself casting spells over a huge black cauldron.

"Maybe she thinks, if the princess is a witch, the people will be more accepting of her clan?"

Cassandra looked up and smiled at Rubin. "You could be right, you know. If that is the case, then I can do something about it and she can release me. I'll promise to support them and offer them shelter and protection."

"I don't think she needs either of those things."

"Then… what? What can I do to release myself from the binding?"

"There isn't anything you can do." The voice came from near the window and both Cassandra and Rubin jumped up in shock, spinning around to find Shona sitting on the window ledge.

"How did you get in here?" Rubin demanded.

"How long have you been there?" asked Cassandra.

"A while," Shona answered, standing up and coming towards them. "Time for you to leave," she said, nodding at Rubin. Rubin instantly bristled, but before he could answer, Cassandra spoke.

"It's fine. Go. I will come and find you later."

Rubin lifted Cassandra's hand and kissed it.

"I'll be in the next room. If you need me, just yell," he said softly before leaving.

"So, once a princess, always a princess," said Shona, sitting down opposite Cassandra.

"What do you mean by that?" Cassandra asked, sitting down herself.

"It's in your blood to boss people about, whether they like it or not."

"That's not true." For a moment, the two women sat looking at each other in silence, weighing each other up.

"I can't release you," Shona said.

"Why not? Tell me what I can do for you instead and I will. But now I need to go and get my son, you've got to release me."

"The only way a binding can be broken is when it is fulfilled," said Shona.

"But who knows how long it will take me to become a witch?" said Cassandra, suddenly full of fear that Shona wasn't going to let her go to Bluedane.

"You'll have to pray you're a quick learner then, won't you?"

"How long does it take for a 'normal' to learn magic?"

"Years."

"YEARS!" yelled Cassandra, jumping up. "I don't have years; I have to protect my son, now." Rage was pouring through Cassandra, mingled with frustration. *I could kill you.*

"And before you think about having me killed, you need to know if I die before the binding is removed, you will die with me."

Cassandra grimaced. She didn't know what shocked her more: that Shona had just read her mind, or this new information, which showed it was now important to keep the witch well and truly alive, despite her longings to throttle her. She started pacing the floor.

"There has to be a way to release me."

"None," said Shona, obviously enjoying the pain she was inflicting.

"Maybe some other witch knows of a way to break a binding?"

"None," repeated Shona.

Cassandra spun round and felt despair swallowing her up as she looked at Shona and begged, "Please release me?"

Shona looked her up and down as if recalculating her view of the princess.

"Even if I wanted to, I'm afraid there is no way to break a binding until the pact is complete." Then Shona sat back in her chair, taken by surprise when Cassandra collapsed onto her knees and started crying. For a moment, pity filled her and, for the tiniest of moments, she wished she could help. Then a picture of her mother came to her, unhappy until her last days that she'd been banished from her home, and suddenly her tender emotions shut down. "Stop your snivelling, you look pathetic," she snapped.

Cassandra instantly pulled herself together and hastily stood up.

"What if demons were chasing your only child? Would you be able to hold it together, knowing you couldn't help or protect them?"

Shona's eyes went ice-cold as she looked at Cassandra. For years she had planned her revenge on the king by destroying the only thing he cared about: his legitimate daughter. She had agreed to Norvora's plans to manipulate the birth of 'the One' with the proviso that Cassandra would always end up being her slave. The stupid woman had so easily signed over her life to her that Shona had hardly believed it. She would turn her into a witch and in the process enslave Cassandra for ever.

"You will come and live in my clan. That way you will learn much quicker than if you remain here."

"But..."

"No buts. We both want this over as quickly as possible, don't we?"

"Yes."

"Then it's settled. Get your things; I want out of this place as quickly as possible."

"I can't come with you now," yelped Cassandra.

"Why not?" asked Shona.

Cassandra searched for a good enough reason.

"Because if I don't say goodbye to my father, he won't stop until he finds me and brings me back."

Shona thought about this briefly.

"Very well, you can have a day to make your farewells, then ride to the far side of Havenshire and wait for me by the Black Pools." Without any warning, Shona made herself invisible.

"Three, can I have three days?" Cassandra called out, but no answer came, and when the curtain moved by the window, she knew Shona had gone.

"Oh dear, Elements, what have I got myself into?" she said, leaning her head against the mantelpiece.

## Chapter 9 – Rodanti

Idi sat looking at his group of friends as the early-morning Grey-moon began its ascent. For some reason, he didn't want to tell them about the Sirocco witch. He knew Marcus would be upset if he found out he had withheld something like this, but he felt it had been a private conversation.

He waited until the birds began their morning songs and then began waking them. The last person he leant over was Katrina, and he paused in midair as he looked at her beautiful, innocent face. *Gosh, I love you, my little Katie.* He gently stroked her cheek and she opened her eyes and smiled at him.

"Morning, Papa," she said, with a big stretch.

"Morning, mischief," he smiled back. She surprised him by throwing her arms around his neck and squeezing him tightly. "Hey, you okay?"

"Yes, Papa. Just happy, that's all."

"Come on, you soppy pair. We've a long walk to Rodanti in front of us," said Marcus, smiling at them.

Valarie and Losia had porridge ready to eat by the time the others had finished packing. The group sat in a circle and wolfed the breakfast down.

"So, all was quiet last night?" asked Valarie, taking a quick peek at Idi, before returning to concentrate on her bowl.

"Yes," said both Marcus and Tanner. After a moment, Valarie looked at Idi.

"All quiet?" she repeated.

"Yes," replied Idi, not taking his eyes off his bowl, "all quiet."

Marcus looked puzzled and asked Valarie, "Did you notice something?"

She looked at Idi and then over to Marcus. "No, I didn't. I was just checking."

Marcus's eyebrows furrowed together as he pondered her answer, clearly showing he now thought something was amiss.

"Is there any more porridge?" asked Gallagher.

Valarie laughed. "Young boys are impossible to fill up," she said. "Here, there is a small bit left; you might as well finish it." Gallagher jumped up quickly and offered his bowl to Valarie for second helpings.

"You must have hollow legs, Gallagher. I've no idea where you put it all," said Idi with a grin.

"I remember the days when you were exactly the same; thought I'd never be able to fill you up," added Marcus.

Idi laughed. "I'm sure I didn't eat that much," he said.

"Oh, I'm sure you did," replied Marcus. The two men smiled at each other, the bond of love between them melded firm over the years.

"Let's get this show on the road," said Tanner, as he closed his eyes and pulled on his magic to change his appearance. When he opened his eyes, the others, except for Katrina and

Gallagher, had also changed. "Can't wait to get hold of some clothes; it will be easier than holding this image too long."

"First chance we get we'll purchase some, so come along and stop your whining," said Marcus.

"I'm not whining," moaned Tanner.

"And I'm not a fairy," chirped in Losia.

"You're not a fairy," said Tanner, confused.

"I know." Losia laughed, leaning in to give Tanner a kiss on the cheek, making him blush.

The group started off in cheerful spirits and set as fast a pace as possible, allowing Katrina and Gallagher to keep up. Idi's appearance kept flickering and his disguise kept fading; he kept muttering to himself in frustration at not being able to hold the magic still.

"First sign of going mad that, you know," said Marcus.

"What is?" replied Idi.

"Talking to yourself," said Marcus with a grin.

"You talk to yourself all the time," said Idi.

"Exactly! You don't want to end up like me, do you?"

Idi looked over at Marcus. "I would be honoured to end up like you, old man. Why do you think I can heal easily but find other magic so hard to control?"

"Lack of confidence."

Idi huffed at Marcus's reply and walked ahead to put a stop to their conversation.

After a few turns of the hourglass, they stopped for a short break and plonked themselves down on the grass for a rest.

When they'd had a drink and caught their breath, they set off again. This time, Valarie and Losia went in their fairy form and flew ahead to check the way.

By the end of the day, Katrina and Gallagher were both exhausted and had extremely sore feet. Neither of them admitted the pain they felt, nor the relief that washed over them when Marcus announced they would make camp for the night.

"We're less than half a day's travel away now," said Losia, while stretching and arching her back, making her green, black-edged wings flutter.

"Why are you so different?" Katrina asked Losia, while looking her up and down. Losia laughed and ruffled her short, black, spikey hair.

"Because of the colours, you mean?" Losia answered.

Katrina looked at the delicate, almost see-through rainbow-coloured wings on Valarie's back and her long, flowing dress. "It's not just the colours. Your dress is tight-fitting and, and… really short."

Losia shook her hips, making her short, petal-shaped skirt swish around her, showing off the full length of her legs. She raised her right knee slightly, and pointed her foot, which was clad in little slip-ons that tied around her legs.

"Men like long legs," she said, winking at Tanner, who quickly looked elsewhere.

"Losia, behave," said Valarie, and Losia lowered her leg and made a pretence of straightening her skirt.

"Do you think human-fairy babies would be pretty?" Losia asked Tanner, as she brushed past him and plonked herself down as near to him as she could get.

Tanner's face instantly flushed, and he coughed before answering. "I'm sure they would be, if you found yourself a handsome man."

"That crosses you off the list then, Tanner," laughed Idi.

"Oy, you! I'll have you know that before Marcus taught me the way, I had ladies chasing after me all the time."

"And they never caught you?" Losia asked, fluttering her eyelashes at him.

"Only when I let them," he grinned back at her. Suddenly, Losia didn't seem so sure of herself, and she shuffled slightly away from him.

"We've noticed the people working on the land around here are wearing different clothes to the travellers we saw. Do you think we should change?" asked Valarie.

"Probably no need to," answered Marcus. "Farmers often wear different attire to the city folk. Now, how's that rabbit coming along? I'm starving!"

They had a quiet evening, with both Katrina and Gallagher falling asleep almost as soon as they'd finished eating. The night watch proved peaceful and the early-morning sun found the group refreshed and eager to reach Rodanti. After a blackberry-laced porridge, they packed up and set off. Valarie and Losia walked with them for some time before taking to the air to check the way ahead.

After a time, Tanner noticed that Katrina was trying to hide a limp.

"Stop a moment," he said, bringing them all to a halt. "Show me," he said to Katrina. There was no disguising the discomfort she felt. So she untied her boots and lifted her foot to show him.

"Katie," said Idi in dismay, when he saw the blistered foot. "Why didn't you say anything?"

Katrina shrugged "We need to conserve the magic, don't we?" she answered.

"Silly girl," said Marcus. "It doesn't use hardly anything to look after your feet. Gallagher, how are yours?"

"Not so good," he admitted.

"Sit down, you pair of silly goats!" said Marcus.

Gallagher came and sat on the ground next to Katrina and removed his boots. Four little, blister-covered feet, oozing pus and bleeding were placed on the grass. Idi knelt down in front of them and instantly pulled on his magic, sending it flooding down his arm and into their feet. Katrina sighed as the pain was instantly gone. Gallagher watched in total amazement as the skin began to grow and cover the wounds, and he looked at Idi in complete awe.

"Thank you," he whispered.

"You're welcome," smiled Idi. Just then, Valarie and Losia came fluttering through the air and, as they landed, transformed into human-sized Bluedanions.

"What are you doing?" asked Valarie. "We could see the magic from miles away."

"I think we're okay," answered Marcus. "We haven't seen a single demon since the others blocked up the Mouth. Maybe we're free of them?"

"We'll never be completely free of the vermin," said Losia. "Who knows how long it will take them to open a new way into Talia?"

"And what about Norvora?" said Valarie. "He's not gone yet. And even without demons, he has a lethal army waiting to attack us."

"You're right, of course. We should try to refrain from using magic as much as possible. I guess these last few weeks have lulled me into a false security. We're so close to 'the One' now, I can feel my excitement rising," answered Marcus.

"I'm sorry," said Katrina, pulling her boots back on.

Valarie looked at her and her irritation vanished. "It's okay, little one," she said, smiling. "I'm a fine one to talk, having made the fish dance for you." Then, to Marcus: "We're nearly there. Over the next hill lies a huge valley that holds Rodanti. We can see it all."

"And the palace, can you see that?" Marcus asked.

"Yes, it lies to the north," Valarie answered.

"Ready?" Marcus asked Katrina and Gallagher.

"Ready," they both answered at the same time.

The group set off at a slow run, eager to see the city. When they came to the top of the hill they stopped and gazed at the view before them. Rodanti was huge, maybe twenty times bigger than Havenshire. The port was full of ships, some docked, some going or returning. Huge, eagle-like birds hovered and glided over the city, cawing shrilly as they surfed on the wind. The city was completely surrounded by a huge brick wall, making the guarded gates the only way in or out. Around the city, organised farms formed a patchwork quilt over the land, and beyond them a great savannah eased into grasslands.

"What a place," said Idi.

"How are we going to reach the palace through all of that?" asked Tanner.

"By the grace of the Elements," answered Marcus.

## Chapter 10 – Hide-and-Seek

Bert and Celestine had moved away from the platoon so that no one could hear them.

"Where do we go from here?" whispered Bert.

"As far away as possible," replied Celestine.

"Yes, but where?"

"We don't really have many choices, do we? We could go to the Tamarind mountains. Apparently the caverns under them are vast, so we could maybe find a corner Bevan wouldn't think to look in?"

"I reckon they'll be the first place he sends a search party to," said Bert.

"Okay, then where do you think we should go?" asked Celestine.

"Bluedane."

"Are you crazy? How would we get across the Silvestre Sea?" hissed Celestine.

"If we found a boat to take us, I'm sure we'd be safe. Bevan would never travel across the sea."

"No ugly human will let us on their boat; they'd kill us on the spot. No, it's too dangerous."

"Not all the ugly humans are evil," whispered Bert.

Celestine looked at him and sighed. It was true, of course. They now knew that not all of them were evil, but they would never be able to tell from a distance which ones were and which ones weren't.

"I think we should go to the Wastelands," said Celestine.

"What! Now you're being crazy. Nothing can live there, not even us, Celest."

"I heard the ruins of Galbastion have an underground fountain beneath them, and if you can find that, you would be able to survive there."

"Myths and legends, Celest. What if we get there and we can't find any water? Do you want to risk their lives on a hand-me-down tale?" Bert pointed to the Fart platoon, who were flopped out on the floor, resting after their exhausting escape from the Gap.

Celestine looked at the goblins she loved and then took hold of Bert's hand. "I think it's our only chance of keeping them alive," she whispered. "And we've lost too many already."

"Okay, Celest. You always seem to know what is best for us, so we'll do it, we'll go in search of the fountain of Galbastion."

She bent forward and rubbed Bert's nose with her own. He blushed and his cheeks turned bright-blue. There was a bit of grumbling from the group, especially from Hurricane, but in the end they all agreed to go.

The Fart platoon was much more of a family than an army platoon, and their progress would be slow, not to mention complete agony for Celestine, who knew Bevan would send his swiftest runners after them. The only thing they had in their favour, she hoped, was that no one would expect them to go to the Wastelands, where nothing but scorpions lived. When they couldn't find them, Bevan might send someone there, but he was sure to look everywhere else first… well, she was crossing her fingers he would.

Knowing the other platoons would only move by night, Bert decided they should walk during the day. This caused tremendous grumbling from the whole group, including Celestine, but he was adamant it would be safer. The sun hurt their eyes after a while, and they kept to the shade of trees as much as possible. They weren't strangers to daylight, but absolutely preferred the dark of night for making long journeys.

"We're being cooked alive," grumbled Obane.

"Hurricane's stomach must be boiling, his farts are toxic gasses," moaned Timo.

"Sure, the other platoon will smell his farts right across Talia and track us down in no time," added Thara.

"I can leave if you like?" growled Hurricane.

"Don't be silly, Hurri. We're only playing with you," said Thara, smiling.

"I'd rather play with the ugly humans right now," grumbled Timo, holding a cloth over his nose. Obane gave him a clout around the ear.

"Don't be rude," said Obane. "Put that cloth away." Timo grumbled as he shoved it in his pocket.

"It's alright for you – your rhinoceros nose isn't sensitive any more," said Timo.

"Your arse won't be sensitive any more if you don't give over your moaning," said Obane, waving his huge hand at Timo. Timo quickly sidestepped and went to walk next to Hurricane. He figured if he wasn't downwind of him any more, the smell wouldn't be too bad.

"I can make bombs with my farts, you know," said Hurricane with pride.

"Really?" said Timo.

"Yes. If I fill a large bag of my air, straight from my backside, and you throw it, when it lands it explodes. Very satisfying it is."

Timo looked up at Hurricane with new respect.

The first day passed slowly and uneventfully and that night they slept in a tight huddle without mishap. It was as the light was rising that Celestine felt the hairs on the back of her neck stand up. She crawled slowly through the long grasses until she came to a bit of a clearing. The Silver-moon of night was dropping, but the Grey-moon of winter was creeping over the mountains, casting its cool reflection down, its watery light pouring down over the Torrean Mountains, lighting everything with its solemn splendour.

As she searched every part of the mountain she could see, Celestine finally found what she was looking for. Movement. She concentrated, honing in on the grey shadows that darted about the mountain face. *Tracker platoon*, she moaned inwardly. They would find them, without a shadow of a doubt, and more than likely it would be tomorrow night when they caught up with the Fart platoon. She crawled back to the group and woke up Bert.

Bert moaned. The Tracker platoon wouldn't attack them, but they would definitely find them and report back to Bevan, who would send others to kill them. It seemed heading to the Wastelands had offered them no security.

"We don't have any option, Bert; we must keep moving forward. Maybe some luck will come our way."

"Yeah, our luck will only bring us something like demons, though," said Bert.

"Don't be like that, Bert. We're still alive, aren't we? That's lucky."

"We lost four of our family in those woods on the mountains, Celestine. I'm not sure that was lucky."

"We're lucky the humans arrived, and saved as many of us as they did," said Thara. Celestine and Bert turned around to see Thara looking at them. "Don't tell the others about the trackers," she said. "They will lose heart."

"What will we lose?" asked Timo, sitting up and rubbing his eyes.

"The game," said Bert.

"What game?" asked Timo, suddenly excited.

"Hide-and-seek," answered Celestine.

"Oh, I love that game," said Hurricane. "Who are we hiding from?" Bert, Celestine and Thara looked at each in amusement.

"From the mighty ogres that live under the ground," said Thara. "We have to run fast and be light on our feet so as not to wake them."

"Let's go," yelped Timo, jumping to his feet.

"Not yet," said Thara, grabbing his ankle. "We need to pack up first."

"That's no fun," said Timo.

"Yes, but very important," said Celestine.

## Chapter 11 – Oops-a-Daisy

Valarie and Losia ventured into the city in the appearance of travellers; however, after many weird and, quite frankly, none-too-pleasant looks, they had ducked behind someone's washing line and transformed their clothes to be more like the people wandering through the streets of Rodanti. Gone were the tight-fitting trousers, replaced by loose-flowing ones that gripped at the ankles. Gone also was all the gold jewellery and the multicolours; now Valarie was dressed in bright turquoise and Losia in brilliant yellow. To complete the change they both wore a strip of cloth tied around their heads.

"I feel like a Daffodil-bandit," giggled Losia.

"Come on," said Valarie, smiling. "Let's buy some children's clothes and get back as soon as we can." They wove their way through the extremely colourful marketplace and it wasn't long before they found a stall selling children's clothes.

"Hello," said Valarie, "we'd like an outfit for a boy and a girl, please."

The stall-seller looked at Valarie bemused. Valarie looked at Losia for help. Losia caught sight of someone buying something on the next stall, handing over three silver bits. She opened up her palm and revealed ten silver bits to the seller. She pointed at them, and then at the clothes, and then offered the silver to the woman, who was now smiling broadly. The woman called to a young girl on a nearby stall, saying something neither Valarie nor Losia could understand. The girl rushed over and beamed widely at them.

"You don't understand Bluetarrian," she stated with a grin.

"No," answered Valarie.

"Where do you come from then?" the girl demanded.

Valarie pointed to the north. "Way on the other side of Bluedane, a small village and everyone there speaks Taliarrian."

"So, what brings you here?" the girl asked.

"Are these clothes for sale, or not?" asked Losia.

"Everything in the market is for sale, for the right price," the girl answered with a shrewd grin.

"And what's the price for two outfits?" asked Losia.

"What size you need?" the girl asked.

Valarie and Losia looked at each other, not sure how to answer.

"They're about this high, a girl and a boy," said Valarie eventually, holding up her hand to just below shoulder height. The girl turned around and started talking quickly to the stall-seller. She turned back with a grin.

"Two outfits, ten silver bits."

"What?" screeched Losia, who had watched the exchange of a whole lamb for two silver bits.

"Okay, we feel generous today. Yours, for eight bits," said the girl, waving at the seller to hurry. The stall-seller dived among the clothes and produced two children's outfits: trousers, tops, scarfs and slip-on sandals. She picked them up and offered them to Valarie and Losia.

"Three bits," bargained Losia.

"You crazy woman," laughed the girl, but quickly followed with "seven bits".

"Five, and if you don't accept we will take our silver elsewhere," said Valarie, quietly but firmly. The woman and girl went into a heated debate for a moment, and then the girl turned back to them, smiling as sweet as can be.

"She accepts," the girl said, putting her hand out for the silver. Losia handed over five bits; the girl then handed four over to the woman and pocketed one herself.

"Commission," she said, then turned and went back to her own stall.

"Shu'hav'larn," the woman said, bowing her head then placing the money in her pocket.

"Shu'hav'lurrn," Valarie said back to her slowly.

"Shu'hav'*larn*," the woman said again, stressing the 'larn'.

"Shu'hav'larn," Valarie repeated.

The woman grinned and nodded, then shoved the clothes into a paper parcel and handed it to Losia.

"Shu'hav'larn," Losia sang with complete ease.

"Everything comes easy to you," Valarie said as they made their way back to the city gates.

"Well, I have just heard the word five times," Losia replied. "Come on, I want to buy some of those pastries over there. They smell amazing."

"We should get back to the others," said Valarie.

"And we will, and we'll take them some pies too."

As they reached the pie seller's stall and started bargaining for the best price, they were watched by an old man, who stopped to lean against the wall of a drinking saloon. His crinkled brown skin was sallow and his eyes were hooded and heavy, his black garb not quite fitting in with the colourful surroundings. As Valarie and Losia finished their purchase and started down the lane, he turned and spat in the gutter. *Stinking fairies*, he muttered, and then, instead of continuing his journey towards the palace, he shuffled after them.

The others were waiting for them in a small coppice, not too far from the city edge. Katrina and Gallagher were sitting on a branch, deep in the foliage, to remain hidden from the occasional passer-by, while the others sat on the grass below them in the shade of the tree. When it looked like the coast was clear, Katrina and Gallagher jumped down to put on the clothes from the market, and eat pies with the others. The clothes weren't a great fit, but from a distance they would blend in okay. Unfortunately, up close was a different thing.

"We could just use a bit of magic and turn their skin brown?" suggested Losia, looking at them and shaking her head. "They'll stand out like sore thumbs as they are."

"If we use magic on their faces they'll be like beacons to anyone in the magic world. I think the risk is too great. We should hide them somewhere around here," said Valarie.

"I agree," said Tanner. "Much safer for them out here."

"I can look after myself," said Katrina crossly.

"Me too," said Gallagher. "We can put our hoods up and keep our faces down."

"I don't want to take that risk," said Idi.

"Papa!" said Katrina.

"Look, today is just a scouting trip. Find our way to the palace, learn the streets and see how we blend in. Maybe even find a tavern for us to stay in tonight. Stay here, up the tree and out of sight, so I don't have to worry about you. Please?"

"Okay, Papa," said Katrina, none too happy.

"Look after her?" Idi said to Gallagher.

"Yes, sir," answered Gallagher quickly.

"I don't need looking after, especially by him," muttered Katrina.

"Don't be a sour-puss," said Idi.

"Let me come with you," she pleaded. Idi raised one eyebrow at her. "Fine," she grumbled and climbed up the tree. "If you're not back by the time the Silver-moon hits the sky, I'm going to come and look for you."

"We'll be back long before then," said Marcus, "and in the meantime look after Gallagher."

"Huh!" said Katrina, giving Gallagher a look that said 'See, Marcus knows who the better fighter is'. As the figures grew small the further they walked, Katrina's shoulders slumped. She hated being left behind. She had to protect Idi, and how could she do that stuck here in the tree, with a young boy to look after to boot?

"Just so you know," said Gallagher, "I can look after myself, thanks."

"Yeah, me too," said Katrina.

Norvora watched as the group made their way to the city, and when he was sure they were inside the walled streets, got up from behind the rock and headed towards the children, who would soon become his secret slaves, after the witches had got into their heads.

Katrina and Gallagher spotted the old man long before he was near.

"Do you think he knows we're here?" asked Katrina quietly.

"He seems to be walking directly towards us, and he's come off the main path," answered Gallagher.

"What shall we do?"

Gallagher pulled his sword out. "An old man is no match for me, Katrina. Don't worry, I'll protect you."

"Really?" said Katrina sarcastically. Gallagher just raised his eyebrows and shook his head at her.

"What do you want?" shouted Gallagher, when Norvora stopped a short distance away from them.

To keep them unaware of who he was, Norvora stayed in his old man's image as he held out a black-velvet bag in front of him. "Would you like to see what I have in here?" he asked, putting on a shaky voice.

"No," said Katrina. "Go away."

"Now, that's not very nice," said Norvora, slowly uncurling his crooked body and standing up straight. Prickles ran up both Katrina's and Gallagher's arms with the realisation that they were in trouble. Norvora gently put the bag on the ground and pulled on the strings to open it up. As the bag fell down it revealed a glass orb with flickering lights inside. Norvora knocked back his hood and shook his head to throw off the last of his disguise.

"Come down and meet the witches, children," he hissed, flicking his forked tongue in and out of his mouth. Both Katrina and Gallagher shrunk back against the trunk of the tree.

"Norvora," Katrina whispered, knowing there was nothing she could do against him without magic.

"For Talia and honour," yelled Gallagher, jumping out of the tree.

"Gallagher!" screamed Katrina, and climbed to a lower branch to jump down after him.

Norvora simply laughed as Gallagher came charging towards him, his sword brandished high above his head.

"Gallagher!" screamed Katrina again, charging after him with her sword in her hand.

"Enough!" bellowed Acacia, from within the orb. Instantly, both Katrina and Gallagher were frozen and unable to move. Fear filled their eyes as they watched Norvora pick up the orb and walk towards them.

"You will be ours," said Desdemona.

"Or you will die," said Abaddon.

"Which do you choose?" hissed Norvora, flicking his elongated tongue over Katrina's face.

"Death," screamed both Katrina and Gallagher in their minds at the same time.

"So be it," said Norvora. "It will be my pleasure to take the most precious thing Idi has away from him."

*I love you, Papa,* cried Katrina internally.

"Love won't save you," said Norvora with glee. "Love is useless and has no place in this world any more." He slowly began transforming himself into a snake, and at the same time started wrapping himself around Gallagher. "So eager to die?" Norvora hissed into Gallagher's ear.

Just then, a howl filled the air. Norvora's death-hold on Gallagher relaxed slightly, as he spun his snake-like head around, just in time to see a huge wolfhound leaping towards him.

"Danger comes," screeched Desdemona.

"Quick, get us out of here," bellowed Acacia.

"We're not strong enough, trapped in the orb. Quick, we must go before she comes," cried Abaddon.

Several things happened at once. As the witches began screaming at Norvora, Katrina and Gallagher were released from their hold. Katrina, who had been running and frozen midstream, went pelting to the ground with a crash. As Norvora went to defend himself against the hound, he loosened his grip around Gallagher, who immediately flung his sword as hard as he could into the quickly disappearing snake-form of Norvora's leg. At the same time, the gigantic hound bit into Norvora's arm, and the Three-witches carried on screaming hysterically. "She's coming, she's coming."

Norvora, assaulted in his leg, arm and head, nearly exploded in anger, and a loud boom reverberated from his body, sending Katrina, Gallagher and the hound flying into the air. In the time it took for them to reach the floor, he had recovered the orb in the bag and hit magic-timing, racing away from whatever was approaching.

Gallagher crawled towards Katrina, fighting the pain in his ears. Katrina lay curled in a ball, her hands over her ears.

"He's gone," Gallagher said, pulling Katrina into his arms. The hound started whining and they looked across to where he lay.

"Poor thing," said Katrina, shrugging herself away from Gallagher and crawling towards him. His head was almost as big as Katrina's torso, but she picked it up and put it on her lap to stroke him.

"He's so big," said Gallagher, who had crawled over to them. "Have you ever seen such a big animal?"

Before Katrina could answer, there came a rush of wind that made them both turn their heads downwards. When they looked up again a woman was standing over them.

"He's a Sirocco hound," she said. "His name is Gulfuss."

"He tried to save us," said Katrina with a frog in her throat.

"He's fine," the woman said. "He's just enjoying your touch so much he doesn't want to get up yet."

Katrina cocked her head to the side to look into the dog's eyes, which seemed to be smiling up at her. "Oh," she said in relief.

"Are you what the witches were afraid of?" asked Gallagher as he admired the red beauty in front of him.

"Come on," she answered, "it's time to be gone."

"Where are we going?" asked Katrina, getting up. The hound immediately jumped up and Katrina couldn't help but jump slightly as he stood well above her head. The hound licked her face.

"Yuk, get off, you soppy thing," she cried, wiping the wet off her face. The woman said something to the dog, in a sing-song voice that neither Katrina nor Gallagher could understand; then the hound was racing away across the fields, in the same direction Norvora had taken.

"Come here," said the woman, with her arms wide. They went to her side without hesitation, and she wrapped her arms around them.

"Saymeetirinathormor-treek-ansolcremarin," she cried, and with the call came a wind that made Katrina and Gallagher close their eyes.

"We're here," she said. They opened their eyes and looked around, no longer where they had been, in the country on the hill, but instead inside a walled garden.

"Where are we?" whispered Katrina.

"In the palace gardens," she answered.

"Who are you?" asked Gallagher.

She smiled at him. "I am Moriya, the Sirocco witch. Now just go and look around the gardens and you will find him soon enough."

"Find who?" asked Gallagher.

"Absalom, the One born to be king," answered Katrina.

Moriya smiled at her and reached out to touch her cheek. "We are all born to be who we are," said Moriya, gazing deeply into Katrina's eyes. "Be sure to always stay true to yourself, dragon-slayer, Pure-queen of Talia." Then, suddenly, she was gone.

"Queen of Talia?" said Gallagher. Just then, they heard a young lad's voice call out in anger.

"I wasn't ready, start again."

Gallagher and Katrina looked at each other.

"Suppose we had better go and meet this born-thingy one," said Gallagher.

Katrina tutted at him but followed him across the grass. As they came around the corner of the crown-shaped hedgerow, they saw two boys fencing. One had pale skin, long black hair tied in a ponytail and wore fancy clothes; the other was an olive-skinned lad who was obviously a servant.

"I'm not trained in sword-fencing, your highness," the servant said, backing away slightly.

"I don't care. I need to practise without anyone noticing, so come on. Come at me again."

The young lad slowly raised his sword and put his left arm behind his back. Absalom did the same.

"Now," he cried, after lunging at the lad. Immediately, he struck the servant with his blunt-ended sword. "You're not even trying," Absalom shouted, and hit the lad with the blunt end of the sword.

"Oy," shouted Katrina.

Both the servant and Absalom froze and turned to look at Katrina as she marched across the grass, pulling her sword out of the sabre as she went. "You can practise with me if you want. I think I can do better than him," she said, flicking her head towards the servant.

"Where did you come from, boy?" demanded Absalom.

"Does it matter?" replied Katrina.

Absalom smiled. "Not at all," he said, taking up the en garde position.

"Umm, I'm not so sure this is a good thing," said Gallagher, rushing over to them.

"Stay back," Absalom demanded.

"As you wish," said Gallagher, and went to stand next to the servant.

Absalom and Katrina weighed each other up. He was a good deal taller than her, but both had the same slim build. Suddenly, he lunged towards her and struck her in the arm.

"Two more points, and I win," he said, raising his chin.

She didn't even challenge the fact that he had lunged before declaring the start. Instead, she lunged, sidestepped and then whacked him behind his legs, sending him falling to the ground.

"Oops-a-daisy," she said, offering him her hand. "I thought you knew we had started."

Absalom glared at the hand offered and then at the face of the young lad who had bettered him in front of a stranger and his servant. As he looked at the freckled face, framed by short-cropped brown hair, it suddenly dawned on him that the boy was a girl. Slowly, when she realised he wasn't going to accept her hand, Katrina withdrew it and looked down at him in disgust. Absalom got to his feet, never taking his eyes off the girl he now hated emphatically.

## Chapter 12 – The Way In

It turned out to be easy finding the way to the palace. The grandiose building lay situated at the highest part of the valley, and all the main streets of Rodanti fell away from the walled palace in straight lines down to the sea. Many little alleys connected the main cobbled streets, giving the appearance from the sky of a huge spider's web.

A group of five men, strangers to the tavern, sat huddled around a table in the corner, looking out of the Blackwood arched-pained, windows, their hands clasped around various drinks. Cherry and vanilla vapour filled the room, rising from the many long-tapered pipes that were being smoked by seemingly wealthy men. Mingling with the sweet white clouds was the strong aroma of aniseed, ascending from delicate glass tumblers.

"Have you seen how many guards there are at the gates?" whispered Valarie. "Peidro must fear for his safety to post that many men. Besides making yourself invisible, I'm not too sure how you will get in."

"The wall around the palace is the highest I've ever seen, and with those spikes on the top we're never going to be able to scale them," whispered Tanner. "Well, not without using magic, anyway."

"We really should try not to use magic until we really need it. We have no idea what kind of magicians Bluedane has," said Marcus.

"You entered Havenshire's castle as mice," said Idi. "Maybe you could be mice again and see if you can find out which part of the palace they are holding Absalom in?"

"Yuk! No. I didn't like being a mouse at all. I kept thinking someone was going to stomp on me," said Losia with a shiver.

"We could be birds, though," said Valarie. "I've noticed that birds fly all over the city. No one would notice us flying over the walls."

"Except anyone adept in magic," said Idi.

"Anyone that soaked in magic would see us for who we are just walking down the streets. It takes no more magic for us to shape-shift into an animal than it does to change our appearance," answered Valarie.

"You're right," said Marcus. "I think our best plan is one that moves swiftly so we expose our magic for as short a time as possible. Birds it is. Can you go now? Once we know where he's being held prisoner, we can work out a plan to get us in and out again, hopefully before anyone realises what's happening."

Losia knocked back the sweet, clear liquid, then licked her lips. "Love this aniseed drink," she said, standing up. She bent down as if to give Tanner a kiss, but he ducked out of the way.

Tanner looked about quickly and straight away spotted the bartender giving them a queer look.

"You're a man," hissed Tanner through his teeth.

"So I am," said Losia, straightening up, scratching her backside, and then heartily slapping Tanner on the back. "See you later then, you ugly mug," she said in an overly loud, deep voice. He scowled back at her.

"We might as well order some food," said Marcus when the fairies had gone. "Draw less attention to ourselves if we're doing something more than staring out of the window." He went over to the counter to speak with the bartender, who luckily spoke some Taliarrian.

"What food do you have on offer today?" Marcus asked with a smile. He was met with a scowl.

"No barter over food," the man practically growled. "You want low-cost, you go downmarket."

"Oh no, sorry. I didn't mean offer as in cheap. I meant, what are you serving today?" said Marcus apologetically.

"We don't cook offal or birds here," said the man, slamming both his hands down on the counter. Marcus looked confused. "Only lamb is cooked here, or roasted vegetables. You want anything else, you go away."

"Lamb, lamb is good. Three lamb, please," said Marcus holding up three fingers.

"I'm no idiot, I know my numbers," snapped the man.

"Of course. Of course," said Marcus, holding up his hands and taking a step away from the angry glare.

"One silver bit," the man said, holding up one finger.

"Yes, of course, here you are," said Marcus, handing the bit over. "Shu'hav'larn."

"Shu'hav'larn," the man responded, more subdued.

"Making friends, Marcus?" laughed Tanner when he returned to the table.

"Very touchy these Bluedanions," he replied as he sat down.

"So much for drawing less attention to ourselves," grinned Idi. "We should have asked Losia to order for us before they left."

"I'd not ask that fairy for anything," said Tanner, "in case she thought it meant I owed her."

"That pixie," corrected Idi.

"Pixie, fairy, whatever the difference is, she is incorrigible."

Both Marcus and Idi grinned at Tanner's discomfort.

"I don't think they let pixies marry humans, do they?" Idi asked Marcus.

"Marry!" splurted Tanner, who had just taken a drink. "Oh, Elements bless us, you don't think she wants to marry me, do you?" Marcus and Idi burst out laughing, and then, amid the laughter, a disturbance reached them. As one, they turned to look at what was causing the commotion.

Guards came flooding into the tavern. A mass of black, flowing trousers and tight-fitting shirts came charging towards them, huge, curved swords waving in the air, as the guards yelled out something which, although they couldn't understand, was obviously 'stay put'. Within moments, their table was surrounded by at least twenty men, all glaring at them with deep-brown, hate-filled eyes.

One of them started barking words at them and was obviously frustrated not to receive an answer. The bartender called something across the room and the captain of the group turned his attention wholly towards Marcus.

"So, you offal-eating peasant," the captain said, with precise, clipped words. "You think King Peidro has too many guards, do you?" Marcus, who had been smiling at the obvious slur on his character, suddenly went cold as the captain finished his sentence. *How did he know? They had been very quiet and discreet, hadn't they?*

"I'm sorry, I think there has been a misunderstanding. We're just travellers on the way to the port who stopped for some refreshments. I don't know what you're talking about."

The captain called out something to the bartender and received a response that included a pointing finger. The captain followed the finger until his eyes came to rest on a very old man, sitting on his own across the room. The captain called out something to him, and the old man nodded and stood up.

"I heard them saying they would need to find a way to scale the walls, and also discussing the number of guards. They are definitely planning to harm the king," the old man said with a shaky voice. He hobbled over to them, sweeping his rich, gold-and-orange-coloured robes around him. He had black kohl heavily drawn around his eyes, which made his long, thin face appear ghostlike. Yet, in sharp contrast to his obviously aged skin, his hair was still vibrant and flaming-red. He raised a thin finger, with an extremely long nail, and pointed at the group.

"Enemy," he spat, before lowering his hand and shuffling out of the tavern. The captain instantly barked out an order and the next moment several guards were grabbing each of them. None too gently, the three were hauled from the tavern, and dragged into the busy street. People stopped to stare as the guards whisked them away into the palace. They tried walking but half the time kept ending up being dragged along the path. They reached a narrow entrance and were taken inside the palace, down several long, cold passageways until they found themselves in the dungeons.

A guard quickly took an oversized ring of keys off the wall and opened a cell. Marcus, Idi and Tanner were thrown harshly inside, where they landed on damp, dirty straw. The captain barked orders at the guard with the keys and then left. The three of them stood up slowly, knocking the straw off themselves.

"I've never been arrested in my entire life," said Marcus, with just a little amused awe.

"Probably the easiest way for us to have got into the palace," said Tanner with a grin.

## Chapter 13 – Reputation

The smell of baking wafted temptingly through the house, causing the witches to lift their noses and sniff in deeply, thinking it was good to have Sheryl back!

As she threw herself into her work, outwardly Sheryl appeared the same, but the turmoil inside made her feel as though her organs were being crushed. To be honest, she didn't know how she was going to carry on. Amber had searched the library, trying to find a spell to get Sheryl back her magic, but it seemed none existed, and she was doomed to a 'normal's' life for ever.

Even the children's basic magic lessons were beyond her and she had stopped going to them because the humiliation was too much. *I'll just stay here, and serve Amber.* Yet that resolution held no joy and she knew that tonight, as every night since she had returned home, she would cry herself to sleep.

She paused in the act of kneading the dough, and a tear ran down her cheek and splashed on the wooden table. She smudged her cheek with the back of her arm, but still managed to cover her face in flour. *Not now,* she scolded herself, and went back to making fruit buns.

"Sheryl?"

She looked up in surprise to find Amber standing in the kitchen door watching her.

"Yes?" she answered, trying to sound chirpy. Amber came across the room, her orange and brown chiffon dress rustling like leaves as she walked.

"I think you should marry Sebastian."

"What?" screeched Sheryl.

"You weren't born to be so unhappy, and I am not sure we will ever get your magic back for you. It is obvious that the two of you love each other. I have been praying to the Elements, and I believe this is the best thing for you."

"He's a Hadrian knight; he won't want to marry *me*!"

Amber smiled. Sheryl hadn't denied loving, or wanting to marry, Sebastian.

"Finish what you're doing, and then get washed up. I want to go to town." Before Sheryl could argue, Amber had turned and walked away. Sheryl stared down at the dough, a bit lost for words. However, suddenly, she didn't feel quite so sad, or lonely.

With Belinda watching the baking buns, Sheryl was free to get ready. Running was frowned upon, so she hurried, as fast as a walk would let her, to her room. She possessed three dresses, so choosing one to go courting in was easy. She pulled the simple, deep-green velvet dress out of the cupboard and dropped it on the bed. She washed at the basin on the table and then dabbed lavender oil around her neck. The dress was too loose but there was no time to take it in, so she took a thick ribbon and tied it around her waist to pull it in. *That's better*, she thought, picking up a comb and pulling it through her long, curly locks.

Amber was waiting for her in the yard with two horses. A pang of pain shot through her as she realised she would never be able to fly again. She hadn't mastered flying really well before going on her quest with Sebastian, and for some reason she'd only been able to fly for the shortest of distances, but she had hoped one day to fly as well as Amber. They mounted the horses and set off for the city. Sheryl was grateful Amber hadn't flown there, as that would only have emphasized her own lack of magic.

*Will he want me?*

Lost in her thoughts, Sheryl was surprised to look up and find they had reached Havenshire already. As the horses clopped over the drawbridge, she was suddenly filled with doubt about this hastily made decision. She drew back on the reins to make her horse stop, determined now to return home.

"No," said Amber over her shoulder, sending a spell through the air which took the reins out of Sheryl's hands and delivered them to her. Sheryl's mouth dropped open. *What, I don't have a choice now?*

Providence delivered Sebastian to them, as two men threw him into the road right in front of them.

"Go back to the barracks, knight. Don't come back again unless you're sober." The tavern proprietor made a show of wiping his hands before going back inside.

"Sebastian!" Sheryl dropped down from her horse and ran to his side. She lifted up his head and wiped his hair out of his face. He blinked and smiled up at her.

"My stinking witch," he said with a slur and a hiccup, while reaching up a now-muddy hand and stroking her face. Sheryl pursed her lips at the reference to being stinky. "I missed you," he said and promptly passed out.

"Seems he needs some looking after," said Amber, getting off her horse. "Here, sir," she called to a passing man. "Could you help us put him over the horse, please?" He gave the situation an appraising glance and tutted.

"We got a city to build and protect and yet these here knights think they're above that, getting drunk and causing trouble. You should leave him in the dirt, miss."

"I would really appreciate your help, sir," said Amber with a smile. He tutted again but came over to help them pick Sebastian up and throw him, a bit roughly, over the horse.

"Thank you," said Sheryl.

"You tell him the city deserves more than lazy drunks when he comes round," said the man before going on his way.

Sheryl and Amber led their horses through the winding streets towards the barracks.

"Do you think he gets drunk all the time?" asked Sheryl.

"Did he get drunk when you were travelling together?"

"No."

"Then the question really should be, why is he drunk now?"

At the gates, two guards quickly took Sebastian from his horse and carried him to his room.

"You stay with him," said Amber. I'm going to find Hamish."

Sheryl went without question. She wanted to make sure Sebastian was okay, while Amber went in search of the king.

With Sebastian in his bed and snoring loudly, Sheryl took a moment to look around his sparse room. *We won't be able to stay here.* The room was tiny, with one narrow bed, a chest of drawers and one rickety old chair. Her hand traced along the washbowl on top of the drawers. Cracked, chipped and in need of replacing, the old china bowl was somehow still beautiful. Daintily painted with magpies in various positions of flight, it was an object you wouldn't expect to find in a knight's room. She picked up the cloth lying next to it and dipped it in the clear, cold water. As she was wringing it out, a sparkle in the water caught her attention. She leant over the bowl, peering into the water. *What was that?* Whatever it was had gone, and Sheryl sighed as she turned around and went to sit on the bed. She washed Sebastian's face, gently wiping off the mud from the road.

He moaned and turned over, and Sheryl was left wondering what she was going to do until he woke. She went back to the dresser to put the cloth down and was drawn to the water, which seemed to be sparkling again.

Sometime later, when the room was dark and cold, Sebastian moaned as he came out of his drunken slumber. He stretched and put his hand on his forehead, moaning again at the throbbing under his temple. Into his uncomfortable rousing, the memory of Sheryl leaning over him popped into his mind. His eyes flew open. *Had she really been here?* He pushed the blanket off and slowly swung his legs over the bed and sat up. *I need a drink.* He stood up and moaned as the pain hit his forehead anew, then shuffled over to the stand to get a drink. His legs knocked into something on the floor.

"What?" he said, puzzled. He crouched on the floor, feeling around for whatever it was, and almost froze in shock when he realised a woman was lying on the floor. He stood up and carefully manoeuvred his way around the body to the stand. His hands hovered over the top, looking for his matches. Once found, he struck one and lit the oil lamp. Lifting the glass and metal lamp up, he turned around to look at his feet.

"Sheryl," he said in shock, falling to his knees. He put the lamp by her head and picked up her hand. She was freezing. "Oh, don't be dead," he whispered. He put his ear over her mouth and listened carefully. After a moment, he sighed in relief as he heard her breathing. He shoved his hands under her body and carefully lifted her and lay her down on his bed.

"What are you doing here?" he asked, pulling the blanket over her. "And what's happened to you?" He gave her a gentle shake. "Sheryl?" She didn't respond and he was filled with panic. He needed help and rushed to the door. Pulling it open, he yelled into the corridor of the barracks.

"Help, someone, help."

"Sebastian."

He swung around to see that Sheryl had opened her eyes. "Elements be blessed, you're alright," he said, rushing back to her side. "What happened?" he asked, taking hold of her hand.

"I think I met your mother," she answered softly.

"You did? No, you can't have. She's dead."

"She said to tell you that you will always be her Seb-the-strong."

Sebastian felt chills roll down his spine. His mother had only ever called him that when they were on their own; it had been her secret name for him.

"She told me how to get my magic back," said Sheryl.

For a while Sebastian was too shocked to speak, and their silence was only interrupted when Myles and Torra came rushing into the room.

"What's wrong?" said Myles, his eyes sweeping around the room, looking for what might have caused the distress call.

"I found her on the floor," said Sebastian, not knowing what else to say. Sheryl pushed herself up and indicated for Sebastian to move so she could stand up.

"I came to visit," said Sheryl, brushing her dress down. "I don't know what happened. I must have fainted."

"It isn't appropriate for you to be here," said Myles, his face stern. "Please keep your meetings to public places." With that he turned and left, indicating with his head that Torra should go with him. Torra threw them a grin and then winked at Sebastian before following Myles. Sheryl crossed the room, shut the door quietly, and then looked at Sebastian, who was still a little lost for words.

"Well, you'll have to marry me now, Sebastian. I feel that my reputation has been thrown to the wind. Probably best we're married if we're to go travelling together again, anyway."

"Travelling again?"

"I tell you two things and the one you want to question is travelling?" said Sheryl, putting her hands on her hips. Suddenly the two were smiling at each other.

"I thought you would get your magic back and not want to see me again," said Sebastian. Sheryl walked over to him and offered him her hands, which he took and squeezed tightly.

"Would you like to be my husband, Sebastian?"

"Do eggs come out of a chicken?"

"Good. Do you think there is any chance we might get married in the morning? I'm eager to be off."

"Ugh, I don't know. Where are we going? I'll need to get permission from the king."

"Back, to see Crannog-Fergal."

"But he took your magic. Why would you go back?"

"Because he's a gate-builder."

## Chapter 14 – No Thanks

The lamps hanging from the walls cast a dim light over the cells and guardsmen's area. The place smelt dank and rotten, and cold wind poured in from the barred windows.

"Well, they know we're here now," said Tanner.

"They do indeed," said Marcus, who cupped his hands to form a bowl then whispered into them. He then called to the young guard, "Young man, could you come here a moment, please?"

"What do you want?" the guard demanded, walking over to their cell, officially upright and stiff with a scowl on his forehead.

"Why, to leave, of course," said Marcus, before blowing across his hands. A wispy smoke sprang from his hands and covered the guard's face.

"What?" yelled the guard, blinking like crazy, while swiping at his face, trying to knock the smoke away. Surprise flashed across his face as he crumbled to the floor.

Tanner, without hesitation, pointed to the ring of keys on the wall, and said, "Come here."

They jangled on the wall for a moment, then shot across the room to land in his hands. Just as he was trying the second key in the lock, two birds came fluttering into the room.

"Ah, Valarie, Losia, nice of you to join us," said Marcus. Instantly the girls transformed into Bluedanions.

"Have you found him?" Tanner asked, turning the key and pulling the prison-barred door open.

"We have," said Valarie. "He's in the gardens."

"The gardens?" said Marcus, puzzled.

"How many guards are watching him?" asked Idi.

"None," answered Losia. The men looked at each other and then turned questioningly to the girls.

"It seems he's not a prisoner," said Valarie.

"And what's more, you'll never guess who he's with," said Losia.

"Who?" all three men asked at once.

"Katrina and Gallagher," answered Valarie.

"And Katrina's giving him a whooping," laughed Losia.

"Well, he won't be happy with that," said a female voice. The group turned around defensively to see Queen Orla walking towards them. "Don't be alarmed, and for goodness' sake don't turn me into a mouse or anything," said Orla, throwing her arms out, palms up, in a sign of peace.

"Wouldn't turn the village bully into a mouse," shivered Losia. "No, if I was going to turn you into anything it would be something like... like..." She looked at the queen, trying to figure out what type of animal she looked like. "A cat," she finally finished.

"Oh, I do hope you mean a regal cat, like a panther or a leopard?"

"Maybe a cougar," Losia answered haughtily.

Besides the crown on her head, Marcus recognised Orla from a painting he had once seen of her.

"Your majesty," he said, bowing with a flourish. The others looked at Orla, and then Marcus, and decided they should bow too.

"The Sirocco witch told me you were coming, and that I should hurry here before you start a war. Come along with me. We will go in search of that husband of mine and get this resolved."

The group looked puzzled but following Orla now seemed like the right thing to do.

"I do hope you haven't hurt, him," said Orla, giving the guard on the floor a quick look.

"No harm done, just a sleeping spell," replied Marcus.

"I'd like to meet this Sirocco witch," Losia whispered to Valarie as they left the prison.

"Me too," said Marcus. Idi kept quiet.

A brisk walk and then Orla was ushering them into their private sitting room.

"Piedro," she called as they entered. The king was sitting at a desk writing, and looked up in surprise when she came in with an entourage of strangers.

"Orla?" he said.

"We have guests, darling. Now don't fret, they've only come to see how he's doing, that's all." Piedro stood, his chair scraping along the floor as he pushed it back.

"Not invited guests," he said, staring at the group as they came naturally to form a line in front of him. Orla reached up and kissed her husband on the cheek.

"Now, dear, this is a time for talking, not for huffing and puffing. They might not have been invited, but they were most definitely expected. Come, let us sit in comfort and discuss matters." Orla waved towards the highly decorative tapestry couches that formed a semicircle around the grand fireplace. "Sit, sit," she said, waving at the slightly stunned group as she went over to the wall and pulled on a silk rope. Within moments, the doors opened and a servant entered.

"Refreshments please, Franco." The servant nodded and left straight away. Dubiously, Piedro made his way across the room and stood in front of the fire.

"I trust you had an uneventful journey here?" Orla asked, placing herself delicately on the edge of the couch nearest her husband.

"We came safely, thank you, my lady," said Marcus.

"We've been expecting you ever since we saw the Talian ship in our waters," she said, placing her hands in her lap.

"Yet despite extra guards everywhere, you still managed to enter the palace," said Piedro, standing straight with his hands behind his back, his irritation at the situation clear to all.

"We were arrested, your grace. So, indeed, your guards did their job well," said Tanner.

"You were?" he said, looking at Orla.

"I didn't think our guests should be put in the dungeons, dear. So I brought them along to meet you." Piedro frowned at Orla. Something odd was going on; this was out of character for her.

"A deal was made with Hamish. Why have you come, if not to break that deal?" asked Piedro.

"Because his mother is full of grief, and a lad belongs with his mother," replied Marcus.

Piedro clearly bristled. "Cassandra is not a worthy enough person to raise him," he snarled.

"Begging your pardon, your grace, but you do not know her," replied Idi. "For if you did, you would know she is a caring and loving mother."

"I understand this must be hard for Cassandra," said Orla, "yet you must remember that whatever pain she feels, it is not a tenth of what I felt when she got our son killed. *My* son will never be returned to me."

"We appreciate the pain of your loss," said Valarie. "However, two wrongs do not make a right. Plus, there is more to this tale of sadness than who should raise him; it is his safety that has brought us all here."

"He is completely safe with us," said Piedro.

"We give him every comfort," said Orla.

Marcus and Valarie stared at each other for a moment, both questioning whether they should reveal the truth of Absalom's birth. Valarie gave Marcus a tiny nod of her head. He turned back to face Piedro.

"Your grace, we believe that Absalom is heavily masked with prophecy, and that one day he will rule all of Talia. Because of this possibility, the dark that moves across the land is searching for him, to turn him towards them. I do not know if you have heard of the Sister-witches, but they still influence men with weak hearts to do their bidding. We believe it is imperative that we keep Absalom hidden from the world for as long as possible."

Now it was Piedro and Orla's turn to exchange glances.

"Bluedane also has a prophecy. The Father of Peace will rise between two nations and rule with a firm hand. His name shall be Absalom, king of all. Imagine the joy that took me when I found out that my grandson, born of two nations, is called Absalom. We understand the importance of keeping him safe and raising him to be a righteous ruler. I assure you, he is completely safe here," said Piedro.

Just then there was a tap on the door.

"Enter," called Orla. The doors opened and Franco returned with maids, all carrying silver trays laden with drinks and tiny cakes. They had just finished laying the trays on the table when Absalom came charging into the room, swiftly followed by Katrina and Gallagher and the poor servant he had been fighting with.

"I'm going to have you thrown in prison," Absalom cried over his shoulder, before coming to a halt when he realised his grandparents had visitors.

"Absalom, whatever has happened?" asked Orla, jumping up and going over to him. She reached out to touch his face but he pulled away. He was very aware that he had several cuts on his face and that he was swelling quickly, and could only imagine the colour that was showing.

"This *girl* insulted me. Have her locked up," yelped Absalom.

"I did no such thing. I simply gave you a lesson that you deserved," said Katrina, raising her eyebrows at Absalom and then winking at Idi.

"Katie, what have you done?" said Idi, standing up, obviously cross.

Katrina lost some of her gusto. Maybe besting the future king with the sword and then punching him repeatedly for being rude wasn't such a good thing to have done.

"Orla, lock her up?" Absalom said with fading confidence.

"I'm sure that's not necessary," said Idi quickly. "Katrina, apologise." Katrina looked at Idi. He only used her full name when he was cross. She looked at the floor and chewed her lip. She hated saying sorry. "Katrina," said Idi sternly.

She pulled herself up straight and looked directly at Absalom. "I'm sorry," she said.

Absalom drew his eyebrows together in temper as he looked at her. He knew no one was going to lock her up.

"You better leave Bluedane quickly, *girl*," he said.

"Oh, I will, and I'll be taking you with us, *boy*," she replied.

"No, you won't," he answered with a snap, then paused and looked at all the strangers. "She won't, will she, Grandfather?"

Before Piedro could answer, Valarie stood up. "We will take you home, if you want us to," she said.

"No, thanks," said Absalom quickly. Orla and Piedro smiled widely, while everyone else just looked at him in surprise.

"Don't you want to go home to your mum?" asked Katrina.

"What a prince wants and what a prince has to do are not always the same thing," he answered, looking at her without expression. "Can I go to my room, Grandfather?"

"Yes, of course," Piedro answered.

Katrina watched Absalom leave with mixed feelings; he was a jerk and a bully, so why did she feel that what he had just said was quite noble?

"As you can see, he is not only well looked after but wants to stay. I trust you report that when you return to Havenshire?" said Piedro.

"If I could get into the gardens and kick his arse, then Norvora could certainly get in and take him away," said Katrina.

"How did you get in?" asked Piedro.

"Who is Norvora?" asked Orla

"Moriya brought us here and Norvora is the wizard who is controlled by the Three-witches," replied Katrina.

"Who is Moriya?" asked Piedro.

"The Sirocco witch," replied Orla. Then, looking directly at Marcus, she asked, "This Norvora doesn't know Absalom is here though, does he?"

"I think he does," Katrina said before Marcus could answer. "He's in Bluedane anyway; he would have killed us if Moriya hadn't turned up to save us."

"He's here?" said nearly everyone at once.

"Yes, he ran away just before Moriya arrived, but I think she sent her hound to follow him," said Gallagher.

"This is bad news indeed," said Marcus, "and your grace, even more reason for us to take Absalom, and go into hiding."

"What does he look like? I will send the army to hunt him down and kill him," said Piedro.

"A snake," said Katrina.

"I'm afraid your men won't be able to catch him, your grace. He is a powerful wizard," said Idi.

Ignoring Idi, Piedro turned to Katrina. "I need a proper description, young lady."

"He was a snake," she answered.

"Look..." began Piedro.

"Your grace, he turned up as an old man, changed into his normal appearance briefly and then shape-shifted into the hugest snake I have ever seen," said Gallagher. Orla sat down.

"How is that possible?" asked Piedro.

The visitors looked at each other in surprise. "Do you not have wizards here, in Bluedane?" asked Idi.

"No, of course not. Magic was outlawed hundreds of years ago. It has been extinct since long before we were born," replied Piedro. "To be honest, I find it very hard to believe that it still exists anywhere, and as for changing into a snake, I will only believe that when I see it with my own eyes."

"Happy to oblige," said Losia, standing up. She smiled at Piedro and then shape-shifted into a green snake and slid across the floor towards the queen. Orla screamed and pulled her legs up onto the sofa. Losia changed back to a human-sized pixie, her wings fluttering behind her.

"I am very sorry to have scared you. That wasn't my intention," she said, looking at Orla.

"You're a fairy!" said Orla in shock.

"A pixie," everyone chimed back before Losia could say anything. Losia sat down on the sofa next to Orla.

"Magic is a wonderful thing when it is mastered by the good. Unfortunately, when evil gets a hold of it, it can be terrifying. You must let us protect Absalom, for we are the only ones who can."

## Chapter 15 – Nowhere to Hide

The Grey-moon hung low in the sky, its pale, cool light emanating across the lands of Talia, throwing shadows throughout the Torrean Mountains. The Fart platoon had kept as high as possible within the range to avoid the Great Plains; a few more hours of running and surely they would reach the Wastelands.

Bert led the way, his uncanny sense of direction constantly taking them on narrow pathways off the beaten track, his nose twitching, leading him on through unknown territory with confidence. The ruins of Galbastion, abandoned for hundreds of years, would be their only hope for a future. Bevan wouldn't risk his men in the scorpion-infested land, so if they could just reach there in time they might have a chance. How they would avoid being stung to death was something they would have to worry about once they got there.

Celestine ran at the rear of the group, ensuring no one fell behind. The Fart platoon had dropped into morbid silence a long time ago and, as their energy began to wane, Celestine knew that, before long, they would have no choice but to stop and rest, approaching soldiers or not.

"We'll rest soon," she said, smiling at Timo. He tried to smile back but stopped halfway there. He was hurting all over and trying his hardest not to cry. Celestine looked at his sorrowful face and her heart broke for him. She reached out and took hold of his hand. He looked at her, a little surprised.

"I'm running out of energy," she told him. "I thought you might help me?"

He squeezed her hand tight. "I'll help you," he said with a smile.

Their leathery feet took a bashing against the stones on the path that ran across the mountains and Celestine began to notice blood marks. Enough was enough.

"Halt," she yelled up through the group. Slowly they came to a stop and instantly sat down, inspecting their feet.

"What is it, Celest?" Bert asked, weaving his way through the group.

"We need a rest," she answered.

"We can't afford to rest. If the Tracker platoon finds us here, with nowhere to run or hide, we're dead."

"Look," said Celestine, pointing at some blood on a stone. "Anyone would be able to find us."

Bert looked down at the blood and then around at the platoon, who all sat dejectedly wiping their feet.

"Right," he announced, "two turns of the hourglass for resting and then we go on." There was a very audible sigh from everyone. Some instantly lay down and curled up in a ball to go to sleep, while others began binding their feet with leather straps. Bert and Celestine walked among the group, checking everyone had water, and bent down to talk to those who were binding their feet. The atmosphere of the group had definitely become more cheerful by the time Bert told everyone it was time to leave.

The last goblin had just got to his feet when a silence fell over the group. As one, they turned to look along the path they had just come by. Clearly seen in the distance was a troop of goblins, leapfrogging their way along the path. Bert searched the surrounding area, looking for somewhere that would offer them a little protection against the oncoming battle.

"There's nowhere to hide," said Celestine, coming alongside him. The v-shaped valley, which they were now in, was too steep to climb; the only way in and out was along the path they were on.

"Hurricane," shouted Celestine.

"I'm here," answered Hurricane, moving towards them.

"You're the tallest goblin alive, Hurricane. Take Timo and Daffy, carry them, and run like the wind. Do not stop until you are miles from this area."

"Celestine, I can't do that. I'm the best fighter we have, besides you. I'm needed here," said Hurricane.

"Celestine's right," said Bert.

"We will probably all die here today. If you don't take our youngest and run, they will die here too, and then the Fart platoon will be gone from the history books *for ever*."

Bert rolled his eyes slightly at Celestine's dramatics.

"Take the children," urged O'bane.

"Please," added Thara.

"I want to stay and fight," said Timo. Daffy started crying and farting at the same time.

"Hurricane, they're coming! Go!" yelled Celestine. Hurricane put his club back in his belt, and then, before the children could argue, he picked them both up at the same time, and with them under his arms, he began running.

"May the spirit of Gurenhok be with them," said Thara.

"May the spirit of Gurenhok be with us," replied the rest of the group. They dropped their bags on the ground and moved together to form a wall. They didn't own shields and only Celestine knew how to fight with a sword. The rest pulled out an array of weapons, including hammers and ball and chains.

Bert and Celestine stood in the front, while the rest shuffled tightly behind them, young, old, male and female.

"I'll see you on the other side," Celestine whispered to Bert.

"I wanted you as my mirror reflection," answered Bert.

"I know," replied Celestine.

They watched as the goblins came charging towards them. Bevan had sent the Brutish platoon after them, not the Tracker platoon. They would be dead soon, but not before they had been made to suffer for their failure at the Gap. Resignation fell upon the Fart platoon. There was no hope, but they would die with honour.

Bert looked at the lust for death on the Brutish goblin faces. He didn't understand them. He closed his eyes for a last call to Gurenhok to help them; then, as he opened his eyes, he saw rocks falling down the mountain face. The Brutish goblins came sliding to a halt, banging into each other, as more and more rocks fell. Within moments, the path between them and the other goblins was completely blocked. As one, the Fart platoon turned their faces to look up the mountain, to where the rocks had fallen from. Standing on a high ridge above them was a red fox, his luscious tail waving slowly. The fox regarded the group for a moment and then howled, lifting his head high, before turning and disappearing.

"He couldn't have pushed those rocks?" said Bert quietly.

"Whatever happened has given us a chance, so come on. Let's be gone before they find a way over the fall," replied Celestine. Without hesitation, the group put away their weapons, picked up their bags and went fleeing up the valley after Hurricane.

"It's not good," panted Celestine, waving at Bert. "Got to get... our breath back." Bert put his hand up and the Fart platoon came to a grinding halt. Half the platoon instantly keeled over and lay gasping for air on the floor. The other half bent over, with hands on knees, and tried to calm their breathing.

Bert anxiously looked down the valley and then up. No sign of the Brutish platoon, and also no sign of Hurricane.

"Do you think we should stop for the night? I don't think the Brutish are after us. If they had found a way over the land fall they would be upon us by now," he said to Celestine.

She looked around at the exhausted goblins, their green faces so pale. "Yes, I think we need to stop," she said.

"I'm not stopping," said Thara, straightening up. "Excuse me Bert, Celest, but I need to find my Timo."

"I'll be going too," said Ogwen. "Daffy needs me."

"We should stay together," said Bert.

"Then let's all go," said Wulfgar. A general murmur of agreement went around as the horde dragged themselves back onto their feet and got ready to run again.

"You take the front," Bert said to Celestine, and then they were running again. Calling on the strength of their survival instinct, they raced through the valley as darkness descended.

## Chapter 16 – The Brothers

It was surprising how quickly the people of Havenshire went around doing their normal daily tasks.

"Don't ya be fooled," said James, who had been watching Caldwin's face. "To carry on, to rebuild, these tasks must be done. Yet beneath their apparent acceptance of everything lies their harrowing pain."

"I feel a need to offer them practical help," answered Caldwin, turning to regard James.

"We all do. The place is in tatters. Matthew and Damien are already out in the fields, designing waterways to help with irrigation. John and Anthony are helping with the new city walls. We're all doing our bit, you muppet."

"Those things are worthy, but I want to do something more long-lasting, something that will benefit them for all of time and not just the here and now."

"Okay, I'm intrigued. What'd ya have in mind?"

Caldwin suddenly grinned. "Come on, I'll show you." The two of them set off down the cobbled streets of the city that was hurriedly rebuilding itself. Sidestepping people at work, they made their way to the far west of the city.

\*\*\*\*\*\*\*\*\*\*

"What do you think of our new garb?" asked Anthony.

"Well, I've discovered it isn't very practical for rebuilding walls in," laughed John. "Still, I was fed-up of washing my only outfit and sitting around naked waiting for it to dry, so I guess I should be thankful to the old king for his gift."

"We're all grateful you don't sit around naked any more!" laughed back Anthony. "Still, I'm not too sure I like it."

"Why's that?" asked John, looking Anthony up and down. "I think the dress quite suits you," he added, with mischief in his eyes.

"It's not the habit per se. I like the soft material, but it's the way people look at us." John scrutinised the habit. Made from the softest grey-coloured wool and adorned with the finest silver embroidery, accompanied with a matching cape, where the edges of the cowl were also decorated with silver patterns, it spoke of riches and mystery, and certainly set the Brothers apart from normal folk.

"They're not designed with manual labour in mind, I'll agree. Yet I don't believe the people look at us any differently due to our attire. I believe it has much more to do with the magic they saw during the battle," answered John.

"You mean they fear us."

"No, not fear. More like respect."

"I never wanted to be set apart," replied Anthony.

"We don't always get what we want, you know that."

"John, I fear we will lose ourselves if we stay here. We should continue our studies, become stronger. We need to find a place where we can both practise magic and spend time building our relationships with the Elements."

John reached out and put his hand on Anthony's shoulder. "If you lose yourself, Anthony, I promise to find you and bring you back." The two Brothers hugged briefly.

"Oh aye. What's going on here then?" They looked up to see Kailin, Raymond and Leona smiling at them. They hastily stepped back from each other.

"Where you off to?" asked John.

"Leona says we are to have a meeting, so we're heading to the west side. Come on, no time for messing about," answered Kailin.

"We weren't messing about," piped Anthony. "We were just discussing keeping our beliefs strong."

"He's kidding, Anthony," replied John. "We were ready for a break anyway. Lead the way."

\*\*\*\*\*\*\*\*\*\*

Thomas threw the quill down in frustration. All morning he had been practising writing with his left hand. The squiggly, barely legible writing was an embarrassment. "Why couldn't I have lost my fingers on my left hand?" he demanded of the empty room. He pushed his chair back from the heavy oak desk and went to stand by the narrow slit windows. It was past noon and the morning noise, of hammer and chatter, had paled, with only the occasional tweet from the birds in the castle gardens below to be heard now, as folk retreated for an afternoon rest. He should have been like the others, and gone to help the people of Havenshire restore their lives and their homes. Yet self-pity had crept into his heart and he battled with his own inner demons.

His left hand absent-mindedly stroked his right stump. *I'm a cripple. What could I possibly do to help rebuild the city?* He shook his head to knock the negativity away. That morning, when the Brothers had discussed their plans for the day, they hadn't asked him what he would do. *That's because they know I am of no use, to neither man nor beast.* He growled a moan and slammed his right stump into the cold, stone wall. Pain charged through his arm and he brought his hand quickly to his chest.

"Earth Element, please, let me be of some use. Help me overcome this, this… lack, help me to be strong, I implore you." Thomas leant his forehead against the wall and breathed in deep.

No answer came. No bolt of lightning or roll of thunder. The ground didn't shake, no vision appeared. Just emptiness. He slid down the wall and sat on the floor, leaning his head back against the wall as he closed his eyes. *Who is this Lon? Will I ever meet him? Can he really regrow my fingers?* Still nothing. Well, except for the arrival of the afternoon songbirds outside, who filled the air with delectable trills. The birds' singing filled his mind and suddenly a passage from the ancient books came to him: 'If we should feed and look after the tiniest of birds in the air, then surely we will feed and look after you.' The metaphor implied that whatever he needed would be given to him by the Elements.

His eyes flew open. *Those who can't, teach. That's what they say. That's what I'll do. I will pour my knowledge of the ancient books into anyone who will listen.* He jumped to his feet, suddenly filled with an urge to be in the gardens. Out of his room, along the corridor, down the spiral staircase, and then out into the fresh air. He breathed in deep; it felt good to be alive. He was just about to head into the rose garden when a gentle probing tapped his mind. He stood still and waited. It came again and he realised Raymond was calling to him. *Coming,* he replied, turning towards the path that would take him to the castle forecourt.

*********

"What do you think then?" asked Caldwin.

"Of what?" replied James.

"Of her, of course," said Caldwin, pointing to the building in front of them. The mansion was old and in a poor state of repair, with ivy climbing all over the three-storey building. Several of the glass windows were broken and the paintwork was peeling.

"She's a sorry excuse for a dwelling," said James. "Shame, really – in its day it would have been beautiful."

"And she can be again, if we do her up," said Caldwin with excitement brimming in his eyes.

"Multiple objections run through me mind. What's going on in that noodle of yours, James? There's work to be done fixing up folks' homes, planting, planning, need I carry on? Besides, what would we want with all them there rooms?"

"To build an Academy, that's what," said Thomas, approaching them.

"Hey, Thomas, how did you find us?" asked James.

"I called him," answered Caldwin. "And here come the others," he said, nodding his head up the street. Sure enough, the rest of the Brothers were coming towards them, with Leona skipping beside them.

"Isn't it wonderful?" said Leona, giving James a big hug.

"What's that, my wee one?" asked James.

"Our new home, of course," she laughed. "Come on," she said, grabbing hold of James's hand. "Let's have a look inside."

"Whoa whoa whoa," said James. "Hold onto your horses a moment. We can't just go barging into a house that's not ours."

"The owner is dead," said Caldwin. "I've been making enquiries. He died three years ago, leaving no family to inherit it, so the house has passed to the king's purse."

"Then if it belongs to the king, we should surely not enter," said James.

"Hamish has no need of it, I've already asked him," said Caldwin, grinning. James just shook his head, at a loss for words.

"What do you want with this elephant of a house, Caldwin?" asked Matthew.

"To build an Academy for the people of Talia." He paused for dramatic effect. "To teach them magic." There was a stunned silence.

"Magic isn't something we can just offer out to anyone, you know that, Caldwin. This is a nonsensical idea," said Damien.

"It takes a lifetime to learn deep magic, and more importantly to train and develop a pure spirit," interjected Anthony.

"I agree," said John. "We need to help people rebuild their lives. Not risk their lives by teaching them magic."

"There is a time and a place for everything under the sun," said Leona. Everyone turned to look at her. "Some will plant, some will build, and others will teach. If you knew what little time lay before us, before the Great Battle arrives, you would not hesitate, but would agree and set to work immediately. We will trust the Elements to guide us in all things, and we will *not* fail."

For a moment, no one knew what to say.

"What she said," said Caldwin, flicking his thumb in Leona's direction. The Brothers couldn't help but laugh.

"Getting children to fight your cause now, are you?" laughed John.

"Aye, well, you know me. I will let someone else do the difficult stuff, if I can," laughed back Caldwin.

"Well, then, what are we waiting for?" said Kailin, stepping forward and trying the handle on the old door. It squeaked as he turned it, but not as loudly as the door creaked when he pushed it forward. Leona, who was wearing a habit that matched the Brothers', hopped forward.

"Me first," she declared and skipped inside.

The house was dark, damp and smelly. Dust flew up from the floor as their habits and cloaks swished over the wooden boards. John pointed to lanterns on the wall of the grand hallway, clicking his fingers at them.

"Light," he demanded. The candles instantly burst into flame and a soft light filtered through the dirty glass. Cobwebs hung like lace curtains across walls and ceilings.

"This will take some cleaning," said Kailin.

"We could use magic?" said Damien.

"No, we can't. Not on something so frivolous as cleaning," answered John. "Buckets of water and mops will soon sort this out. It is the repairs that will take more effort."

Caldwin went to the doors on the far side of the hallway that opened up into the gardens. He pulled down the blankets that had been covering them and the afternoon sun came pouring through. He turned a huge key in the lock and then pushed the doors wide open. Fresh air flooded the hallway and all of a sudden the place didn't look so bad.

"The garden is huge, we can grow our own vegetables here," he said, turning around and going to the next set of doors. He pushed open a large wooden door and walked into the library. Leona ran to the windows and started pulling down the blankets. He smiled at her and helped her push the paned-glass windows open.

"This room is for you, Thomas," he called over his shoulder, as he started looking at the books on the shelves. Thomas came and stood beside him and looked in awe at the floor-to-ceiling bookcases that were jampacked with books.

"I won't have enough years to read all these," he whispered.

Caldwin put his hand on Thomas's shoulder. "Just read the important ones," he advised with a smile.

"Good heavens, look at this kitchen," cried James. They turned and headed back into the hallway to see which way the kitchens were. They heard a clanging to the right and went in search of the others. The kitchen was almost as big as the one in the castle and was fully equipped with pots and pans of all shapes and sizes. James checked inside the big metal oven and came up quickly as the stench nearly knocked him over. "Well, we won't be eating in here tonight," he declared.

The group meandered slowly from room to room, in awe at how big the place was. They came upon the ballroom and gazed admiringly at the beautiful tapestries that still hung on the walls.

"I hope we're not too late to preserve them," said Raymond, gingerly touching the silk pictures.

"This will be the classroom," declared Caldwin. "What say you, Thomas?"

Thomas turned around slowly, taking in the huge room with its high ceiling. "It's perfect," he finally answered.

"What shall we call it?" asked Leona.

"Call what?" asked John.

"This place, of course," she answered, with a smile that said you silly thing.

"Selwin Academy," said Thomas straight away. The others looked at him.

"Now *that* is perfect," said Anthony.

"Hear, hear," said John. "A fitting tribute and memorial to a man who delighted in watching things grow."

"Hear, hear," resounded the response from all the Brothers.

"Hear, hear," said Leona. "Can the wolves come and live with us too?" The Brothers laughed.

"I don't think that would go down too well with the people of Havenshire, Leona. Best they stay in the wilds, that's their home," said John. Leona's face dropped in disappointment.

"I'll take you out to see them whenever you want, though," said Caldwin, and her smile sprang back.

## Chapter 17 – Crannog's Gang

"That must have been the quickest marriage ever to take place," said Sebastian as they approached the stables.

"Are you moaning already, husband?" Sheryl answered.

He put back his head and laughed heartily. "Never. I hate spectacles."

"So do I, but a little bit of a celebration might have been nice, although obviously not appropriate, in times like these."

Sebastian touched her shoulder gently, and then, as his hand dropped away, he asked, "So, are you going to tell me why we need a gate-builder, wife?" Having never thought he would ever marry, he was surprisingly happy to be so.

"Your mother told me he can build me a gate to a place where unicorns live, and they can give me my magic back."

"I don't know what's harder to believe, that you spoke with my mother or that unicorns exist."

"But you don't find it weird that other places exist?"

"No. I think I would find it harder to believe Talia was the only place there is. Tell me about my mother, did she look well?"

Sheryl threw him a sideways glance. *How much to say?*

"Well, it was kind of a blurred vision and she came fading in and out. Really, it was her voice that came through clearly, and that was sweet and gentle."

"She was always gently spoken, my mother. Everyone loved her. Do you remember anything specific?"

"Only her flaming-red hair," Sheryl said with a sigh. "It was beautiful."

"My mother didn't have red hair," said Sebastian, stopping mid-stride.

"Oh? Maybe it wasn't her then?"

"But you said…"

"What she told me to."

"But you realise, don't you, that if this spirit lied about being my mother, she could also have lied about getting your magic back?"

"I am not sure who it was, Sebastian, but I have to hope in this."

Sebastian put his hands on her shoulders and made her look up at him. "Sheryl, what if this place doesn't exist?"

"Then I promise to accept my situation, but until I know for sure, I want to have hope."

He looked at her for a moment, and then nodded. "Okay, hope it is. For now."

The stablehand had two horses waiting for them. "They're the best we can spare," he said as they approached. "Running short on horses, we are. So if you would be kind enough to return them in good health, well that would be appreciated."

"We'll certainly do our best, Jack," said Sebastian.

Sheryl climbed on her horse and then looked at Jack with a twinkle in her eyes. "We'll try not to let the scorpions kill them," she said, nudging her horse to move away.

"She's only joking," Sebastian added quickly.

"Thank goodness for that," replied Jack, wiping his brow.

Once over the drawbridge the two nudged their horses into a canter. As they sped through the lands surrounding Havenshire they were amazed to see that farmers were in the fields ploughing.

"Amazing how life carries on after what we've been through," Sebastian called to Sheryl.

"We need to eat, and people need a reason to go on," she answered.

They rode in silence for the rest of the day, both eager to reach the Treegothin ogre's home. When the light began to dim, they searched for a place to rest for the night.

"Do you think you could ride through the night?" Sebastian asked. Sheryl looked at him, his tense body and hushed words revealing his worry.

"Yes," she nodded at him. He smiled slightly in relief.

"We'll go slow for the horses' sake, and rest as soon as we can. I just think it would be best to reach the Wastelands as soon as possible and, to be honest, we have no idea what kind of reception we'll receive if seen by anyone in Rhayador or Ilfordton. I'm hoping, if we go swiftly through the night, we might pass without seeing anyone at all."

"Why do you think they ignored the king's call for assistance?" asked Sheryl.

Sebastian scratched his head. "We don't know. They may have been attacked before us for all we know; either that or they chose to protect themselves behind their castle walls. We never received word from them. Whatever the reason, I want to skirt around their lands as much as possible without delaying us too much."

They headed south along the River Haven until Ilfordton was left behind them. As the Grey-moon of winter slowly began her morning ascent, showering the lands in her watery light, Sebastian pulled on the reins and brought them to a stop.

"We'll stop here by the river for a while and rest the horses, then head to the south of Rhayador as far as possible and hope for the best." His dismounted and reached up to lift Sheryl off her horse. She winced as he put her on the ground.

"Eee, what I wouldn't give to have a bit of magic in me now," she said, shaking her body and trying to straighten up.

"It's a piece of dung being normal, isn't it?" Sebastian laughed, then, seeing Sheryl's sad face, stopped abruptly. "I'm sorry," he said, wrapping his arms around her.

She lay her head against his chest and let his love comfort her. "It's not all bad," she said with a smile, looking up at his chin.

They rested longer than Sebastian would have liked, and the Grey-moon was already starting her descent when he woke Sheryl and told her it was time to go. They skirted around the farmlands south of Rhayador, keeping to the wild as much as possible. Although it was a relief not to come across anyone, Sebastian began to worry as to the reason why.

The Grey-moon had dropped behind the horizon and the Silver-moon twinkled down on them as they reached the edge of the Wastelands.

"I never thought I would come back here," said Sebastian.

"Nor me, not so quickly anyway," answered Sheryl.

"We'll stay on the borderlands as much as possible, following the Gothin River, and head north until we reach the Elleon Ripple. If we stay in the shadow of the Elleon Mountains, we should be clear of the scorpion-infested parts. Hopefully, Crannog-Fergal will come out to meet us before we get ourselves into trouble."

\*\*\*\*\*\*\*\*\*\*

The Fart platoon tumbled to a halt, most of them instantly collapsing on the floor while both panting and farting simultaneously. The disappearance of the Grey-moon made the icy wind of winter feel bitter.

"We should have found them by now," panted Bert, bending over with his hands on his knees. Celestine remained upright but her chest hurt with each breath as the icy-cold air mingled with her hot breath.

"How can he have run so far when he's carrying Timo and Daffy?" asked Celestine.

"Well, you did pick the fastest runner to take off with the young ones," said Bert, straightening up.

"Right, so this is all *my* fault, is it?" demanded Celestine, her face turning blue in anger.

"Oh, don't get all dramatic on me now," sighed Bert.

"Right, so who was it that wanted to help the stinking humans in the first place? You were so quick and eager to desert our own kind, you brought this down on us. You knew Bevan wouldn't stop until he'd killed us." Suddenly the anger fell away from her and she looked at Bert in shock. "I'm sorry, Bert, I didn't mean it. I'm just so worried, that's all. What is to become of us? We are so few and Bevan's army is countless. We have nowhere to live or hide. Talia isn't that big and wherever we go he'll find us." There was a catch in her voice and Bert took a step forward and reached up to touch her face.

"I will find us somewhere safe to live, I promise." For the first time in his life, Bert watched a tear roll down Celestine's face. As he brushed the tear away with his finger, a stink wafted through the group. Bert smiled.

"Hurricane!" said nearly all of them at once. Within seconds, they were all on their feet and trotting in the direction of the smell. They followed it a short distance and had no trouble at all finding the source of the stinking fart.

Hurricane lay on his back, Timo and Daffy on top of him while he pinned them to his huge chest with his arms. He had manoeuvred himself under tall ferns but his boots were clearly on display for all to see. Bert gave them a gentle kick, and Hurricane was awake and sitting up instantly, pushing Timo and Daffy behind him, declaring, "You'll not have the last of our clan. By all that I have, I will kill you first!" He sprang to his feet, thrusting his dagger at them.

"Wahoo, Hurricane, it's alright. It's only us," yelled Bert, stepping back just in time to evade the swinging dagger. A moment's surprise crossed Hurricane's face and then he was throwing himself around Bert and squeezing the breath out of him.

"Put him down," said Celestine. "Before you break his ribs." Hurricane dropped Bert, who crumpled somewhat, then he reached over to hug Celestine.

"You're okay, thanks. I'll keep my breath in me," said Celestine, putting up her hands and backing away. Hurricane dropped his hands to his side and gave a kooky grin. Thara charged at him and threw her arms around him, and he patted her on the top of her head while still smiling at everyone.

"Thought I was never going to see you again," he said.

"Oh, ye of little faith," said Celestine. "Thought you knew I could fight off an army?" Hurricane's eyes nearly popped out.

"You killed them?" he asked.

"Actually, we didn't fight anyone," said Bert. "It seems the Elements were with us, for there was a landslide that miraculously fell so as to separate us from, and hopefully kill, the Brutish platoon."

Bert looked around at everyone. "I know you're all tired," he said in a tone of authority, "but we need to keep going. The Grey-moon has set and who knows what will happen before it rises once more? We need to reach the Wastelands as soon as we can and take our chances there with whatever happens."

There was no grumbling, even from the oldest of the Fart platoon. They knew if there was a way through the mountain path, the Brutish, and maybe other platoons, would find it and come after them.

They formed a single line and set off at a trot through the last part of valley before reaching the edge of the desert.

\*\*\*\*\*\*\*\*\*\*

He wasn't sure he liked the red-headed woman who stood before him, and he definitely didn't like the news she'd just given him.

"But I likes it here," he protested, banging his huge, stone-like hands on the table.

"Crannog-Fergal, don't be childish. Why would you want to stay here for… what, maybe another hundred years? The loneliness is too much for anyone to bear. I thought you would be happy to have a new family around you?"

"Humans and goblins are *not* family, they're irritating flees that need to be eaten or crushed," Crannog replied sullenly.

"Really? Why did you help Sebastian and Sheryl then?"

"Cos I wanted her magic, that's why."

"Yet you helped them before you knew she had magic."

"How do you know?"

Moriya smiled at him. "I just do. The same way I know that these humans and goblins are going to become your new family and that you'll grow to love them."

"No ogre and goblin has ever been friends before in the history of Talia."

"History has gone. Today is here and tomorrow will be however we choose it to be."

"Uggh?"

"Do you choose the history of the Treegothin ogres to be… Crannog-Fergal died alone and miserable and will never be remembered or written about in the books of Shyne? Or would you prefer… Crannog-Fergal, the great ogre, who helped save the world of Talia, much loved and talked about among the humans and goblins alike."

"Much loved?"

"Which would you choose?"

"Well, I think, as the last living Treegothin ogre, that it is my duty to ensure we are remembered."

"Good, that's settled then. Sheryl and Sebastian arrive first, coming from the south. The Fart platoon will arrive shortly after, coming down from the north. Take them to the place where the Avrintarian ogres lived and keep them safe."

Crannog opened his mouth to ask questions but she had disappeared.

"Women," he muttered. "So rude, so demanding." He pulled on his old leather waistcoat, picked up his staff and went charging through the tunnels.

As soon as he was in the open he could smell the humans. Boy, but they stank of soap and body odour. How was he going to live with that? His stone-like body stomped across the desert and sent vibrations rippling through the cracked earth. He heard the horses neighing in fear before he caught sight of Sheryl and Sebastian, who were fighting desperately to keep their mounts under control.

Both Sheryl and Sebastian slid off the horses and held them by the bit while stroking their heads and whispering to them. By the time they had finally calmed down, Crannog was standing in front of them.

"Well, you survived the scorpions then," declared Crannog. Sheryl was about to make a sharp remark about not having her magic to help them but changed her mind. She needed this gruff ogre to build her a gate.

"Nice to see you again, Crannog-Fergal, Oath-Keeper and Gate-Builder. I trust you are well?" said Sheryl, with a sweet smile.

Crannog sighed. "This isn't going to be easy for me. You humans smell awful and you women always want so much. With your smiles and pleasantries comes a "can you just", to be sure. Come on then, let's get back." Sheryl looked at Sebastian, puzzled, but he was just grinning.

Back at the entrance to his underground labyrinth, Crannog pushed open the door. He swung his head towards it, indicating they should enter.

"You haven't asked why we are here," said Sheryl.

"Plenty of time for talking later. I'm having a very hectic day. Come on, hurry up."

Sebastian nodded at Sheryl that they should go in. Once they had led the horses into the tunnel, Crannog let the door slam behind them.

"Hey!" yelled Sebastian, banging on the door. "What's going on?"

"Got another tiresome errand to deal with. Back soon," said Crannog. They heard the boom of his steps as he went marching away. With no way of opening the gigantic door, the two of them led the horses down into the open caverns that served as the ogre's home.

"Sweetness and light, I forgot how much it smelt down here, and Crannog has the audacity to proclaim we smell!"

said Sheryl, looking around the huge room that hadn't changed one iota.

"He didn't seem surprised to see us, did he?" said Sebastian.

"No, in actual fact it looked like he was out looking for us," replied Sheryl.

The Fart platoon heard the ogre approaching long before he came into sight. Celestine was excited beyond belief that she was about to meet an ogre, all of whom were considered to be long since dead. Bert pulled her sharply downwards when the sound announced the ogre had reached the mouth of the valley opening.

Daffy clenched tight, but it was no good – fear always made her tummy sizzle with wind. Pip, pip, pip. Little particles of smelly air made their escape; she covered her head to hide, believing for sure that the ogre would come and eat her when he knew how good she smelt.

"Geez, you guys, do you think you can honestly hide from me smelling like *that*?" sighed Crannog. One by one the goblins all began popping their heads up over the tops of rocks and ferns where they'd been hiding.

"Who did that?" hissed Obane, glaring at Timo.

"Wasn't me," piped Timo. "Why do you always think it's me?"

"Wasn't me," declared Wulfgar, coming out from behind his rock.

"Nor me," chirped in Bert, also standing up.

"Honestly, Bert," said Celestine, giving him an annoyed look. "It doesn't matter who did it – he could smell us anyway."

Ogwen, who had been hugging Daffy tightly, gave a very audible sigh, which instantly gave away the fact that either she or her daughter were responsible.

Hurricane came up behind them and ruffled Daffy's hair. "Have to say, Daffy, I've never heard such dainty farts," he said with a large grin. Daffy got the giggles and tried to hide her face behind her hands.

"Well, this is all… a bit too much, if I'm honest. I wish you'd get a move on, I want to be home," grumbled Crannog. The goblins slowly emerged and came to assemble in front of him. They weren't even as high as Crannog's knees and had to lean backwards to look up at him.

"What is it you want, ogre? If it's not to eat us?" asked Bert.

"Apparently, you're my new family, although to be honest I was doing very well on my own. I don't really know why she thinks I need the company of smelly little green things."

"Actually, you don't smell so good yourself," said Timo, screwing up his nose.

"What?" said Crannog, in total surprise. "Ogres don't smell."

"Well, maybe not among your own kind, but I'm afraid you really do smell to us," said Wulfgar.

"Smell like what?" asked Crannog, looking hurt.

"Bad compost," shouted up Bert. Thara gave him a quick flick on his ear. "What?" he said, looking at her miffed.

"Manners, child, that's what," she answered.

"Better than smelling like rotten eggs," replied Crannog, winking down at Bert. Bert grinned up at him, instantly liking this ogre.

"So, can we get going, or what?" asked Crannog.

"And you're not planning to eat us?" asked Bert.

"Can't eat family. Family is family. Got to stick together, got to love each other. Anyway, the red-headed lady said we'll make a good family." Everyone was puzzled, even Crannog, who was rubbing his forehead with the back of his hand as if bewildered. "Can't remember the last time I ate anything other than roots anyway, so don't know what you're worried about."

"Who is this red lady?" asked Celestine.

"Ooo, *crazy* lady with fiery red hair. One minute I was on my own, then the next she was there. And then, puff, just like that she's gone again. Anyway, she sent me to fetch you, so are you coming?" Bert and Celestine looked at each other.

"Yes," said Bert, with sudden hope rising in his chest. "Yes, we will come with you, great big ogre. Lead the way!"

"Name's Crannog-Fergal, Oath-keeper and Gate-builder," said Crannog, squatting down. "Anyone need a ride?"

"Yes!" screeched Timo and jumped up onto the ogre's outstretched hand.

"Timo," yelled Thara in sudden fright the ogre would eat Timo after all. But Timo was laughing as Crannog lifted him up onto his shoulder.

"Anyone else?" he asked. Suddenly there was a surge forward from everyone except Bert and Celestine. They stood back in amused disbelief as one by one the entire Fact platoon scrambled onto some part of the ogre's body.

"I have space in my waistcoat pockets still, if you want to climb aboard?" Crannog asked.

"Why not?" said Celestine, who hadn't admitted to anyone that her feet were killing her. Crannog reached out and picked them up, gently putting them in his top pockets. They were taller than the pockets and, to stop themselves falling out, crouched down and held on tight. They both felt a bit wobbly as they looked down at the ground so far below.

It wasn't long, with his huge strides, before they were back at the Treegothin door. Crannog crouched down and the goblins jumped off, laughing at the speed with which they had just crossed the desert.

"That's put some distance between us and the Brutish platoon," whispered Celestine.

"Yes, and with any luck they'll think the ogre has eaten us as our footsteps disappear when his arrived," said Bert. For the first time in a long while Celestine smiled, and Bert so wanted to rub

her nose.

## Chapter 18 – Knowledge Is Power

The greenery had long gone. In its place, the lands were shrouded in the white reflections of ice-covered greys and browns. If it hadn't been before the cock's crow and so cold, Idi might have appreciated the Grey-moon's handiwork. Instead, pulling his warmest woollen cloak around him, he groaned.

"I'm never going to be able to do this, Marcus. Let's go back before we freeze to death."

"You have the power of words inside you, Idi. Release them and set that old lightning tree on fire, then you'll be warm enough."

"I've tried, I can't do it."

"You mean you don't want to do it."

"I'd like to be tucked up in bed if I'm honest; I don't know why you dragged me out here before dawn. What does the early hour have to do with learning magic?"

"Attitude."

"You'd have an attitude too, if I was making you do something you didn't want to do."

"The early hour is to reveal your attitude." Idi ground his teeth. He was tired of always being tested, tired of Marcus always looking at him to 'be' more than he was.

"We've been in Bluedane for an entire cycle of the Silver-moon and yet your magic is no stronger than it ever was."

"I'm sorry."

"What for?"

"Disappointing you, of course."

"You do not disappoint me, son." The two men looked at each other, their breath swirling in freezing puffs before them. The fire lesson was over; there would be no changing Idi's mind today.

"So, you don't want to set fire to the lightning tree, but you *do* want to go back to the warmth of the palace?" said Marcus.

Idi grinned. "I sure do."

"Go!" demanded Marcus, and the two horses that had carried them miles across the plains north of the city suddenly fled.

"Hey!" yelled Idi, raising his hand as if to stop them. But they were gone, galloping across the frozen earth, steam flying from their nostrils.

"What did you do that for? It will take two days to run back to Bluedane."

"Not for me," grinned Marcus, who turned to face the city. "I'll see you back there. Don't be long or there'll be no breakfast left for you." With that, Marcus hit magic-timing and became a blur as he streaked across the lands, overtaking the horses and disappearing from sight. Idi groaned, dropped his head for a moment in defeat, and then started running. *Faster*, he yelled at his magic, and his legs did fill with strength and enable him to run faster than he'd ever gone before. But he couldn't catch up with the horses. *Faster*, he demanded again. He felt his magic surge through his body and, for a moment, excitement hit him as he thought he was going into magic-timing. Instead, his legs lost their coordination and sent him tripping over his own feet, crashing to the ground.

"Damn!" he yelled, pushing himself up. He looked down at his knees. There were rips in his trousers and his skin was cut and bleeding. Without thinking, he put his hand over them and sent healing power into them. The cuts began to shrink and then were gone.

"Why do you think it is, that you can heal so easily, and yet find other magic so hard?" Idi spun around in shock to see a red fox looking at him. He looked beyond the fox to see who had spoken, but no one was there, meaning only one thing: it was the fox who'd asked the question.

"Who are you?" Idi asked.

"That's a very good question. Who are *you*?"

Idi pushed down with his hands to push himself upright, but something was wrong. He looked down at his arms to find they had gone. In their place were the legs of a fox.

"What?" he yelled, trying to stand up. Instead, he found himself on all fours; he spun his body round, trying to see all around him. A big bushy tail flicked in the air near his face as he spun. "What have you done to me? Who are you?" Just then, the sound of a hunting horn bellowed across the land.

"Oh dear, I thought we had longer to talk than that. Quick, we best get going before the hounds are upon us." With that, the beautiful red fox turned and started running northwards. For a moment Idi thought of running back to the palace, but he could see the hounds, their legs bouncing as they raced towards his scent. He looked beyond the dogs to the equestrians. *Maybe they don't intend to kill, just catch and release.* The adrenalin of fear was making his heart pound fast in his chest, almost hurting his ribcage. He tried for a moment to turn himself back into a man, but he couldn't do it.

They were getting close now; he could hear their panting and smell the scent of the hunt. Idi turned and ran. *Faster,* he cried, and his paws fell in front of themselves in rapid succession, speeding him across the plains faster than any other fox had ever run. He was too fast for the hounds and, as he realised he was leaving them behind, his heart started slowing slightly and the fear began to subside. In the distance he could see the red fox waiting for him. *What else should I do?* He raced towards her, with the sudden thought that he wanted to fight this talking animal, and bring her to her knees.

As soon as he thought he was almost upon her, she seemed to sense his intent, for she turned and started running across the plains towards the Abscindo river. *I'll get you. Faster, faster.* Magic flowed through his limbs and he ran so fast he became a blur. The fox had stopped by the river, and seemed to be waiting for him. Just as he was about to reach her, he came out of magic-timing and leapt at her. As he crashed onto the ground where she'd been, she disappeared. Idi landed hard on the earth and skidded towards the river. He managed to scramble around and just stop himself before he went in. The river would be ice-cold and the possibility of the shock killing him, when he was so hot, was great.

He made himself stand up and turn around to look for her. A short distance away stood the Sirocco witch. *I should have known.* He felt a tingling in his body and then he was himself once more.

"Why do you not call on your magic like that all the time?" she asked.

"I don't know."

"That's a lie." She pointed at him and suddenly he was rising off the ground. His arms and legs flapped about in the air as he tried to get himself back down. Moriya flicked her finger at him, and he was picked up and thrown into the icy river. The shock was horrendous and he thought that alone might kill him as his head burst through the water and came up for air. He gasped deeply and then swam as fast as he could to the bank, where he scrambled out a shivering mess.

"What did you do that for? I'll get pneumonia."

"Oh dear."

"What?" snapped Idi. He started coughing and his chest was racked with pain. His eyes became sore and itchy and his nose began to run. He coughed again and the sound, even to his own ears, was deep and rattling. He was bent double coughing and looked up at the witch from his contorted position.

"No one gets pneumonia that quickly!"

"But that was what you declared over your life, so you brought it upon yourself."

"I didn't bring it on myself, you're doing this."

"That's a lie." Again his body was picked up and dropped into the lake. It took him much longer to get to the bank this time; coughing kept making him sink and his body ached badly, making movement hard. He crawled out of the river. He lay there, his body shaking violently as he coughed and shivered. Sweat ran off his forehead and mingled with the icy river drops that were forming tiny icicles all over his body.

"Stop," he pleaded with chattering teeth.

"Speak, the truth, boy."

"I… am… healthy," he stammered. Instantly the fever left him, but he was still freezing and his teeth were knocking. He clutched his body, rolled onto his side, and forced himself to stand up. He was shaking from head to foot.

"What are you?"

"Iiiii ammm healthyyyy," he stuttered. His magic raced through his body, returning warmth everywhere it touched. His shivering stopped and he stood up straight.

"Why do you not speak your magic all the time?"

"I don't know."

"That's a lie." Once again he was sailing through the air and unceremoniously dropped into the river. This time he was at the bank and climbing out in moments. He stood before the Sirocco witch with anger mounting. He glared at her and didn't notice that his clothes were instantly dry.

"What do you want of me?" he demanded.

"Tell me why you don't use your magic."

"I don't know!" he barked back. A moment later he was storming out of the river again.

"Tell me why you don't use your magic!"

His eyes were blurred as anger swirled inside him. His hands curled into tight fists, but he didn't answer straight away. He'd had enough of the icy water.

"I'm afraid," he finally said.

"Of what?"

"Of losing myself." One moment she was across the clearing from him; the next she was standing right in front of him, her face kind and gentle.

"Tell me," she said softly.

"The day Katrina killed the dragon I nearly lost myself." He looked into her speckled green eyes and felt her love seep into him. "The magic was too strong; it wanted to take control of me." He looked at her, the shame he felt at fearing magic lying heavy in his heart, but her look was one of understanding. "I have come to like the person I am, and I don't wish to be consumed by something larger than myself. I fear I will lose everything, that nothing, not even the love I have for Katrina, will remain should I submit to it." Idi dropped his head feeling crushed by his confession. The Oracle had told Marcus that he was going to save the 'One', but he didn't want to do it if it meant losing everything else. For the first time in his life, he felt loved, and the fear of losing that was too great. Moriya reached out to touch Idi's face and make him look back at her.

"Fear is a necessary and complex emotion, but fear should never be the reason why we don't progress. If you don't wish to be on the path the Elements have set before you, simply pray and ask them to remove you from it. But Idi, I must remind you that you promised to dedicate your life if the Elements helped the people of Havenshire survive. Do you wish to take back that pledge?" Idi looked at her and knew in an instant that he didn't.

"No," he said softly, shaking his head.

"Why do you think the Elements would give you the love of Katrina and Marcus only to snatch it away from you again?"

"I don't understand their ways. Why do they let Norvora live? Why weren't the Sister-witches killed when they were caught? Why did so many have to die from the touch of the demons?"

"These are fair questions. Yet, this is not the time to answer them. One day you will come before the Elements and see why all things fall the way they do. Until that day they ask that you trust them."

It was illogical and annoyingly abstract, and yet acceptance flooded through him and with that came peace.

"I will tell you this much. The reason why you live, is to learn how to love and to accumulate knowledge. Knowledge is powerful, Idi. Mix the right proportions of love, knowledge and the magic of words together, and then, who knows what you might accomplish?"

Idi looked at her, puzzled, trying to absorb her meaning.

"Your breakfast is getting cold."

Idi looked up and realised they were standing in the palace gardens.

"Will I see you again?" Idi asked.

"Yes." Then she was gone. Idi's stomach grumbled and he chuckled. *Really? I've been abandoned in the middle of nowhere, turned into a fox, chased, nearly drowned, and still I want feeding?* The smell of cooking came wafting through the air and his stomach growled louder. He laughed and set off at a slow run to the kitchens.

## Chapter 19 – Family

The last of the goblins had climbed off Crannog and now an awkward silence filled the huge cavern, everyone just slightly unsure what was going to happen next.

"You're not going to eat us, are you?" piped Timo. Thara hastily covered his mouth with her hand; nevertheless, she looked up, worried, as she waited for the ogre's reply.

"Not today, young man." Crannog laughed at his own joke, but no one else saw the funny side and so he stopped. "Been a very long time since I've eaten any meat. I don't think it would be to my taste any more."

"We are very grateful to you for bringing us to the safety of your home, Crannog-Fergal, but do you mind if I ask why?" said Celestine.

"Like I said, you're my new family," answered Crannog. Everyone looked puzzled, including Sheryl and Sebastian, who both thought that maybe the ogre had lost his marbles. "We're going on a trip," announced Crannog, seemingly oblivious to everyone's bewilderment.

"I like trips," announced Daffy. "Can we go to the sea? I've never seen it before."

"Ugh, no," answered Crannog. "We have to go to the far east of the Torrean Mountains."

"Why?" asked Sheryl.

"To build a gate, of course. That is why you've come, isn't it? To help me build a gate that's large enough for you to pass through to another world."

"How do you know that?" asked Sheryl.

"Irritating redhead told me, that's how."

"A-hum," coughed Bert. "That's very interesting. However, us goblins can't go with you, I'm afraid. If we go back out towards either the Torrean Mountains or the Great Plains, we'll be set upon by very angry platoons, who will take great delight in ripping this new family of yours to shreds."

"Family is family," said Crannog. "We take care of each other. So no platoon will reach you, without reaching me as well."

"That is a wonderful thing to say," said Celestine, "but you should know that there are thousands of goblins who want to kill us."

"What they have in numbers, I have in knowledge. Do they know the pathways through the Rainbow caverns?"

"No one knows them," replied Bert.

"But you see, I do," said Crannog. "I know many things that the creatures of Talia have forgotten, for I have been here since the beginning. The Treegothin and the Avrintarian ogres once worked together to build the pathways under Talia so that we might travel without being seen."

"Oh, I love secret things," chirped in Timo.

"Why do we need to go east to build the gate?" asked Sebastian.

"You humans do make me laugh. How you have lived so long when you lack brains has always been a mystery to me. Because there are no redwood trees left around here, of course; in fact, there are very few trees left at all. Now, if you don't mind, I am exhausted. I've not spoken so much in near on twenty years, and I need some sleep." He paused for a moment, looking around at everyone. "I don't have anything to feed you with, but there is fresh water in the trough over there. You should get some sleep because we will be walking for many days and I am not too sure you will want to stop to rest in the Rainbow caverns." Then, with no preamble, Crannog dropped to the ground, curled up in a ball and went to sleep. Within moments his snores were racketing around the room.

"I wish I could go to sleep that quickly," said Sheryl. As one, the goblins all turned around to look at her. Sebastian put his hand on the hilt of his sword. Celestine and Bert moved forward to come before Sheryl and Sebastian. For a moment, they eyed each other with suspicion.

"I'm Sheryl, and this is Sebastian," said Sheryl.

"I'm Bert, and this is Celestine." He paused for a moment, weighing them up. "If someone had predicted that I would call a human family a short time ago, I would have killed him for insulting us. Yet, you are not the first humans we have come across, and the others I would have been quite happy to take into our family, so my eyes now see things differently. And you, big fighting man, how do you see things?"

For a moment, Sebastian was lost for words. Goblins were the bane of Talia, mutilating the countryside, killing cattle, causing havoc, and seemingly just for the fun of it. Up until this moment, he would have been happy slicing off the head of any goblin he came across.

"We live in strange times," he answered, "where our enemies become our friends, and our friends are hard to find. I believe in family. We…" He flicked his thumb between himself and Sheryl. "…Have just become husband and wife, and one day I hope very much to start a family together." Sheryl looked at him, quite surprised; she hadn't known that. "But family is more than blood, it is bond. An unseen agreement that we'll look out for each other and a silent pledge always to protect one other. So if Crannog is right, and we are to become one family, then I say my eyes have also been opened, and I hope they will never be closed again." Sebastian held out his hand. "It is a pleasure to meet you." Bert reached up and, taking Sebastian's hand in his, brought it to tap against his chest. Sebastian gently pulled back on Bert's hand and, leaning down, tapped it against his own chest, in the symbol of welcoming someone new to the family.

A short time later the goblins were also asleep; the relief of being safe, mingled with total exhaustion, had sent the group into a snoring, farting heaven. Sheryl and Sebastian moved out of the room into one of the great hallways to get away from the overpowering smell. They lay curled up on a blanket, Sebastian's arms wrapped tightly around Sheryl. He kissed the top of her head.

"You know I can't come with you, don't you?" he said.

"Yes, I understand."

"I am sworn to Hamish. My honour demands that I return to his side. He granted me a short leave of absence, but my oath as a Hadrian knight binds me to always be by his side until he releases me."

"I know. It's going to be alright. I will return to you as soon as I can."

"I hope that won't be too long, my love."

"So do I."

\*\*\*\*\*\*\*\*

The journey through the caverns had inspired a mixture of awe and fear. The beauty of the colours in the deepest realms of the earth had been breathtaking, especially the red caves where stalactites looked like they were dripping blood. But the cold had been unbearable and Crannog had been right – they hadn't slept through one night. They had taken short, sharp rests and carried on as quickly as they could. An eeriness seeped off the walls and Sheryl couldn't help but let her imagination run wild as she dreamt of all manner of monsters lurking down there. Silly, really, to think anything could survive in such cold, but more than once she was sure she heard shuffling in different tunnels, and sometimes she was positive she saw the reflections of eyes watching them. One thing was for sure: she was extremely relieved when at last Crannog brought them to a door to the outside.

It took all of Crannog's strength to push the door open, and when he finally did they could see the reason for the resistance. Heavy growth now covered the Avrintarian entrance and a plethora of ferns and ivy acted better than a lock. Still, after a lot of pushing, and a great deal of mutterings, Crannog was finally able to push it open wide enough to go through. The rush of fresh air stung Sheryl's chest and for a moment she went dizzy and found herself falling. Celestine and Thara were instantly by her side.

"It will be fine in a moment; your lungs are adjusting to the air, that's all," Celestine told her.

"I didn't realise there had been such a lack of air down there," said Sheryl when she began feeling normal again.

"It's because you lose the air slowly the deeper you go and your lungs adjust, and because it is gradual you don't really notice it," said Thara.

"Does it not affect you?" asked Sheryl, noticing that no one else seemed to be suffering.

"No, most of us were born in the depths of the ground," said Bert, who had come to join them. "Do you think you can manage a bit further? Crannog says he wants to get us to some place before the day breaks."

"Yes, I'll be fine," answered Sheryl, getting up to find her feet rather wobbly. Her head was hit with a thumping pain, causing her to wince.

"It'll ease in a few hours," said Thara with sympathy, taking Sheryl's bag off her.

She wasn't sure how she managed to get as far as she did, but suddenly Sheryl was fainting. She opened her eyes to find a multitude of goblin faces peering at her.

"I'm okay," she said and tried sitting up. She was aware that her body was shaking and lifted her hand out in front of her. It shook for all to see, and she dropped it down by her side. *I miss my magic.* She felt her chin wobble and tried snapping herself out of it. Then Crannog's face appeared above the heads of the goblins, and they shifted out of the way. He reached down and lay his hand on the ground next to her. Without hesitation, she climbed onto his hand, and the next moment she was sailing through the air as Crannog stood up straight and she clung to his sleeve.

"The forest used to cover all these parts of the mountains," said Crannog as he started walking. "It seems the forest has shrunk, but I can see it in the distance. Once we are there we will stop and rest."

Sheryl wasn't the only one who was glad to hear what Crannog had just said, and more than one goblin was heard sighing. The Silver-moon was dipping and the Grey-moon rising when they reached the edge of the Tremblin Forest. The huge redwoods that towered towards the sky were covered in frost and tiny icicles. It was a winter wonderland and breathtakingly beautiful, but Sheryl wondered where they would sleep. When they had gone a short distance into the forest, Crannog put Sheryl on the floor, then reached up and snapped a branch off the tree. He plonked himself down on the ground, where he sat crossed-legged and began munching on the wood. Thara passed Sheryl her bag and then went to help the others, who were setting up camp with lightning speed.

Sheryl pulled the strings on her bag and dived in looking for some dried beef to eat. She found the muslin bag and, with shaking hands, pulled out a piece of beef and started munching away, in much the same way Crannog was eating.

A fire was lit and sprout stew cooking before Sheryl even finished her piece of beef. She pulled her leather-quilted blanket from her bag, wrapped it around herself and lay down.

"Not here." Sheryl opened her eyes reluctantly, to see Celestine standing by her head. "In there," Celestine said, pointing at a tree. Sheryl pushed herself upright and looked at the tree, which was almost the width of a small barn. "It has a section hollowed out, so you can sleep in there," said Celestine before turning and walking away.

"Thank you," Sheryl called after her, then scrambled up and went gingerly into the tree. Luckily, the freeze had either killed off the bugs or sent them into hibernation, because, after a brief look around, she realised she didn't have to share her bed with insects.

The next morning, Sheryl was woken by the flickering light of the Grey-moon as it bounced down through the branches of the trees. She was obviously the last one to wake as she could hear Crannog laughing with the goblins.

"Afternoon," laughed Crannog as she came to join them around the fire.

"It's not afternoon yet, is it?" said Sheryl, searching above the treetops to see where the Grey-moon was.

"Nearly," said Thara. "Here, have some stew." She pushed a wooden bowl towards Sheryl, who hesitated only a moment before reaching up and accepting it with a smile.

"Thank you," she said. After a quick look at the others revealed there were no spoons, Sheryl lifted the bowl and took a mouthful. She was pleasantly surprised. The strong taste of sprouts was there, but so was a mix of herbs that surely included tarragon and rosemary.

"It's good, no?" said Crannog with a wink.

"It is," she said, smiling back. As she ate her stew, she looked around the camp and took in the different characters around the fire. It was strange because, although they might look different, they acted the same way any family would.

"Why do you need a gate?" Crannog asked.

"If I can find a way into the world of the unicorns, I can ask them to give me my magic back."

"And, as I took your magic away, it seems only fair that I should build you a gate," Crannog said, looking at her closely. She didn't know what to say.

"How long will it take you to build?" she asked.

"Umm, let me see," said Crannog, starting to count on his pebble-dashed fingers. When the counting went on and on, Sheryl began to be alarmed.

"About fifty-nine years," he declared.

"What?" yelped Sheryl. "I'll be dead by then."

"Ah yes, I forgot you humans don't live very long."

"Can't you do it any faster?" she asked with a sinking heart.

"I could maybe knock it down to fifty years, if I work a few rest days," he answered.

"You should have told me this before."

"Why?"

"Because I would have gone home with Sebastian."

"But then you wouldn't know where the gate it."

"What good is a gate to me when I'm an old woman? Will you take me home, Crannog?" He looked at her and she could tell by the sorrow in his eyes that the answer was no.

"Can anyone take me home?" she asked. Everyone looked down. "I'll never find my way back through all those caverns," she said, looking at Crannog. Crannog was just about to say something when, all of a sudden, there was a shaking of the earth. Everyone jumped to their feet and the goblins pulled out their weapons. Crannog sniffed. *That's a funny smell, a bit like…*

"Hello!" he yelled out in sudden excitement, spinning around looking for something. "Hello," he called again. From different directions, five ogres came in and surrounded the group. "Hello," he said for a third time, now with a big smile on his face.

"Rakindar," said one of ogres.

"Rakindar," responded Crannog.

"Helin crafee tu lin sai?"

"We're here to build a gate," beamed Crannog, obviously not bothered that the new ogres all seemed to be extremely bad-tempered-looking with each carrying a club the size of a small tree.

"Si in tullin cre manker?"

"Oh, I'm ever so sorry, please excuse me. My name is Crannog-Fergal, Oath-keeper and Gate-builder, last living

Treegothin ogre of Talia." There was a sudden buzz in the air as the new arrivals began talking among themselves. They seemed to come to some agreement.

"Why do you sit among goblins and humans?" one of them asked.

"They are my new family. Where I go, they go."

"Can they build gates?"

"They can help me build a gate." The five ogres went back to discussing something between themselves and then addressed him again.

"Where will you build your next gate to?"

"I cannot predict the destination behind the gate, but we are hoping it will be to the land of the unicorns." Now the ogres spoke excitedly among themselves.

"We will help you," said one of them. Crannog stood up.

"Dak in tar min crebar," he said with a bow.

"You are welcome, Crannog-Fergal, last living Treegothin ogre of Talia. For we five are the last of the living Avrintarian ogres in this world. We wish to seek out husbands in other worlds, should there be any out there."

"Have you built yourself a gate?" asked Crannog.

"No, none of us has the magic needed to make a gateway to another dimension, but we are skilled carpenters and will carve as you direct us, and we hum pretty good."

"This is good news for you, Sheryl," said Crannog.

"Why?" she whispered, not wanting to bring the attention of the new ogres her way.

"Because many hands make light work." Crannog winked at her and she was filled with hope as she realised what he was saying.

## Chapter 20 – Group Hug

Katrina felt the constraints of the palace walls as tightly as bars in a prison. To keep herself from going bananas she had taken to running around the entire palace at least three times every morning, well before the servants woke. This was her solitude time and, as she ran, she allowed the absence of people and chatter to bathe and restore her peace. However, she was on edge this morning and, as she ran her circuit, the cold, grey mist of dawn was thicker and heavier than she had ever seen it. If Idi and Marcus had known she was out on her own there would have been fireworks, but she was dangerously independent and adventurous for a young girl. However, today she was feeling vulnerable and on edge.

She kept feeling as if someone was watching her, so she would stop mid-pace and spin around. There was never anyone there, but the feeling wouldn't lessen. She slowed her pace, allowing her breathing to slow. As she controlled her breaths, she was able to make them silent and so sharpen her hearing to what lay beyond her body. There! She knew it. She span around again and glared into the mist behind her. Nothing. But she knew she'd heard a footstep. She slunk back against the wall and searched her brain for the best thing to do. Sense told her she should enter the palace as quickly as possible and call the guards. Nevertheless, she was curious.

Who was out at this time in the morning, and were they following her or up to something else?

Feeling inquisitive, she pushed herself away from the wall and began very slowly to retrace her steps. She couldn't see anyone and was slightly disappointed. She decided her run was ruined and decided to go back inside. As she approached the small side door she always used to sneak out, a chill went down her spine as she realised it was open.

Not wanting to run with the biggest key she had ever seen, she always locked the door and placed the key behind the nearest bush. Now the door was open and the key was in the lock. Her heart started pounding. Who had entered the palace? Was it Norvora? Fear for Idi and Marcus suddenly made her brave and she charged into the small hallway. She hesitated slightly; the wall lamp she had left on had been blown out. That wasn't a good sign; it meant whoever it was definitely didn't want to be seen. She began running down the corridor, but after only a moment pulled herself to a stop because her boots were echoing on the stone floor. She pulled them off, dropped them on the floor and started running again in her woollen socks.

She got to the split in the corridor where she would normally turn right to go back to the sleeping quarters. A slight noise down the left corridor informed her someone was active down there. What should she do? She pulled her sword out of the strap she carried on her back; she couldn't run with it tied around her waist, but she never went anywhere without it. She glanced quickly to the right, knowing she should go and get Marcus and Idi, but instead she started creeping down the left passageway in search of the intruder.

A low, guttural growling echoed up the corridor. Katrina paused; only one thing could have made that noise: Absalom's tiger. She had seen Absalom with it several times as he walked her around the palace gardens, but she had never ventured anywhere near it. The growl came again and Katrina almost retreated. But the stranger's secretive entrance into the palace made her realise that he must be up to no good. She carried on down, going more slowly. When she came to the end of the passageway, a stone staircase led downwards into a cellar. She crept down the stairs, her sword ready in her hand. The thudding of her heart and a slight sweat on her forehead were, she knew, signs that she should turn around.

She tiptoed down the last couple of steps and peered into the large room that was lit up by several wall lamps. The ceiling was fluted like a huge fan, supported by decorative marble pillars. Piles of crates were stacked all around and shelves along the walls were filled with boxes. *Storage. Maybe he's a thief?*

"I am going to kill you and take your strength."

Katrina froze, at first thinking someone had spoken to her. Then she heard the tiger snarl and realised someone was about to kill it.

Her hands were shaking and the sword was wobbling. She should run back and get help, but that might be too late. Afraid of what might happen to her, but more afraid for the tiger, Katrina went charging forward with the loudest war cry she could muster. The would-be tiger assassin was in the process of throwing his spear. Her cry shocked him and his throw was off by a distance, his spear landing on the floor at the back of the cage.

"Get away from him," Katrina demanded, throwing a quick look at the cub to make sure she wasn't hurt. Coming to his senses the man charged towards Katrina. She dived to the floor and covered her head, expecting him to stab her, but instead he raced past her and back up the spiral staircase.

In that moment of wondering what to do, Katrina heard people shouting and obviously coming her way. A few seconds later, Absalom and two guards came bursting into the room from the far right-hand side of the cellar.

"You," Absalom said in shock when he saw Katrina.

"He went up there," Katrina said, pointing to the staircase. Absalom just stared at her. "He was here to kill the tiger. Don't you want to chase him?" Katrina asked. Absalom seemed to come to.

"Don't let him get away," he yelled at his guards, who went charging after the intruder.

"What are you doing here?" demanded Absalom.

"I thought I heard a noise and came to investigate. It was lucky I did, for he was just about to put that spear in your cub." Katrina pointed to the spear on the floor inside the cage. Absalom opened the cage and went inside. The cub was instantly by his legs, rubbing her head against him. He bent down and picked the spear up, looking it up and down.

"It's a Bluedanian spear," he said, coming back out of the cage.

"And?" shrugged Katrina.

"I just assumed it would be a foreigner come to kill him."

"How did you know someone had come to kill him?" Absalom just stared at her, his face unreadable. The cub chuffed and Absalom turned to look at her. He smiled and threw her a piece of meat from a nearby bucket. When she had finished eating it the cub came up to the cage bars and pressed her head against them. Absalom put his hand in and scratched her ear. Katrina watched, fascinated by the love the two obviously had for each other. Then, no longer wanting to intrude, she started backing up.

"Erm, glad she's okay. I'll just get going now. See you later."

"Wait."

Katrina froze. Had he sussed out that she was to blame for the intruder's entrance? She turned around to face him. The cub ambled back to her bed and lay down. Katrina felt the blood in her temples pounding and knew she had gone red.

She was just about to open her mouth and confess all, honesty being the best policy and all, when Absalom spoke.

"Thank you. I think if you hadn't been here we would have arrived too late." The tension dropped out of Katrina's shoulders as she realised he hadn't worked it out.

"You're welcome… your highness." Absalom had his stony face back in place and just stared at her. She felt uncomfortable. She had never called him that before, because she knew it irritated him so much that she refused to, and that it doubly upset him that she insisted on calling him boy, whenever they met. So why was he unhappy now she had given him the respect he'd been demanding since the first day they arrived?

"My name is Absalom."

"Erm. Okay, Absalom. I really should get going so I can wash before they serve the morning meal."

"Yes, you really should. You stink."

Katrina had forgotten that she had been running in her multilayered outfit and that she must indeed smell. She gave Absalom the briefest of smiles and then went running up the stone staircase as quickly as she could.

Later, when she was in the halls eating, she heard that the intruder had got away. A part of her was relieved, for he'd surely have told everyone how he got into the palace if he'd been caught. Suddenly starving, she went up to the cooks to refill her plate.

"Especially hungry today?" Marcus said, sitting down next to her with his plate full to overflowing.

"I'm not the only one, it seems," said Katrina, pointing her fork at his plate.

"Ah yes, but I have been up since the time you went to bed."

"How come?"

"Took Idi out to do some training."

Katrina pulled a face. "And how did that go?"

"Not so good. In fact, I've left him in the middle of nowhere, to either pull on his magic and get back or face the humiliation of me having to ride out and fetch him later."

"Oh dear, that won't put him a good mood. Think I'll be stearing clear of Papa today," laughed Katrina. "Ooh," she said, in surprised shock.

"What?" asked Marcus, turning around to see what she was looking at. When Marcus saw Idi striding across the room towards them, his heart surged with joy. *He's found it.*

"Idi, son," he said, lifting out his arms to him.

"Don't you son me, old man," barked Idi, who pointed at Marcus and then the ceiling. Marcus was picked up by magic and left to float near the high ceiling. Idi went to stand underneath him as a hush of shock descended in the room.

"Do you know how many times I was dunked into that icy river this morning?" demanded Idi, bending his head back so he could look at Marcus's face. Marcus started chuckling.

Hanging in the air like a puppet, his shoulders began to shake as the joy inside him found its way out. Soon he was laughing so hard that his eyes watered and dripped on Idi.

"What's so funny?" demanded Idi, "I nearly caught pneumonia!" This just seemed to amuse Marcus even more as his body shook with laughter. Katrina couldn't help it and started laughing too. Idi threw her a puzzled look. "He left me to die in the cold," he said.

"Papa, you're making Marcus fly!"

Idi looked at her face and smiled. "That's not flying," he said with a wink. "This is flying." Marcus shot across the room, his long grey hair and purple gown streaming behind him. Then Idi beckoned to him, and Marcus was flying back to them, where Idi brought him down gently to stand in front of them.

"Oh, son," said Marcus, "I'm so proud of you." Then Marcus threw his arms around Idi and held him tight. Idi returned the hug and Katrina wiggled her way in so she could become a part of it.

"Group hug," she chirped. Everyone in the room, realising at last that something good had happened, started yelling and clapping. As the room began to quieten down, Katrina noticed Absalom walking towards them with his cub on a lead.

"Join us?" Katrina asked him.

"I think I will," said Absalom and sat down on the end of the bench, where the cub instantly sat on his feet.

"Have you given her a name yet?" asked Tanner, sitting down opposite Absalom.

"Her name is Fluke," answered Absalom.

"That's a good name," replied Tanner. "May she always bring you good luck."

"I think it's a silly name," muttered Gallagher to himself. Katrina gave him a kick under the table and scowled at him. "What?" he said, shrugging his shoulders.

Just then, they were joined by Valarie and Losia, who were both in their fairy form, but of human height.

"Room for two little ones?" said Losia, batting her eyelashes at Tanner and squashing in next to him on the bench.

"Not really," Tanner grumbled.

"How did it go?" Marcus asked, looking at Valarie, shuffling along the bench so she could sit next to him. When she'd sat down, she waved her arm and put the group in an invisible bubble so no one could hear her reply.

"We didn't find him but we did come across the Sirocco witch's hound. He told us that Norvora has taken the witches and returned home."

"So we have a reprieve for a little while, but who knows when he'll come back?" said Marcus.

"Maybe he won't come back," said Katrina.

"Yeah, I mean those witches seemed really scared of the Sirocco witch, so maybe they've given up," said Gallagher.

"Or maybe he's waiting until I'm sixteen," said Absalom.

"Why sixteen?" asked Losia.

"Because that is when I return to Havenshire, to take my rightful place there."

# Chapter 21 - Seven Years of Peace

## As noted in Marcus's diary

There have been seven years of peace, a full cycle and one.
Passing seasons marked time, but left only a blur.
We became wiser, older and a tad less tolerant.
Some argued, others debated, most seemed not to care.
No wars, no dying in battle, no pulling together.

Events drove us from place to place, together then apart.
Katrina blossomed, on that we all agree.
Tall she's grown, and beautiful too. But fierce, relentless.
Her skill with the sword is known to all. She rides a white stallion that races the wind, and wears her feelings on her sleeve, for all to see.

Idi hides among the books, searching, ever seeking.
I coax him out whenever I can, but he's swift to return
The Brothers protect Leona, and school a multitude.

What is Talia coming to, that 'normals' may learn?
Why does my heart yearn for this melancholy end?

The Oracles have been silent, curse their selective appearances.

Absalom struts like a baby lion, fearless, knowledge-less,
yet eager to learn and to improve.
I fear Katrina has caught his eye.
His spirit shifts like the seasons. Will he come true? No guarantee, we'll have to wait and see.

Then there are the witches. Elements bless, what to do?
They mock and taunt and keep the past ever present.

And me? I've grown old. Tired of this false utopia.
Turtledoff shares with me his dreams of what approaches.
Will we be ready? Will the fat of peace have ruined us all?

Well, not the girl, woman she is now, Pure-queen to be.
Will she save us from ourselves?

So diary, old friend, I lie to you not.
I quake when looking to the future and sigh at the past.
We've had our rest, a little repast.
Now the day hastens, challenges in store.
I hope I'll still be talking with you, in another seven-year score.

## Chapter 22 – Coming of Age

For the past seven years, Katrina and Absalom had grown very close and were often seen together. They started each day in the yard, practising sword-fencing. Much to Katrina's annoyance, Absalom had long since passed her skill level, but she enjoyed the challenge of trying to best him. In the afternoon, when Absalom's lessons with his educational tutors finished, they would go together across the plains and let Fluke run wild.

"Why do you think she never runs away?" Katrina asked. Absalom smiled as they watched Fluke racing across the plains.

"She's not ready yet, but have no fear – the day is coming when she will want her freedom more than my love."

Katrina looked down at her hands and felt the colour rise in her cheeks as she contemplated the fact that she would always choose Absalom's love over her freedom. To hide from her sudden thoughts she changed the subject.

"So, tomorrow's the big day. Are you ready for all the pomp and ceremony?"

Absalom groaned. "Save me from my grandparents' doting, please," he pleaded, and Katrina chuckled.

"Oh, you poor thing," she mocked. "To be loved so much must be simply awful."

He playfully punched her in the arm. "I should make you stand next to me while I greet all the guests," he said, turning to grin at her.

"Oh, no thank you, your highness," she said, giving an awkward curtsy. "I'd rather do anything else but that."

"Kiss me, and I will let you off?"

Katrina blushed deep as Absalom reached up to touch her face. She closed her eyes as he came in and planted a tender kiss on her lips.

"Eee, for goodness' sake," said Gallagher as he approached. "Can't leave you two alone for five minutes." Katrina stood back quickly and squared her shoulders. "I've been sent by Marcus to come fetch ya both to his rooms."

"What does he want?" asked Absalom.

"I dunno, I'm just the messenger boy these days, it seems." Absalom put two fingers in his mouth and whistled. Within seconds, Fluke was charging towards them. Gallagher took a few steps backwards.

"She'd never hurt you, Gallagher," said Katrina, ruffling Fluke's ear.

"Yeah, well, that may be, but I won't push me luck by getting too close," replied Gallagher, eyeing up Fluke with honest suspicion.

"Come on, beautiful," said Katrina, slapping her hip and launching into a sprint back to the palace. Within seconds, both Fluke and Absalom were running with her. Gallagher, who had on more than one occasion been floored by the playful tiger, hung back somewhat and kept his distance.

Once at the palace, they walked with Fluke to her enclosure. The cage in the cellar had long since been abandoned and replaced with a new home especially built for the tiger in the gardens. It was massive, with plenty of space for her to roam about, and completely enclosed by bars, more to stop would-be killers from taking her life to claim her power than to keep her locked in. Once she was safely locked up, they made their way to the north entrance, which was the closest to Marcus's rooms.

Absalom gave a firm rap on the ornate door and instantly they heard Marcus call out, "Come in." They opened the heavy door and stepped inside the room Marcus had set up as his 'home-from-home'. He was standing with his back to the fireplace and smiled at them as they came in. Idi was sitting on a chair near to the hearth.

"Papa!" exclaimed Katrina. "It's so good to see you out of the library. Are you going to stay out long enough to attend Absalom's birthday party?" She leant over and kissed his forehead before plonking herself down on the arm of his chair.

"I do hope you will, sir," said Absalom, coming to stand near them. "I would very much like all of you to enjoy the day."

"Yes, we are all, in fact, planning to attend your coming-of-age party, Absalom. Turning sixteen is a very special moment in anyone's life. But probably more so for you."

Absalom just nodded slightly to acknowledge Idi's statement, although he had a feeling he knew what was coming next.

"Piedro has announced that your party shall last three days," said Idi.

"Stupid amount of time to celebrate your birthdate, if you ask me," interjected Marcus.

"Luckily, no one *is* asking you," said Katrina, with a soft smile at the old magician, who was (as everyone had noticed) becoming grumpier by the day. Idi quickly knocked her leg with his hand as a warning to be quiet.

"At the end of which," continued Idi, "we shall set sail for mainland Talia and return to Havenshire."

Absalom wished he could pour himself some honey-mead. He had been dreading this day for a long time. Bluedane was his home now. He was happy here, and although he wanted to see his mother again, he had this knot in his stomach every time he pondered on the thought that he might never be able to return to what he now considered to be his home.

As if reading his mind, Katrina spoke up. "You will always be free to return here, whenever you want."

"We must ask you something," said Idi, standing up.

"Ask away," replied Absalom.

"We ask that you will always, at all times, have Tanner, Marcus or me by your side," said Idi.

"You seem to have a knack of always knowing where I am," replied Absalom. "It hasn't gone without notice that, even if I sneak off by myself, you are close by me at all times. I have been aware of your shadow for years now. I am accustomed to it and do not get irritated about it like I used to. Why are you now asking my permission to do what you have always done?"

Idi and Marcus exchanged glances.

"We have been able to give you some freedom here in Rodanti, but once back on the mainland… well, things will need to be different," said Marcus.

Idi, who could see the annoyance wash over Absalom's face, jumped in. "It is for your protection, your highness. Evil rises and its head is searching for you."

"You mean the wizard, Norvora," said Absalom.

"Yes. But more than that, there have been reports that the demons have once more found a way into the land of the living and are getting bold once more in their movements," said Idi.

"And, with them, the goblin army also builds in strength," said Marcus. "If the three should group together again, as before, there will be many deaths, for their numbers have grown unnaturally high."

"So, you wish to be with me, every waking moment… what, to protect me from magic and demons?"

"Not just your waking moments, your highness," replied Idi.

"That is preposterous; you want to be with me while I sleep too?"

"Yes, your highness. We will be able to see things your eyes cannot, and we will be able to defend you in ways you can't protect yourself," said Idi.

"The prophecy says…" began Katrina, but Absalom cut her off.

"I know *exactly* what it says. That if evil can seep into my heart then I will be the one to bring about the destruction of Talia."

"And that if love rules your decisions, then peace will come for a thousand years," finished Katrina.

"I understand all that. What irks me so is that any of you, who know me so well, would think for a moment I would let evil ever be a part of who I am."

"Our souls are like sponges," said Marcus. "If we surround ourselves with good people, it is easy for us to remain in the light. Should those people be removed and replaced with others full of hate and revenge, then we may absorb things which, from a distance, we would want to avoid. Evil is clever, Absalom. It doesn't confront you and say, 'I'm evil, let me in.' No, it comes to us in disguise, saying, 'I'm not so bad. In fact, with me you could do great things.' Slowly, then, are we seduced into changing and becoming something else."

"You speak of weak people, Marcus. I am not weak. I would not be tempted. In fact, I am insulted that you have such little faith in me," said Absalom, his hands burning as his temper built. Suddenly, a rope appeared from nowhere and began to coil itself around Absalom until he was held tight. Yelling and fighting against it, he was lifted into the air.

"Papa, put him down," yelled Katrina, shaking Idi's arm like mad. Idi looked up at Absalom, his eyes fully black as his magic oozed from him. "Papa," Katrina yelled again, tugging hard. Idi's eyes reverted to normal and Absalom was lowered to the floor, where the rope loosened and fell to the ground.

"Everyone is weak," said Idi. "Only a foolish man would think he was stronger than everything else. But my faith is in the Elements; they sent the Oracle to Marcus to tell him that we need to protect you. Do you think they would have sent us if they thought you could protect yourself from magic?"

Absalom's face was like stone and Katrina was unable to read his thoughts.

"Norvora would have turned me to evil if Moriya's hound hadn't arrived when he did, and I am a strong person, Absalom. You know how strong. Sometimes we need help, that's all," said Katrina.

"You are correct, of course. I know you all mean me well. However, tomorrow I come of age, and I need to make my own decisions and not have the wishes of others thrust upon me. For, if I did that, what kind of king would I make? Now, you will excuse me, for there is much I must attend to." Absalom nodded at each of them and then left.

"That didn't go so well," grumbled Marcus.

"What did you expect? You can't ambush him like that, demanding to be by his side for the rest of his life, and have him not react. You are wonderful men, but you really need to learn how to approach him with more respect," said Katrina, who, without waiting for a response, flounced out of the room.

"Did we not treat him with respect?" asked Marcus. "Could have sworn I was very polite to him. Was it you, young man? Were you rude to him?"

"I don't think so, Marcus."

"I think his pride will be his downfall," said Marcus.

"Retract that," Idi demanded, looking at Marcus sharply.

"I hope wisdom will rule his every decision," said Marcus, and Idi sighed.

"We have to be careful to only speak positively of him, Marcus. Or evil will take our negative words and use them against us, and against him."

"I think I like it better when you're engrossed in your books," said Marcus with an exaggerated sigh.

"My book days are over, old man." Marcus looked at Idi questioningly.

"I have absorbed everything I could. I have read until I felt my mind would burst with information, but there is no more time for gathering knowledge. In four days' time we set sail and must be ready for everything Norvora plans for us."

Marcus laid his hands on Idi's shoulders.

"If ever a man was ready for his destiny, then that man is you."

\*\*\*\*\*\*\*\*\*\*

The drummers beat a steady thud. Bevan found this helped the goblins work at a even pace. He stood on one of the high pillars and looked down at the platoons working away like ants. It had been the witch's idea to rebuild Olecranon, but now they had started, he was filled with pride to see his ancestral palace being rebuilt. A direct descendant of Gurenhok himself, Bevan was true heir to the throne. He had never dreamt of being king and restoring the monarchy; he'd always been happy that everyone bowed to his word. But now he wanted more. Demanded more. The Sister-witches fuelled his greed, and his pride – he knew that. He knew they wished to manipulate him. But he was willing to make that small sacrifice if it meant the time of the goblins could come again.

The mist that always covered Olecranon was ice-cold, and he knew his soldiers were complaining among themselves. Let them. When they were great once more, when they ruled the lands, they would thank him, respecting him and acknowledging his wisdom.

The stones that had laid splattered across the Great Plains for hundreds of years were still soaked in magic. Magic he would use to keep them safe, when the war was over.

He had no doubt that Norvora would win. The Sister-witches guided him and the demons responded to his summons. Norvora would crush all who stood in the way, and the boy would be made to release the witches from the orb. But what happened then? That was the question that had kept him pacing at night. Who would protect the goblins against Norvora and his demons, and, more importantly, from the destruction the Sisters wanted to bring? So, while the Sisters might want Olecranon restored for their own purposes, Bevan would make sure the magic here bent to no one's will but his own.

## Chapter 23 – The Gate

Sheryl was woken by a none-too-gentle shake.

"What?" she barked, squinting upwards to find a huge, stone-like face in front of her. "For goodness' sake Gwynn, don't come so close. I can smell what you had to eat last week coming off you!" Gwynn's massively long eyelashes fluttered, causing a small wind to wash over Sheryl. "Back up, back up. I'm getting up, for goodness' sake." A sound like grating stones came as Gwynn shuffled backwards on her knees and backed out of Sheryl's hut. Sheryl pulled her clothes on and wrapped her huge fur coat around her, and headed outside to see what Gwynn wanted.

"I've told you not to come into my hut," snapped Sheryl. "I'm fed-up to death of having to rebuild it."

Gwynn chuckled, and a deep, thunderous sound bellowed all around. "It's funny watching your house fall down," she said.

"What do you want?" demanded Sheryl, bending down to lift up the pot near the fire.

"Crannog wants you," Gwynn said, fluttering her eyelashes like crazy, while clutching her hands in front of her and rocking her enormous hips. Sheryl rolled her eyes. It was mostly funny that all five female ogres were in love with Crannog… well, most of the time it was, anyway.

"Is that a tree in your hair, Gwynn?" Sheryl asked, trying not to laugh.

"It's a Crimson-Acer, do you like it? Do you think it makes me look pretty? More importantly, do you think Crannog will like it?" The sigh that came out of Gwynn was a blast of wind that nearly knocked Sheryl over.

"I'm sure he will find you enchanting," replied Sheryl, as she turned around and started heading towards the cave where the door was being built. She could hear Crannog humming as she approached and smiled. He was such a placid ogre and always optimistic, and she had grown awfully fond of him.

"You want me, Crannog?" she said, as she entered the cave.

Crannog stopped humming and stood up straight as she approached. The gate was massive and filled a great deal of the cave. The ogres had gathered huge stones and the door lay on top of them, giving the appearance of a banquet table. Intricately carved with the image of a thousand trees, edged with silver plating, and adorned with two silver-dragon handles in the middle – where one day the gate would open up – the gateway looked like two huge doors lying next to each other.

"Give me your hand," he said, when she reached his side. She offered her hand to him. Crannog took it carefully between two of his enormous fingers and laid her hand on the door, then stared at her. She wrinkled her nose as she tried to puzzle out what he wanted from her. Then she felt it. A shot of heat surged through the door and she snatched her hand back. Crannog smiled.

"It is coming to life," he said with a nod.

"The door is?"

"Well, I don't mean the cave walls," chuckled Crannog.

"I didn't know it would be alive," Sheryl said in a whisper.

"It can't hear you," Crannog whispered back.

"So, this means… the magic is working?"

"Yes, it also means we are nearly finished."

Sheryl stiffened, her heart suddenly beating wildly in her ribs. She had waited so long to hear this news. "How long?" she whispered.

"No more than one more cycle of the Silver-moon." Sheryl wobbled and Crannog picked her up and sat her on the door.

"Is it okay for me to sit on it?" Sheryl asked, getting ready to jump off.

"It still sleeps," replied Crannog, tracing his finger along the door edge with obvious affection. He automatically began humming to the door as he traced his fingers along the extraordinary carvings that had taken him seven years to complete. Sheryl got down and traced her finger along the pictures in the wood. Crannog and the other ogres had made sure that, from the first moment the outline of the door had been crafted, at least one of them was with the gate, humming to it and calling forth its magic.

Sheryl felt overwhelmed with emotions. Many of her nights had been spent inventing different scenarios that all ended with Sebastian telling her he didn't love her any more.

"I have to go home," she said.

"But it's nearly finished," said Crannog in surprise.

"I can't go to another world without Sebastian. If he can't come with me, I shall live out my life as a normal and stay with him."

"That is wise."

Sheryl looked up at Crannog-Fergal and felt love for the huge, guileless ogre. "Will you go through as soon as it is finished?"

Crannog thought for a moment, while grinding his teeth.

"I am not sure I wish to go to another world, Sheryl. My life has been here, in Talia. I have had a good life and my days left are numbered. I think I will stay here with my memories and let the others go. I should remain to protect the gate, anyway. If it was ever destroyed, they would never be able to come home."

"If they wanted to come home."

"True, there may be better places to go. But not for me. I am too fond of Talia. So, when will you leave?"

"Today. Without magic and without knowledge of the underground caverns, I will have to travel through the forest on foot. Maybe once I reach the open lands I will find someone to help me get home quicker, but I am thinking it will take me a long time."

"You haven't asked if I will take you through the caverns."

"I know your place is here, with the door and looking after the goblins."

"I love my new family," Crannog said with a huge grin.

"You will miss them if they go through the gate."

"Celestine has said she will remain by my side always, so even if the others go, she will stay and keep me company."

Sheryl wasn't too sure what Bert would have to say about that, but no doubt they would work it out.

"Go and fetch Gwawr. She can tend the gate and I will carry you as far as I can. At least until you're out of the mountains."

"Thank you, Crannog."

"Try and come back to us, if you can. I have grown rather fond of you."

Timo, who had grown a full three inches in the last seven years, was turning into a strapping goblin youth, and trying his hardest to get everyone to stop seeing him as the infant. Although, right now, as he hid in the shadows and listened to Crannog and Sheryl, he felt like a baby because he wanted to cry. He burst out of his hiding place and ran to Sheryl, throwing his arms around her.

"We're family now, please don't go," he said.

"Hey, hey," said Sheryl, pushing him back a little so she could look down at his face. "I'll come back."

"Do you promise?"

"We shouldn't make promises unless we're sure we can keep them. So no, I don't promise that I will come back. But I do promise I will do everything I can to return as quickly as possible. Keeping my fingers crossed I will remember how to, that is."

Timo stood back and wiped his nose, which was quickly becoming identical to his father's rhino-sized hook nose, with the back of his arm. "Can I come with you, Crannog, when you take her through the mountains?"

"If you'll stop spying on people?" said Crannog, squinting at Timo, whose cheeks were turning blue.

"I wasn't spying. I just came to see you and then I heard you talking and didn't want to interrupt."

"Awfully polite of you, Timo," said Sheryl, with a wink. "Right, well, I need to go and make my farewells to everyone. Can we go straight after that?" Sheryl asked, and Crannog nodded.

Sheryl headed towards Gwawr's cave to fetch her for Crannog. Each one of the female ogres had their own cave and, when the storms raged, Sheryl and the goblins would take shelter in them. For the rest of the time, Sheryl lived in her house of logs that kept falling down, and the goblins had dug a warren to shelter in.

"Gwawr, are you here?" Sheryl called.

"Yes, just making patta-cakes. Come in."

Sheryl grimaced and gave a little shudder. She had been about to take a bite out of a patta-cake when they first arrived, until Crannog pointed out that they were made from ground bones. Although the ogres had all stopped eating human flesh a long time ago, they were still partial to the flavour of bones, so whenever they came across a skeleton they would bring it home and get excited over baking cakes.

"Crannog says can you take the next shift with the gate, please? He's going to take me through the mountains, down to Tremblin Forest."

There was a brief silence, then the floor vibrated as Gwawr took a few quick steps across the cave. "You're leaving?" she said, bending down to be near Sheryl's face.

"I need to find Sebastian, and see if he still considers me his wife before I can go through the gate. I've missed him so much. I know I've been waiting all this time to go through the gateway, but now that time is nearly here, I realise I can't go without him."

Gwawr stood up straight. "I understand. Do you plan to come back, really?"

"Yes, of course. I miss my magic and if the unicorns can help me get it back I must try and find them."

"Do something for me, human?"

"Yes, of course. You have been very good to me. What do you want me to do?"

"Well, when people die they are no longer in their bodies, right? They go to the Elements, that's what you told us."

"Yes, that's what we believe."

"Then, when you come back, bring me six human skeletons. I am fed-up with deer bones; they do not taste the same."

"I, I..." stammered Sheryl.

"...Will of course do this small thing for you, Gwawr," said Gwawr, raising her eyebrows. Sheryl had no idea how she was going to bring back six human skeletons to the ogres, and she wasn't too sure encouraging their taste for humans was a good thing to do. Still, they had kept her alive these last years and been kind to her.

"I will try my hardest to find them for you, Gwawr."

"Good, and if you could make it ten, that would, of course, be much better."

"I don't know how I would carry ten skeletons."

"Get a cart, girl. Use your noggin. In fact, if you have a cart, you could bring back twenty?"

"Six, Gwawr. You said six."

"I know, but now I'm thinking of it, thirty has a much better ring to it, don't you think?"

"Six," said Sheryl, already on her way out, with a smile on her face.

"You could just round it up to a hundred?" Gwawr called after her.

A short while later, everyone gathered in the clearing to say farewell, with the exception of Gwawr, who was humming like a thousand bees over the door.

"I hope you get back to us before the gate is finished," said Thara.

"I hope so too," Sheryl said, giving Thara a quick hug.

"You won't be long, will you, Crannog?" asked Gwynn, batting her eyelashes at him. Crannog just shook his head in mock despair at her.

"Come on, then," said Crannog, laying his palms down near the floor. Timo hopped onto one and Sheryl sat down on the other. He lifted them up to his shoulders, where leather straps had been stitched on his coat. Timo and Sheryl used these to secure themselves and settled in for the ride.

"Look after each other," Sheryl called, as Crannog set off. The ogres and goblins waved until they were out of sight.

Crannog marched as fast as he could, and whenever there was a bit of a clearing he would speed up. One time, though, he went a bit too fast.

"Stop!" yelled Sheryl towards his ear, fearing she and Timo would be thrown from his shoulders.

"What's wrong?" asked Crannog, trying hard to look at her on his shoulder, but not quite able to. Sheryl put her hair back into place and took a deep breath.

"Please don't go so fast; it's more than a little frightening up here as it is."

"Nooo," piped up Timo, "it's sooo fun. Do it again, do it again!"

"On the way back, Timo," answered Crannog. "I'll keep to a brisk walk for now."

"Thanks," said Sheryl, grabbing the leather strap and holding it so tight her knuckles turned white. Crannog set off again, at a slightly slower rate, and Sheryl found to her relief that her bum lifted off his shoulder much more sedately.

They came to a bare part of the mountainside, which had obviously been washed away by a landslide, leaving only a pile of shale.

"Do we need to find another way down?" asked Sheryl.

"Hold on," replied Crannog, who sat down on the edge of the slope.

"Oh no, you're not going to... Arrgghh," screamed Sheryl as Crannog suddenly pushed himself over the edge and went sliding down the mountainside. At one point, Sheryl was lifted off Crannog's shoulder for a full minute and was sure she was going to die, but eventually they came to a very bumpy halt at the bottom.

"Elements bless me," Sheryl said, reeling from the slide.

"Again, again," yelled Timo.

"Ooo, me bum's on fire," yelped Crannog, jumping up and whacking his backside. Timo burst into unstoppable laughter and, before long, Crannog and Sheryl joined in. When they eventually stopped laughing, Crannog began walking towards the ridges that would take Sheryl to the Tremblin Forest. Not long after, he reached up his hand so she could get down.

She stood on the ground, looking up at the huge ogre.

"Thank you for everything, Crannog."

"You're welcome. Now go and fetch that husband of yours and come back as quickly as you can. I'll keep looking for you, so if you manage to get his far, you'll know I'll soon be with you."

"Thank you, Crannog, you really are wonderful. I will return as soon as I can, although I'm worried the height of winter is now upon us. Bye, Timo," she called, waving up at him.

"Bye, Sheryl," he answered, waving back like mad from his great height. Sheryl watched them for a few moments as they began their journey home.

"Can we do the slide again, Crannog?" Timo asked.

"Not today."

"Awww. I can't wait to tell everyone, they're going to be so jealous. Come on, Crannog, let's go fast." Crannog began to run and Sheryl could hear Timo laughing in glee. She was going to miss them. She turned slowly and looked at where the trees began to thicken. The Tremblin Forest. She couldn't believe she was about to enter it on her own.

## Chapter 24 – Destroyer of Souls

Cassandra felt exhilarated. This was the longest she'd gone before getting caught. She could hear Shona's heavy breathing as she began to tire, and the sense of accomplishment made Cassandra want to yell in jubilation.

For seven years, Shona had tirelessly, and sometimes cruelly, instructed Cassandra on the ways of magic. Cassandra's body was covered in scars from magic-whippings and all the falls she had taken. This was their monthly hunt, where Cassandra was given the amount of time it took for the sand to run through an egg timer to run and hide, before Shona started hunting her. The quicker Shona found Cassandra, the more beatings were inflicted on her. As Cassandra's magic grew stronger, she was able to hide for longer. Today she was almost back at the camp, the first time ever. If she was able to remain hidden until the Silver-moon was high in the sky and managed to get the silver bell, Shona would declare her a witch. More important than the name was the freedom that went with it. For Shona had promised Sheryl that the day she became a witch would be the day she released her from her bond and let her go home.

Cassandra froze, the hairs on her neck standing up as she felt the breath of Shona right beside her. She closed her eyes and concentrated on her inner strength, calling her magic to keep her calm, silent and, most importantly, invisible. It worked. Shona moved away, herself invisible, listening for sounds that would give Cassandra away. *Not today*, thought Cassandra, as she slunk into the bark of the tree and called on her 'empty space' to calm her mind. She heard Shona move off and let out a tiny sigh of relief. But still she would not move. Instead, she would wait until the moon was high and then run for the camp.

Shona came close to being able to reach out and touch Cassandra two more times before the time was right. *Now. It has to be now, before she heads back herself.* She waited as long as she could, ensuring Shona was as far away as possible, and then picked up her skirts and ran, full-pelt, towards the camp. Concentrating on speed now, Cassandra's magic covering dropped slightly and her head became visible. But it was the sound of running steps on leaves and twigs that alerted Shona to the fact that Cassandra was making a sprint for home. She also hitched up her skirts, dropped the invisible spell to release more magic into her muscles, and went charging after Cassandra.

"They're coming," cried out Kylie, who had been keeping watch. The Fire-clan witches began pouring into their communal area. The bell Cassandra had to ring was tied on one of the high branches of the tallest fir in their midst. There was a buzz of excitement, for the hunt had normally finished way before now.

"She's coming," yelled Kylie, jumping off her post and running down to join the others. Cassandra's chest hurt as the cold, icy air filled her lungs. "Faster," she cried to her magic as she heard Shona catching her up.

Shona decided to cheat and pulled her wand out of her pocket.

"Over you go," she yelled, pointing the stick at Cassandra. Cassandra heard the words and pulled on her magic to shield her as she ran. The little lightning bolt bounced off her shield and Shona yelled in frustration. Cassandra was smiling. She felt amazing as the magic charged through her veins.

"High," she cried, as she approached a fallen tree, and with the next step she was leaping way into the air above it. Just a little too high, as her head bashed against another tree branch. "Oww," she yelled, holding her head as she came to land on the ground again. She heard Shona laughing and almost stopped to take her on in a fight. Almost. She had never won a battle against Shona and, today, getting her freedom was the most important thing.

She heard some of the witches whooping and stamping their feet, so she knew she was getting close. She felt them willing her to succeed and it pushed her on, even as her legs began to tire.

Not able to hit Cassandra with her magic, Shona decided to try and block the way, pointing to the top of a tree near Cassandra.

"Tumble," she cried. As the lightning hit the top of the tree, the high branches instantly cracked and came tumbling down in front of Cassandra. She just managed to pull back in time before it fell on her. She risked a quick look behind her and scowled at Shona. This was meant to be a game of hide-and-seek, not hurt-or-kill.

Shona looked crazy, her long black hair billowing out behind her as she raced across the clearing towards the camp. Even from where she stood, Cassandra could see the blacks of Shona's eyes, and a sudden shudder of fear went through her. It was what she needed. She turned and leapt over the fallen tree and went charging into the centre. She might be here first, but she still needed to get the bell.

As she charged towards the tree, she didn't think twice but leapt at it in a mighty jump. She reached one of the middle branches, where she hung precariously for a moment, before finding a foothold. Then she began to climb. She heard Shona whish through the air as she leapt at the tree, and felt it shudder as she landed on a branch. She was so close – she had to get it, had to get home. Panic began to settle in and she dropped her magic shield in her rush to climb the tree. Shona didn't hesitate and flicked her wand at Cassandra. Pain went coursing through her body as the lightning hit her back. For a moment she was blinded by pain. She was going to fall, there was no doubt in her mind. This was it. She started to plummet through the air. As she was falling backwards, she cupped her hand and pointed it towards the bell.

"Here," she demanded. With a ping, and a trickle of tiny clangs, the bell dropped out of the high branch and fell into her hand, as she went crashing towards the ground.

"Stop," cried Margot, pointing her wand at Cassandra's body. A short distance from the ground, Cassandra's body did as Margot's magic commanded, and hung suspended in the air for a moment before coming to land gently on the floor.

"Hurray," went up the cheer, and witches raced over to help her up and offer their congratulations. Cassandra felt dizzy, and kept looking at the bell.

"Oh, well done," chirped Kylie, throwing her arms around her. Cassandra smiled and hugged her back.

"Congratulations." Cassandra looked up to find Shona in front of her. The other witches began falling back.

"You cheated," stated Cassandra.

"I'm the head of the clan," Shona said, with a shrug.

"That's not fair," answered Cassandra.

"Hardly anything in life is fair. I thought you knew that by now?"

"Yes, but you made the rules, so why make them if you're going to break them?"

"Because I can."

Cassandra felt anger building up.

"Maybe we should go to your cabin, Shona?" said Margot. Shona glared at Cassandra, willing her to challenge her in front of everyone. But suddenly, Cassandra smiled. Shona had made her promise in front of the entire clan seven years ago. She would have no choice now, other than to let her go.

"I need a drink," she said. The tension fell off Shona's shoulders and she smiled back at her.

"Me too, come on."

"I wouldn't mind a drink myself," added Margot.

"Not now, Margot. Cassandra and I need to talk." The smile slid off Margot's face and a flicker of hatred crossed her features before she quickly pulled her face back under control.

"Yes, of course. I will be in my cabin if you want me." As Margot's chubby body wobbled its way back to her own domain, Cassandra shook her head and looked at Shona.

"You will have to keep her in check, Shona."

"I know."

When they were inside Shona's cabin, she poured two large glasses of brandy and passed one to Cassandra.

"Cheers," she said, raising her glass.

"Cheers," answered Cassandra, clanging her glass into Shona's. As was their custom, when they were on speaking terms, they went to sit by the log burner.

"The heavy snows of the Grey-moon are nearly upon us. It is good you have reached the bell now, for travelling will soon be difficult."

"Wouldn't be if you would teach me to fly," said Cassandra hopefully.

"Although you became a witch today, you still have a long way to go before you have enough magic for that." Shona swished her drink around in the glass and then took a large glug. "Will you continue to learn?" she asked quietly.

Cassandra looked into her drink to try to get her thoughts in order. When she had first come to the home of the Fire-clan, deep in the Tremblin Forest, she'd thought she would hate Shona for ever. Funny, but with the passing of time, and getting to know each other, they'd actually become friends. More than that, the bond of sisterhood had formed between them. But as for magic? Well, she hadn't even made up her mind whether she was going to tell her father about it yet. She enjoyed using magic, as doing even the smallest thing filled her with a sense of power.

"Stay here with us," said Shona, leaning forward in her chair. "You're one of us now, and you know it. Your life will be boring if you go back to sitting on a throne and twiddling your thumbs."

"For your information, I have *never* twiddled my fingers."

"Stay?"

"I need to find Absalom, Shona. You must understand. He's my son."

"I am your father's daughter, but he never searched for me," said Shona, sitting back in her chair and taking another drink.

"You are too hard on him. You need to forgive him."

"I can't do that. As far as I am concerned, my mother died because he banished us to the far corners of Talia and left us to rot. She could never get over it, being torn away from her family by the man she loved, who she thought loved her. What kind of man does that?" Shona got up and went to refill her glass.

"He may be foolish and make mistakes, but he holds a great responsibility for the people of Havenshire. Duty has always come first to him, before even my mother and I."

"Then why did he sleep with a maid, if he's such an honourable man?"

"I don't know. Maybe he did love your mum but couldn't risk causing a scandal when she became pregnant?"

"So he tossed us aside like garbage."

"Well, from what you've told me, he ensured your mother had enough money to set up a new life, a comfortable one at that. So maybe throwing you away like rubbish isn't a good comparison."

"My mother's heart was broken. All the money in the world wasn't going to make it better, and only a fool would think it would."

"You know he banished me when I fell in love with Rodanti, and I am the only heir to the throne."

"Then help me punish him?"

"I can't do that, I love him."

"But he cast you away, the same as my mother and I."

"I understand why he did it. Even though I know it must have been one of the hardest things he's ever done, he put the lives of many before the life of one. Anyway, we all make mistakes, Shona. None of us goes through life without doing something we regret."

"Don't go Cassandra. Please stay with me. True, I brought you here to turn you against him, but I would rather keep your friendship than lose you by never giving up. Geez, I've tried hard enough through the years, so if I've not succeeded by now, I guess I never will."

"Turtledoff is full of wise sayings. Two of them pierced my heart and remain with me always." Cassandra pause and took a small drink. "Anger is an acid that can do more harm to the vessel in which it is stored than to the person on whom it is poured, and... unforgiveness is the destroyer of souls. Let it go, Shona, before it ruins you."

"So, that's a no, then? You're not going to stay?" Cassandra looked at Shona and the two of them started laughing. "I will miss you," Shona said.

"And I, you," replied Cassandra. "Why don't you come to the castle with me?"

"My responsibilities are to my clan, and I'm not ready to let go of my hatred towards our father just yet."

"And mine are to my son and the people of Havenshire."

They clinked glasses together with a nod and took one last drink together.

Before the Grey-moon had done little more than raise its head above the mountains, Cassandra was dressed and ready to go. Despite the early hour, most of the Fire-clan had come to say goodbye, and she was surprised at how sad she felt at leaving them.

"Are you sure she said I can take a horse?" Cassandra asked for about the tenth time, while scanning around, hoping to get a glimpse of Shona.

"Yes, I'm sure," answered Kylie with a smile. The stable only had three horses in it, three huge Shires. These were used for many tasks and Cassandra knew the loss of one of them would be felt by the clan.

"Maybe you could bring him back to us one day?" said Kylie. Cassandra was still looking around. "She's not coming – she said she has important matters to deal with," said Kylie, touching Cassandra's arm. Cassandra turned around and gave her full attention to the young woman who had helped her adjust to life with the witches.

"I am not sure I would have coped without you," Cassandra said, her tears building up. "When I arrived, you were the first person to speak to me and treat me like a friend."

"Of course you would. You're a strong woman."

"I will bring the horse back – probably not until the Yellow-moon of spring draws near, though."

"Good," said Kylie, giving Cassandra a hug. Cassandra shook hands with lots of the witches and hugged a few. As far as she could see, only Margot and Shona had stayed away.

Eventually, when all the goodbyes had been exchanged, Cassandra climbed on the horse.

"I'll miss you," she said to everyone.

"Well, we won't be missing you," someone shouted back. Everyone laughed, for of course they would miss her; she had become a witch and a member of their clan.

She looked back often as she set off, waving behind her until she couldn't see them any more beyond the trees. As she meandered through the thick forest, it started to snow. Huge white flakes came fluttering down, turning everything frosty-white. She pulled the hood of her cape up, thankful for the thick fur lining and gloves Briac had made for her.

The huge horse clopped his way down the valley that had been Cassandra's home for the last seven years, leading them into the deepest parts of the Tremblin Forest, where the witches ventured as little as possible.

Cassandra recalled another time she'd fled into this forest, only entering from the south that time. It seemed like an eternity ago now, and as she recalled being young and pregnant and racing through the trees, it felt as though she was looking at someone else. That had been a terrifying experience for her, but in it, she had given birth to Absalom. She closed her eyes for a moment as a rush of emotion ran through her: love for her son, terror at losing him, and anger at not being able to protect him. Then, through her rush of memories, appeared the image of the rainbow of lights. They'd filled her body and mind with strength, but also given her the image of her son as king. Why did she ever doubt the Elements? Their 'will' would be done.

She'd left the clan far behind when the horse suddenly pulled back on his reins and snorted. Cassandra's eyes flew open, looking for the cause. She heard a whoosh in the sky above and instantly slid off the horse so she could hold it by the bit and keep it calm. As she stroked the horse's mane, she searched the skies for the thing she feared to see. All the witches had witnessed the flying Delphics (as the witches had named them, not knowing what they were) circling in the skies.

Half man, half dragon, the Delphics filled the witches with fear every time they flew overhead. So far, the beasts hadn't ventured into the forest where the witches lived, but their presence brought a feeling of foreboding and menace into the clan. As she searched above the treetops, they suddenly came into view, and Cassandra automatically threw an invisible spell over herself and the horse.

"Sssh," she urged the horse, sending a calming spell into him until he stopped his fidgeting and stood still. Cassandra counted six of them soaring above, circling as if searching for something. *What kind of evil created these creatures?*

The 'body' was much the same as a human's, with a head, torso, arms and legs. However, halfway down their backs, a dragon's tail flowed, thick, long and reflecting colours from its multiple plates. They had no hair and most of their bodies were covered in scales. Along the tops of their heads, and down their arms, ran a band of spikes. Instead of hands and feet, they had claws, and their skin was like that of a snake. From their shoulders, two huge wings spread out, many times larger than the human-looking body, so from the distance it looked like a dragon carrying a human.

They didn't stay long, much to Cassandra's relief, and the moment they were gone she climbed back on the horse and set off again, more eager than ever to have this journey over with.

She'd travelled through the first day and night with only a few very brief stops to rest the horse. The light was just rising, announcing the birth of a new day, but Cassandra was barely aware of it, her head bouncing and nodding as she kept falling asleep. Eventually she surrendered and let her chin drop to her chest as she sank into sleep. She awoke some time later to find the horse coming to a stop, and opened her eyes begrudgingly to see why.

Standing on the path a short way in front of her was a woman. Her face was white and thin, and she clutched a huge fur wrap tightly around her.

Cassandra soothed the horse and got him to take a few steps forward.

"What do you want?" she asked as she reached the woman.

"Your help, please. You're heading south. Take me with you?" Cassandra looked at the woman and saw she was cold and exhausted and the strangeness of the meeting was overtaken by pity.

"Where have you come from and why are you so far from home?"

The woman pointed northwards, higher up the Torrean Mountains. "I have spent a long time on my own up there, but the Winter-moon is here and I must head home to the Lowlands."

Snow was still falling and the stark, bare branches had become completely white. Cassandra watched a snowdrop fall on the woman's nose and had an urge to wipe it away and warm her up.

"Climb up," she said, offering the woman her hand. The briefest of smiles flickered across the woman's face as she muttered, "Elements be blessed." As the woman swung around her, Cassandra threw a protective shield around her body – just in case.

"Oh," said the woman, "you're a witch." Cassandra felt the woman behind her stiffen in sudden fear.

"You have nothing to fear from me," replied Cassandra, "but tell me, how does a normal know when someone is a witch?"

"I felt something tingle... I just assumed."

Cassandra thought about the woman's answer. She was sure she was lying, yet Cassandra could feel no magic coming off her, so she couldn't be a witch herself.

"What's your name?" Cassandra asked.

"Sheryl," replied her new companion.

## Chapter 25 – Name Day

She'd never worn a dress and had never wanted to, but as she looked at her reflection in the mirror she couldn't help but smile.

"Do you like it?" asked Orla, and Katrina turned around to smile at her.

"Thank you," she said, giving the queen a quick hug. "I don't recognise myself."

Orla reached up to fiddle with the flower band on Katrina's head. "Such a pity you won't grow your hair long. Having it cropped short like a boy's was fine when you were young, but you're a young lady now, and you really should start behaving like one. You'll never get yourself a husband if you insist on wearing trousers and acting like a man."

Katrina blushed. Did the queen know she was in love with Absalom? Was that why she was telling her this?

"There," said Orla. "You look beautiful. The dress brings out the blue in your eyes to perfection."

Blue poppies and harvest-bells adorned not only her head but her right wrist. Her sky-blue, crushed-velvet dress clung to the top part of her body and then flowed away from her from the hips down. She felt like she was floating. And she also felt giddy. No one had ever called her beautiful before and she wondered if Absalom would think her beautiful. As if reading her thoughts, Orla reached out and took hold of Katrina's chin gently.

"He can never marry you, you know?"

"Who?" asked Katrina, surprised at the statement.

"Absalom. He will be king, not only of Bluedane but the whole of Talia, and as such he must take a... suitable wife."

"I am sure he will marry whoever he loves," said Katrina defensively. Orla laughed and dropped her hand away.

"I am sure you are right. He is very headstrong, just like his father. But I am warning you, the odds are stacked very high against it being you." The joy of the moment washed out of Katrina, much as if someone had thrown a bucket of ice-cold water over her.

"Come along, my dear, don't look so crestfallen. It never does to let a gentleman know your feelings for him. That only evokes sadness when the inevitable rejection comes."

Katrina didn't answer. She felt like crying, but she followed Orla out into the hallway anyway.

"That Gallagher is a very nice young man, and he wears his love for you on his sleeve, clear for everyone to see. Why don't you put him out of his misery and become his betrothed?"

"Gallagher's not in love with me, and even if he was, I am certainly not in love with him," Katrina snapped. As if saying his name aloud had summoned him, Gallagher suddenly turned up in front of them. Katrina turned beetroot-red.

"Absalom sent me to find you," Gallagher said quietly, his face like stone. Katrina kept her eyes down.

"We're coming, young man. Here, why you don't you take Katrina's arm and lead her into the great hall?" Orla tapped Katrina's arm with her fan. He did as he was asked, and took a step closer, putting his arm through Katrina's. She sneaked a look at him from under her eyelashes, hoping against hope that she hadn't upset him.

"You look very handsome," she whispered at him as they started walking. "Hardly recognise you in those clothes." He didn't answer and she felt crushed, firstly because she must have hurt him indeed if he wasn't talking to her, and secondly because he hadn't returned the compliment, and now she felt worried that she didn't look as nice as Orla had stated.

As they walked into the room, she started searching for Absalom. She found him, laughing at something Loreiei had said, and her heart dropped. Making an effort to hide her unwelcome newfound emotions, she squared her shoulder and lifted her chin. Loreiei looked beautiful in a silver-and-red gown, her hair lifted into soft curls in a cascading bun. *I have no chance against her.*

Absalom turned and saw her. He froze, the shock of seeing her on his face. *What's he thinking? Is it good shock?* Then he was striding across the floor towards them. Her hands were shaking and she clasped them together to hide it. She dropped her eyes for a moment, fearful of his first words.

"You look… beautiful," Absalom said. Gallagher let go of her arm and moved away. Orla rolled her eyes and flapped her fan in irritation. Katrina looked up, her stomach full of butterflies, and as she looked into his eyes, the two of them froze, suddenly unaware of the room and all the people around them. The noise faded and time stood still as the two of them, without words, acknowledged their love for each other.

"Oh, for goodness' sake," snapped Orla, breaking them out of their trance. "Absalom, you have guests. Go do the regal bit that is required of you and greet them, please."

"I want your first dance," Absalom said, not taking his eyes off Katrina. She nodded. He turned and scowled playfully at his grandmother before heading towards the main entrance to join his grandfather. On his way, Loreiei caught up with him and slipped her arm through his.

"Don't you think my grandson and Loreiei make a lovely couple?" said Orla. Instant irritation flooded Katrina.

"She may look as pretty as a picture on his arm, and perhaps she is able to greet the guests with all the proper etiquette I obviously lack…" Katrina paused for a moment and turned to look Orla in the face. "…But Absalom's enemies are not the courtiers in this room, nor are they normal humans. They are powerful and evil, and when they come, I shall be standing beside him, putting my life before him to protect him. Tell me, when that day arrives, where will Loreiei be?" Katrina didn't give the queen a chance to answer. She took a small amount of pleasure at the shock she saw on Orla's face, then turned and went in search of the others.

The queen knew how to organise an event to perfection, and today was no exception. Once the guests had all arrived, the entertainers began their shows, the best wine flowed, and the tables were laden with perfect delicacies. Katrina felt detached through it all and would have left, but she refused to let Orla know she had got to her.

"You don't look like you're having fun," said Losia. Katrina smiled and then gestured to her dress.

"It's not really my thing, is it?" she answered with a grin.

"You should dance," said Marcus. "Gallagher, why don't you ask the lady to dance?"

"What lady is that?" said Gallagher, looking around as if searching for someone.

"Oy," said Katrina, playfully punching him.

"Oh, you," said Gallagher with a smile. He gave a deep bow. "Care to dance?" he asked. The smile fell from Katrina's face.

"I'm sorry, Gallagher. I, I…"

"No problem. Of course you don't want to dance with me." He turned and stalked off across the room and out into the gardens. Katrina went to go after him.

"Leave him, lass. He'll get over it," said Marcus.

Katrina turned back to Marcus, feeling sad. "I don't mean to hurt him, but I seem to be doing that a lot lately."

"Come and sit down, Katie," said Idi, patting the chair next to him.

"Actually, I want to get out of this dress. I think I will go back to my room."

"You'll miss his crowning if you leave," said Idi. Katrina looked across the room and saw Absalom dancing with a comely young woman in a bright-yellow dress.

"He looks like he's dancing with a bowl of custard," said Losia with a giggle. Katrina couldn't stop herself from laughing.

"He's asking who's stolen his whole mustard?" asked Marcus, puzzled. Katrina nearly collapsed in laughter. She gave Marcus a hug. "What was that for?" he asked.

"Just because. Move up then, let me sit down." Idi moved up a chair so Katrina could sit between them. "How long will it be before they crown him, do you think?"

"They'll do it at midnight," answered Idi.

They enjoyed the jugglers and the dancing ladies, and clapped along to various melodies played by the orchestra. Valarie and Losia spent the entire evening dancing with different partners, their beauty obviously causing quite a stir. Losia kept coming back to the group to entice Tanner to dance with her, but he wouldn't be moved from his seat. Katrina was surprised when a drumroll announced it was time for the coronation. She searched the room, hoping to see Gallagher.

"I wish Gallagher was here," she said.

"I am," said a voice behind her ear. She jumped and span around.

"How long have you been behind us?" she asked, smiling up at him.

He grinned. "Most of the evening."

"Please be upstanding," declared the master of ceremonies. Everyone who had been seated stood up. Three drummers beat a steady, quiet drumroll as Absalom walked up onto the throne platform. Piedro and Orla were already up there, smiling as they watched their grandson, pride pouring from them.

Piedro gave a long, traditional speech, naming all the new titles Absalom would acquire now he had come into manhood at the age of sixteen. When he had finished, the master of ceremonies passed him a golden ring on a purple cushion. The king picked up the crown and held it for a moment over Absalom's head.

"I'm proud of you, Absalom," he whispered to Absalom before putting the crown on his head. He turned to face the crowd and declared, "I give you Absalom, your crown prince." A deafening roar came from the crowd as they not only cheered, but clapped and stomped their feet. Katrina wiped away a tear, surprised at how emotional she felt. When the cheering had stopped, Absalom addressed them.

"I am grateful for your acceptance of me. I may not be fully Bluedanion but I hold on to my birth right with fierce pride and I promise you, I will serve Bluedane to the best of my ability. Now go, enjoy the rest of the evening." Another cheer went up and Absalom came down and started shaking hands with everyone.

"He'll make a good king," said Gallagher. Katrina turned to face him and give him a smile.

"Thank you," she said, reaching up and planting a kiss on his cheek.

"Will you die with me, Katie?" asked Marcus.

"Die with you?" answered Katie, shocked.

"No, of course not. I said dance with me. What's wrong with your hearing, girl."

Katrina looked at Idi, worry written over her face. Idi shook his head, indicating she should let it go.

"I will dance with you later, Marcus," she answered. They decided to get some food and sit in the gardens for a little bit of quiet and cool night air. They had not long finished when Absalom turned up.

"Are you ready for your return to Talia?" asked Idi.

"Yes, sir. I am extremely eager to see my mother once more, and if we can go to Tamarind, then to see Turtledoff and Martha as well."

"When do we go?" asked Gallagher. Katrina looked at his excited face and realised he would also be looking forward to being reunited with his mother.

"In three days' time," answered Absalom.

"You must be excited, young man," said Marcus.

"I am."

"You know you must always have either myself or Idi beside you wherever you go?" said Marcus.

"My grandfather has advised me that is what you have requested, but I don't believe it will be necessary."

"It will indeed be necessary, for we return home, not only to King Hamish, but to all your enemies, including Norvora."

"I have become, thanks to Katrina and Gallagher, one of the best swordsmen in Bluedane. I will be able to defend myself against my enemies."

Marcus tutted. "You have not been listening, boy," he said, annoyed.

Idi jumped in before Marcus had a chance to offend Absalom. "We'll have the journey home to discuss all these matters," he said. "Let's enjoy some merriment while we can."

"I agree," said Absalom. "Katrina…" He offered her his arm, which she took, feeling shivers of excitement rush through her at the contact. As Absalom took them back into the great hall, he kept his face looking straight ahead, but said in a quiet voice so only she could hear, "You haven't danced with anyone?"

"No, I've been waiting for you."

"Good."

When they reached the dance floor, he held her hand and promenaded her around in a full circle. Everyone else on the floor stopped and began to edge backwards, making space for their future king. Katrina's heart thudded hard against her ribs, making her feel breathless and giddy. Absalom pulled her into his arms and she was surprised at his strength and confidence.

"I've been having lessons," he whispered in her ear. Her head rocked back as she laughed. They glided around and around the room until everything became a blur. She thought she'd never been so happy in all her life.

"I love you," he whispered into her hair, and her insides exploded with happiness.

## Chapter 26 – Leona

Both her hands and her right ear rested against the knobbly bark of an ancient oak tree. She had been here for a while and the wolves, which at first had lain down to wait, now paced around. Snow was falling thick and fast, and the icy wind howled through the forest. However, the huge white, alpha wolves, Singarti and Bleddyn, stood statue-like on either side of Leona, their only movement an eye-blink as snowflakes fell on them.

Leona sighed, and at last moved away from the tree. Singarti and Bleddyn instantly moved to walk one on either side of her, the rest of the pack following behind. She reached out both her gloved hands and rested them on top of the alphas. She was sad, for the Earth Element had confirmed it would soon be time for her to return home – the place that hovered in the back of her mind yet refused to be clearly remembered. Feeling her sadness, the two wolves nuzzled in close against her long, white fur coat.

Turning her face towards the sky and letting her huge fur hood fall back, Leona let the snowflakes land on her without wiping them away. She wanted to capture every moment and hold it like a treasure. She made her way slowly back to the cabin that had become her home during the last few years.

She loved it here, far enough away from Havenshire to be quiet, and close enough to see the Brothers after a few hours' ride. It had taken her a long time to convince the Brothers that she no longer needed looking after and to let her live in the forest.

She pushed open the door and stepped inside. Only Singarti, the female alpha, came inside with her. The others waited until they heard her drop the bar across the door before racing into the forest. Elk cries had come to them on the wind and they were hungry.

The fire had burnt itself out so she piled some new logs on and then blew on them. Instantly, they burst into flame, crackling and sparkling, emitting the sweet aroma of pines. Singarti made herself comfortable in front of the fire and Leona went to prepare herself some food.

"Hello, Leona." Leona put down her knife and ran across the room, throwing her arms around the Sirocco witch.

"It's nearly time," Leona said, stepping back a bit so she could look up at Moriya.

"I know, child," Moriya answered.

"Will we be able to save all of them?"

"No."

Leona's multicoloured eyes filled with tears. "I will miss them when I return to the ground to sleep."

"Until you come again," said Moriya.

"Until I come again," Leona repeated. "I was about to make some supper, will you join me?"

"No, thank you. I came only to check that you were ready."

"I am."

"Good. The Earth Element is concerned that you are not yourself today, that you are… lonely."

"I am. I wish very much that I wasn't the only one of my kind."

"Maybe I can do something about that. But for now, before the passing of three days, you must return to live with the

Brothers in the Academy." Leona nodded. "I must go now, for there is much to put in place." Moriya went over to Singarti and rubbed her ears. "You look after my little eleven princess for me," she whispered to the wolf. Singarti bowed her head.

"One last thing," said Moriya. "Two women come your way. They are important to the prophecy and Norvora has sent demons deep into the forest to kill them. Save them." Then, as suddenly as she had appeared, the Sirocco witch was gone.

Without hesitation Leona reached over for her fur cloak. By the time she had flung it around her shoulders, Singarti was growling by the door. "Call the family," Leona told her. "I think we may need them." Leona knew the demons had found another entrance into Talia, for she had seen several demons, and some creatures she called Dragon-demons, flying through the forest in the night. What she was unsure of was how many had returned. Singarti lifted her head and howled.

Then Leona and Singarti were racing into the forest, which was fast becoming dark.

\*\*\*\*\*\*\*\*\*\*

Sheryl was glad not to be walking, but the continual sitting was allowing the cold to seep into her bones and, some time ago, she had wrapped her arms around Cassandra, trying to keep them both warm.

Her fingers and toes stung with the cold, but her nose hurt the most without any protection. Every now and then, she would rub her nose on Cassandra's back to make sure she still had it.

"You'd better not be wiping your nose on my cloak," muttered Cassandra.

"I wouldn't dream of it," answered Sheryl. There was silence for a little while.

"Cassandra?"

"Yes?"

"I have only ever heard of one other Cassandra, and she is the princess of Havenshire. Are you one and the same?"

"Does it matter who I am? Have I not offered you help, not knowing who you are?"

"I was just curious."

"Hush," Cassandra suddenly whispered, pulling the horse to a stop.

"What is it?" whispered Sheryl.

"I'm not sure, it's too far away. But whatever it is, is getting close. We should hide. Quick!" Both women slid off the horse and Cassandra whispered into the horse's ear, "Home, go home." The horse turned around and galloped away.

"What did you do that for?" hissed Sheryl.

"Instinct. I think whatever comes our way would kill him. I'm just trying to give him a chance to outrun it." The two of them scrambled through the bushes, looking for somewhere to hide.

"And what is *it*?"

"I don't know, but I'm afraid. Now hush, it's nearly here."

'It' turned out to be 'them', as several black shadows darted through the forest, sniffing out the humans.

Cassandra put her arm around Sheryl and threw an invisible spell over the pair of them. "Whatever you do," she whispered, "don't let go of me." She wriggled her nose towards the clearing where they had dismounted and a little gust of wind whipped up the dry red leaves and covered their tracks. As they watched the black blobs jump and fly from ground to tree to bush, she realised they were following their smell. Some horse dung lay a little up the way and she beckoned it and made it weave all over the earth where they had stood.

Suddenly, there was an ear-piercing screech as a demon dropped out of a tree and attacked the moving dung. On its cry, other demons descended into the clearing in front of them and started sniffing the ground like hounds. Sheryl slipped her hand into Cassandra's and was glad to find that she was trembling as much as she was.

A demon that looked like a cross between a pig and a dog jumped towards them. The women leant back and stiffened.

Cassandra lifted her finger to her lips in a silent hush, and then strengthened the invisible spell around them. The demon came into their bush. Sheryl's lip trembled as the demon's head came within inches of her. She nearly gagged on the vile, sulphur-like smell that came from it. It stopped and seemed to be waiting for a sound. Sweat dripped off Cassandra's face and her palms became sticky. She knew that, if they were discovered, she wouldn't have time to kill all of them before the demons had them.

Just then, a wolf's howl echoed through the forest. The demons all stopped moving and waited. Another howl filled the night and the goblin near the women jumped out into the clearing. In the moment it took the demons to decide to flee, Leona appeared. Her long blonde hair flew behind her, as she raced towards them with a pack of wolves at her heels.

The demons finally responded and started darting onto the trees or up into the air. Wolves leapt high into the air and caught demons in their mouths, pulling them back to the ground and ripping them apart. The ones that did make it into the air fared no better, as Leona came to a whirlwind halt in the clearing and started firing arrows of light at them, from her fingertips. One by one the demons were hit in quick succession, and instantly exploded into black dust.

It was over in a moment, only splatters of black dust marring the white snow and the lasting stench of sulphur revealing that anything had happened. Leona turned and looked towards their hiding place.

"You can come out now," she said.

Cassandra and Sheryl crawled out of the bush and stood up.

"Thank you," said Sheryl, eyeing up the wolves cautiously.

"The forest is not a safe place. We should return to my cabin as quickly as possible," said Leona.

"No argument there from me," said Sheryl. "Please lead the way." Leona turned around and started walking away.

"How did you know where to find us?" Cassandra called.

"The Sirocco witch sent me," answered Leona, without turning around.

"Come on." Sheryl took hold of Cassandra's hand. "She said 'cabin'. It will be a warm place to spend the night. By the way… thank you for saving my life."

"You're welcome," said Cassandra, giving Sheryl's hand a quick squeeze. They hastened after Leona and the wolves through the thick, falling snow.

"Who do you think she is?" whispered Cassandra.

"I don't know, but I'm glad she found us," answered Sheryl.

"So am I."

Not too long afterwards, the three women were sitting around the fire, holding empty bowls that had been full of vegetable soup.

"That was lovely," said Sheryl.

"Yes, I agree. Thank you," said Cassandra.

"You're welcome, ladies," replied Leona.

"Aren't you a bit too young to be living out here in the forest on your own?" asked Sheryl.

"I'm not on my own, though," said Leona, nodding her head towards the alpha wolves that lay curled up together in the corner.

"Wolves can't protect you from everything," said Cassandra.

"I know. But I also have my magic to protect me."

"You were pretty awesome out there," said Sheryl. "What I wouldn't give to have my magic back and to be as powerful as you."

Cassandra looked at Sheryl in surprise. "You were a witch?" she asked.

"I was. Until an ogre decided he wanted to take it from me."

"Which clan?" asked Cassandra.

Sheryl looked at her. "Earth," she replied after a moment, and waited for Sheryl's response. It was not what she expected.

"I am of the Fire-clan," she said. "We must be, like, cousins, or something."

"Or something," Sheryl answered with a smile.

"And what of you, Leona, what clan are you?" asked Cassandra.

"I'm not a witch," she replied.

"Oh, then how do you do magic?" asked Sheryl.

"I was born with it, it flows in my blood."

"Where do you come from and where is your family?" asked Cassandra.

"I can't explain where I come from," Leona answered. "I feel like I know, but when I try to speak of it, it becomes like a blur and fades. As for family, I am the last of my kind. Although, I do consider the Brothers to be my new family."

"Marcus's Brothers?" asked Cassandra.

"Yes, do you know them?" asked Leona, smiling.

"I know Marcus and Idi, and Marcus has mentioned the Brothers many times."

"How did they become your family?" asked Sheryl.

"They found me in the woods and looked after me, until I came to live here a few years ago."

"And they let you live here?" asked Cassandra.

"They took a great deal of persuasion, but yes, eventually they understood I needed to be here with the wolves."

"Aren't you afraid the demons might come into the cabin at night?" asked Sheryl.

"I am mindful of them when I am in the forest, but they cannot come in here. There is an enchantment on the cabin that enables only those I invite to enter."

"That is powerful magic," said Sheryl. They all sat quiet for a while, staring into the fire, lost in their own thoughts. Leona absent-mindedly tucked her hair behind her ear. A moment later, she caught Sheryl staring at her, puzzled, and quickly let the hair fall forward again. People looked at her strangely when her pointed ears were on show, and she had long since grown into the habit of hiding them behind her long locks.

They were up and dressed early the next morning, all for their own reasons in a hurry to reach Havenshire. They broke their fast with bread and cheese and camomile tea and little talking. When the cabin was clean, they went outside where Leona walked off a little way with the alphas. She bent down and spoke with them and when she stood up her eyes were sad.

"I can't take them with me," she said as she led her horse out of the stable adjacent to the cabin. "We should take it in turns to ride the horse. Cassandra, you're on first."

Cassandra didn't argue. She put her foot in the stirrup and sprang up onto the horse. They might be letting her ride first because she was the oldest, but she would show them she was still perfectly agile. They set off, going south towards

Havenshire. They would have plenty of time to get there before dark if they could run some of the way.

As they came out of the thickest part of the forest, and reached the part where the trees grew much further apart, Leona turned to Sheryl.

"Are you up for a run, Sheryl?" she asked.

"Sure am," she replied. They set off at a slow run so as not to tire too quickly. Sheryl knew that Leona held back, going slowly to enable Sheryl to keep up. Although the snow had stopped falling, the ground was covered quite deeply and it wasn't long before their dresses and boots were wet through. They had been running for several hours, and Sheryl's energy had gone and she was close to collapsing, when Leona called them to a halt. Cassandra climbed off the horse and passed the reins to Sheryl, who only nodded, not having the breath to talk. Seeing the state of Sheryl's dress, Cassandra hitched hers up and used her belt to hold it in place. With it now only reaching her knees, she would be able to run much faster without the added weight of a wet dress.

"Ready?" asked Leona. Cassandra nodded and they set off again. Cassandra pulled on her magic to strengthen her legs and she ran faster than Sheryl could have. After they had stopped for a light lunch, Cassandra insisted she wanted to run and let Sheryl get back on the horse. This time, though, they went at a fast walk as Cassandra's energy levels were dropping.

"Won't the horse be too exhausted if we don't rest a while longer?" asked Sheryl.

"Her name is Lightning and magic runs through her blood, thanks to Selwin who filled her and her brother, Thunder, with magic a long time ago. She'll be fine."

Full of excitement at the thought of seeing Sebastian again, Sheryl began to sing. Her voice lilted and dived, rocking between highs and lows, and Leona was reminded of a running stream. Leona didn't know the words but picked up the melody and began to chant her own sounds alongside Sheryl's. Cassandra thought it the most perfect sound she had ever heard and was deeply moved. When the song had finished the three women exchanged glances; this had been a special moment and none of them would ever forget it.

"Climb on the horse, Cassandra. She can carry both of you the last part," said Leona. Sheryl offered Cassandra her hand and helped swing her up onto the horse behind her. "Come on, girl," Leona said to the horse, stroking her face. Then they were off, the horse galloping and Leona racing like the wind beside her.

They made it to Havenshire well before dark, and as Leona led the horse over the drawbridge, the three of them felt safe and at home.

## Chapter 27 – Homecoming

Although she loved them, Katrina was finding Idi and Marcus's chaperoning overbearing and couldn't wait for the ship to dock. They had always been protective, but their constant shadowing of her left her feeling as if she couldn't breathe, and irritated at not being able to spend time alone with Absalom.

She'd only been allowed to attend the first day of Absalom's name-day celebrations. After that she had been inundated with numerous tasks, including packing. She had consoled herself with the thought that they would be spending three days onboard ship (with Loreiei left behind in Bluedane) and that she would have plenty of time to talk to Absalom about his declaration of love. Alas, it wasn't to be. Wrapped up warm against the biting wind, Katrina circled the deck repeatedly in an effort to keep active. It was Marcus's turn to watch her, and he sat in the shelter of the bridge, observing her through the window.

She had almost finished her exercise stomp when Absalom appeared. As soon as he saw her, he came to her with big strides, knowing their time alone would be brief. Katrina glanced quickly at the bridge, relieved to see the back of Marcus's head as he engaged in conversation with the captain.

Absalom reached up his hands and pulled Katrina's cold face towards him. He kissed her gently and then let her go.

She blushed, feeling shy, embarrassed and elated all at the same time.

"We reach Hamlyn Bay tomorrow and I wanted to talk to you before we do." Absalom threw a quick look towards the bridge.

"He's still talking," said Katrina.

"They are going to do their best to keep us separated. I am to go to the palace and they are talking about taking you to something called the Academy. My grandparents have signed an agreement with Trytellen, saying that I will marry Loreiei when I turn eighteen. I have told them I will do no such thing, but I can see they believe they will convince me… for the good of the people and all that. I need you to know, no matter what people say, that the only person I intend to marry is you. Wait for me, Katrina. I don't know how long it will be before I am allowed to choose my own wife, and I think it may not be until I am twenty-one. But wait for me, please. I promise I will never love another the way I love you."

"Katie?" They turned around to see Marcus coming towards them.

"I promise," Katrina replied.

"There you are, girl. Come on, let's go inside before we freeze to death out here," said Marcus, wrapping his cloak tightly around his body.

"I'm coming, Marcus," she said, smiling at him.

*Oh no*, thought Marcus, as he saw her sparkling eyes. "Come on, come on. I'm too old to be out here." And with that, he turned and headed for the door.

"I love you, too," mouthed Katrina, taking a last look at Absalom's deep-brown eyes, before hurrying after the grouchy magician.

Katrina sang a lullaby as she packed her bags the next morning, and Idi and Marcus looked at each other and grimaced.

"My singing's not that bad," Katrina said with a mock scowl.

"Oh, yes, it is," said Idi, and then ducked as Katrina threw her pillow at him. He picked it up and put it back on the bed.

"Katie, we need to talk," said Idi, standing in front of her.

"Oh, yeah? What about?" Idi threw Marcus a quick glance.

"I'm just going to say my farewells to the captain," he said, and hurried out of the room.

"You were talking with Absalom, yesterday."

"Talking isn't a crime, is it?"

"Don't be insolent, Katie. It really doesn't suit you."

Katrina sighed and sat down on the bed. "Sorry," she said.

Idi sat down next to her. "We just don't want you to get hurt, Katie. That's all."

"Absalom would never hurt me, Papa."

Idi took hold of her hand and absent-mindedly stroked it with his thumb. "My little girl is all grown up," he said with a smile.

"Is that what's wrong? Are you worried I will leave you, or that I will love you less? You know that will never happen. This space here…" She tapped her chest with her free hand. "…Will hold my love for you and Marcus, always."

"No, that's not what worries us. Absalom is betrothed to another and we fear, if you continue to love him, that nothing but heartache awaits you."

Katrina was caught off-guard a little by the fact that Idi knew she loved Absalom.

"He's told me he will never marry Loreiei."

"Kings don't always get everything they want, and in the tradition of marrying to secure alliances, I'm afraid all kings normally end up with a wife not of their choosing. Even Absalom's grandfather, Hamish, had to send the woman he loved away when his father announced he must marry Cassandra's mother. It is said, though, that they grew to love each other very much after their marriage and that he swore to never love another when she died. So even arranged marriages can be happy ones and Absalom will come to realise this in time."

"He's promised he will marry only me," said Katrina, but all her fight had gone and her shoulders stooped.

Idi wanted to hold her and tell her everything would be alright, but he had never loved like this and didn't know what to say. He wanted to tell her Gallagher would make a fine husband, for it was true – he was a lovely man – but he knew she didn't want to hear that. So instead, he wrapped his arms tightly around her and squeezed her tight.

"You always give the best hugs, Papa," she said, nuzzling into his chest.

A few hours later, they were standing on the docks watching their crates being loaded onto wagons, which Hamish had sent to pick them up.

Katrina had walked her horse, Snowflake, carefully down the aisle. She was obviously pleased to be on solid ground once more, and shook her mane and neighed. Katrina rubbed her head against Snowflake while stroking her.

"She managed that journey better than I did," said Gallagher.

"Yes, she did. I know it wasn't great for her being cooped up like that, but I just couldn't leave her behind."

"You go over with Marcus; I'll tie Snowflake to the back of the carriage."

Katrina smiled at Gallagher and passed him the reins before joining the others.

"We'll make our goodbyes here," said Valarie. "We need to return home straight away."

"It's been a pleasure being in your company these past seven years," said Tanner, giving a tiny bow before her.

"It has indeed been the same for us," said Valarie. "I feel like I'm saying goodbye to family."

"Yes, but I'm sure we will meet again, won't we?" said Losia, looking at Valarie.

"With the Elements' blessing I'm sure we will," answered Valarie.

"That's good," said Losia, taking a step to stand in front of Tanner. "I'll miss you, magician," she said, reaching up to kiss him. To everyone's surprise, instead of pulling away, Tanner bent his head down and returned the kiss. Losia pulled back with the biggest smile on her face.

"Thank you for your company and for your added protection. I can assure you it's been gratefully received and not unnoticed, and we'll be sure to tell King Hamish how valuable you've both been in keeping his grandson safe," said Idi.

"It's been an honour," said Valarie. "Time to go home now, though, Losia." The two of them transformed into their fairy size and, like fireflies, went darting and sparkling through the air and were gone.

"Not sure the folk back home will believe I've been living with fairies," said Gallagher.

"A fairy and a pixie," corrected everyone at the same time.

A short distance away, the royal guards were greeting Absalom.

"They're leaving straight away. I'd best be off. See you in Havenshire," said Tanner, before going to join Absalom. Katrina watched as Absalom mounted a huge black horse and went galloping off, surrounded by Hadrian knights and Tanner close behind. She caught Idi and Marcus staring at her and plastered a large, 'pretend' smile upon her face. Not convinced by her 'happy face' Idi took a step towards her.

"So, are we ready then? Shall we go?" she said, cheerily.

Idi hesitated, but then decided that if she was trying to pretend nothing was the matter, he should go along with it. "Yep, let's get going," he said.

They were jolly as they climbed into the carriage; the footman closed the door and climbed on top to sit next to the driver. Marcus suddenly sat up straight and smiled.

"I can't wait to get back to the Homestead. You know, James cooks the most excellent mutton stew. I hope he's made some for us. I think he knows it's my favourite."

"We're not going to the Homestead, Marcus. We're going to Havenshire," said Katrina, with worry creases on her face.

"Why would we go to Havenshire? No. We're going home to see the Brothers, aren't we, Idi? They'll be missing me, you know, I've been gone for weeks."

Katrina looked at Idi and he shook his head as if to say 'let it alone'. She moved up close to Marcus and put her arm through his. "So long as we're together, Marcus, then I'm happy," she said.

"Me, too, my little darling. Me, too," said Marcus, looking out of the window.

The sky was alive with reds and oranges as the light began to fade, throwing a golden glow over the snow-covered farmlands of Havenshire. Katrina felt a bubble of excitement as they crossed over the drawbridge and into the town. The smell of evening meals wafted through the streets and they could hear people singing, probably in a tavern somewhere in the distance. Two old men walked the cobbled streets and lit the oil lamps that cast jumping shadows all around. As they alighted the carriage, Katrina looked around at a part of town she wasn't familiar with.

"Where are we?" she asked. "Aren't we going to our rooms in the castle?" Just then, Thomas, James and Raymond came rushing out of a building.

"You're here at last," cried Thomas, throwing his arms around Marcus. James and Raymond joined in the hug and patted Marcus on the back. Just then, more Brothers came charging out of the building with whoops and yells.

"We've missed you, old man," said Caldwin. It became obvious that Marcus seemed a little disorientated.

"Come, let us go inside, everyone. Out of this cold night air," said Caldwin, taking Marcus by the arm and leading him inside.

"Is he alright?" Anthony asked Idi.

"Age has crept up on him. He seems to have got old all of a sudden," he answered.

"You made stew! See, I told Idi you'd remember it was my favourite, Oh, tis good to be home."

They all smiled at each other as they heard Marcus and James discussing food inside.

"Well, it's good to see he's not lost his appetite," said Thomas.

"Come on, everyone. Let's get inside," said Raymond. A rush to unload the coach ensued, and as soon as it was empty, the driver left to return to the castle. Gallagher and Katrina stood looking at each other, holding their bags.

"Your ma will be pleased to see you," Katrina said.

"And I her," answered Gallagher. "Look after yourself, Katie. And if you ever need me, you know where to find me." Katrina dropped her bag and threw her arms around him. At first he didn't respond, then, after a few moments, he relaxed and returned the hug.

"You're a good friend," Katrina said when she let him go. He nodded at her before turning and walking down the street.

"Come on, Katie love. It's cold out here," said Idi, who was standing behind her. She bent down, picked up her bag and put a smile back on her face as she looked up at him.

Once inside, the warmth of the building washed over her and Katrina quickly untied her cape and took it off. She gazed around the hallway, trying to take in all the quirkiness of the place.

As soon as the Academy had opened its doors to students of magic, the Brothers had been inundated with requests to join; the volume of applications had taken them by surprise. Another thing that had astounded them was the number of books that had been donated to the Academy – so much so that the library had long since started overflowing into the hallway, where quick, makeshift shelving had sprung up to accommodate them all. The result was that the hallway now looked like the most higgledy-piggledy library ever seen.

"I'll take you to your room," said Raymond, offering to take Katrina's bag from her.

She was a little surprised when he took her bag; she wasn't used to being treated like a lady. At the age of sixteen, she still dressed in leather breeches, men's shirts and a close-fitting waistcoat. With her hair cut short, she was often taken for a boy. Although, she had to admit, those occasions were becoming fewer and fewer as her body not only grew upwards but also become more feminine.

They were just about to climb the stairs when a bell rang out from the kitchen.

"Step back a moment," said Raymond, leaning back against the wall. Idi and Katrina copied him and stood with their backs to the wall. There came a rumble of activity from all over the house, and then people came charging out of rooms and running towards the kitchen.

"Slow down," Raymond called out. Several close by dropped into a hurried walk, but others coming down the stairs did so at maximum speed. Raymond's hand shot out in front of him and the next lot of lads to come charging down the stairs crashed into an invisible wall. "I said go slow," said Raymond, frowning at them. There must have been about fifteen lads on the stairs, aged from seven to seventeen. They instantly shuffled into an orderly line, knowing Raymond would hold them there until he was sure they would walk.

Raymond lowered his hand and the gang of lads walked past, reasonably slowly, nodding at him as they went. Katrina couldn't help but smile as the last one went by and gave her a wink.

"Are they always so boisterous?" she asked.

"Only at mealtimes," Raymond answered, before heading up the stairs. They went up two levels and walked down a long corridor, which itself had a short flight of steps, first down and then up. "I'm afraid you will have to share. We have moved our two youngest out of here to share with some of the others. It is the only space we can offer you, I'm afraid."

"That's wonderful, thank you," said Idi.

"We're used to sharing," said Katrina.

"Yes, she likes it really. She gets me to check under her bed for monsters before she'll go to sleep," said Idi.

"Papa! Don't fib."

"As soon as you're ready, come back downstairs and join us for supper," said Raymond.

Supper turned out to be a jolly occasion. Two enormously long tables completely filled the annex to the kitchen, and around them on benches sat about fifty people of mixed ages. It was noticeable that there were only three girls, and Katrina made a note to ask the Brothers about this later. She had expected the Brothers to all be sitting together, but they weren't. They were dotted around the tables with the students, and everyone was talking fifteen-to-the-dozen, the noise quite deafening.

After the meal, cleaning and washing up was a joint effort and magic was practised all over the place, with plates and cups often flying through the air to land in the two huge sinks in the kitchen.

"Stop practising with my dishes," yelled James several times, before eventually giving up and heading to the parlour.

The parlour was small, cosy and jampacked with comfy chairs in a semicircle around the fireplace.

"This is where we come for a bit of peace and quiet," said Caldwin, pouring himself a cup of tea and taking a chair by the hearth.

"Strictly no students allowed," said Anthony, going to the sideboard and pouring himself a tea. Idi made a drink and went to sit down next to Caldwin; Katrina came and sat on the floor by his legs and leant back against his chair. Ginger and mint incense burnt in the corner of the room, and that aroma mixed with the crackling wood-fire made the room feel so relaxing that Katrina closed her eyes and just listened to the Brothers talking.

Idi gave an account of the past seven years in Bluedane, with Marcus adding the occasional 'that's right'.

"So then, you are happy he is of the light?" asked Raymond.

"Yes, most definitely," replied Idi. "We've watched him closely for signs that the dark might be calling him, but none have been noted."

Katrina pricked up her ears to listen as she realised they were talking about Absalom, and half opened her eyes to see who was talking.

"We heard the fairies planned to kill him, if they had any doubts about him," said Thomas, as he stuffed his long clay pipe with tobacco. Katrina shivered.

"Well, they didn't kill him, so they also must believe he has chosen the light," said Idi.

"I didn't know that was why they came with us." said Katrina. "I always assumed they were there to help us protect him."

"The prophecy states that if he turns to the dark he will release the Sister-witches and they will destroy Talia, so I can understand why they might have wanted to kill him," said Anthony.

"How could he release the witches?" Katrina asked, sitting up straight.

"The 'One' will have dominion over everything in Talia, including the witches, and... quite unfortunately, he will also have the authority to release all prisoners. And, as the Sister-witches are prisoners of the orb, he could pardon them and set them free," said Caldwin.

"He'd never do that," said Katrina.

"Let's hope you're right," said Kailin.

"Tell me about Norvora," Marcus said. There was quiet for a moment, with the Brothers looking at each other. "Spit it out, we need to know everything."

Kailin stood up and went to stand with his back to the fire.

"The news is not good, Marcus," he said.

"I didn't think it would be," Marcus replied.

"Since you've been gone, Norvora has been building his army. We don't understand why men are joining him and we think he might be using his magic to control them in some way," said Kailin.

"Some of our scouts have reported back, saying his army no longer looks normal – that their eyes are completely black and they don't talk any more. They've nicknamed them the soulless ones," Caldwin interjected.

"His army is so large that he can't contain them within his three towers any longer, and they camp permanently around the fortress instead," added Anthony.

"We believe his magic has become extraordinarily powerful and we're sure he's ready to attack," said James.

"We believe he's been waiting for Absalom to return, and now he has, we think Norvora will make his move," said Kailin.

"We must go to him," said Katrina, jumping up. "He's in danger without any of us around him."

Kailin reached out to touch her arm.

"It's alright, lass. We have not been idle ourselves in the last seven years. We have created a shield around Havenshire and spent years researching ways to make it impregnable."

"So Norvora can't get to the castle?" Katrina asked him.

"Well, not without us knowing, nor without giving us plenty of notice. So you see, so long as Absalom stays within the boundaries of Havenshire, he'll be safe." Katrina turned to look at Idi, searching his face for what to do.

"He'll be fine, Katie. Besides, he's not alone – Tanner is with him. Come and sit back down," Idi said, patting the side of his chair.

"If you don't mind," Katrina said, "I think I will take myself off to bed. I feel shattered." As she left the parlour and entered the hallway, the front door opened and, with a gust of howling wind, two women walked in.

"Leona!" cried Thomas, jumping out of his chair and rushing into the hallway to hug her.

"Thomas," she said tenderly.

Cassandra hesitated before knocking on the door. She was unsure of the greeting she'd receive from her father after having left him for so many years, yet again. She took a deep breath and tapped gently on the door. A brief moment later, she heard a quiet 'come in' and turned the handle.

Her eyes went straight to Hamish, who was sitting by the fire. Shock at how much he had aged hit her. He looked like an old man, with bent shoulders, thin grey hair and a wrinkled face. However, when he saw her, his eyes lit with joy and he got straight to his feet. She ran to him, throwing her arms around him, and they hugged for a long time. When they separated, Hamish sat back down and Cassandra launched into her prepared speech.

"Father, I am sorry I have been away so long, but…"

Before she could say anything more, Hamish interrupted her. "Cassandra…" he said, holding up his hand to stem her words. She looked at him, worried. "…There is someone else in the room.

Cassandra slowly turned around, looking for the other person. A young man stepped forward, coming into the light. Cassandra felt her heart heave and pain gripped her chest so tightly she thought she might die.

"Hello, Mother," said Absalom. Cassandra burst into tears and started sobbing uncontrollably. Absalom took a few quick steps across the room and put his arms around her.

"Here, here," said Hamish, offering her his hankie, "come sit down, child." Absalom manoeuvred Cassandra and helped her into a chair next to Hamish.

"How? When?" Cassandra finally managed to mutter when the crying eased off.

"By ship, and today," answered Absalom.

"You're sixteen," said Cassandra and started sobbing again, for all the lost time, and all the missed birthdays. Absalom looked at Hamish, a bit uncertain what to do.

"I think your mother needs a brandy, lad."

Absalom quickly went across the room to the drinks table and poured a glass full of rich-smelling brandy. Cassandra accepted the drink with shaking hands.

"Sorry," she said. "I will be alright in a moment."

The three spent the next few hours exchanging news and getting to know each other all over again. There were a few points when Cassandra couldn't stop the tears from flowing, mostly because she realised that, although Absalom still obviously loved her, a gap imposed by years apart was obviously present. And then there were other moments when they laughed together, and as the night grew long, Cassandra was filled with a quiet joy at being reunited once more, not only with her son, but also with her father.

"I am so happy to hear you've been well looked after – and more, that you've been loved. It means everything to me," said Cassandra, reaching out to touch Absalom's arm.

"Yes, I have been well looked after. Think I might even be a bit spoilt with all the attention I've received. There is, however, one thing that saddens me."

"What's that?" asked Cassandra, sitting up straight, worried about what he was about to say.

"They want me to marry some girl called Loreiei, and no matter how many times I tell them I'm not going to, they ignore me and continue with their plans. I love them both very much, but I won't agree to this."

Cassandra sat back, relieved. "You will not have to marry her until you are twenty-one," said Cassandra. "You will have grown used to the idea by then."

"What? You've not met her and you would encourage my marriage, even though it's not what I want?" said Absalom, moving his arm away from her touch. The movement showed Cassandra exactly how much her son was opposed to the idea of marrying Loreiei, but still, he was to be king of Talia.

"We are of royal blood," said Cassandra. "We often have to do things we wouldn't choose to, but we do it for the good of the people. We have responsibility and that comes before our wants and likes."

"You haven't even asked why I don't want to marry her," said Absalom, standing up and moving to stand in front of the fire.

"Why don't you, Absalom?" asked Hamish quietly.

Absalom bent down and put a few more logs onto the waning fire. When he stood up again he turned to look at them, standing tall, with his shoulders back. Cassandra was struck again at his resemblance to his father.

"Because I am in love with Katrina, and she is the only woman I will marry."

"Little fighting Katrina?" asked Cassandra, shocked.

"She is not so little any more," smiled Absalom.

"But she's the magician's daughter?" said Cassandra, trying hard to work out her feelings.

"And? What does that mean?" snapped Absalom.

"Does this girl love you in return?" asked Hamish.

"She does."

"Then you are right. This Katrina is the one you should marry," replied Hamish.

"Father!" snapped Cassandra.

"Hush, my dear," said Hamish, reaching over to take her hand. "Love is the most important thing in this world. We are here to grow in knowledge and in our ability to both give and receive love."

"But you had to marry the woman your parents chose for you," said Cassandra.

"And so I did, to strengthen the ties between Havenshire and Ilfordton, but where are they now in our hour of need? I did love your mother deeply, Cassandra, but I must tell you I loved another before her and my heart broke when she was sent away."

"Rhianna," said Cassandra.

"How do you know that?" asked Hamish in surprise.

"It's a long story and I'll tell you another day, for we should all be to our beds now."

"So you agree I can marry Katrina?" said Absalom.

"I think we need to talk about this when we're not so tired," said Cassandra.

"Yes, you can marry her so long as you really love her," said Hamish.

"Father," said Cassandra with a big sigh.

"Sweetheart, you're not listening to me. Love is the most powerful defence we have against the world of evil that perpetually seeks to destroy us. If the lad and this Katrina love each other, we should give them our blessing and rejoice with them. Let their union make them strong."

Outnumbered by the two people she loved most in the world, Cassandra succumbed to them and nodded. Absalom smiled in relief. He would, of course, marry Katrina no matter what they said, but their blessing would endorse his marriage. A servant carrying a lantern showed him to his room, and despite the late hour, he walked with lightness of step and of heart.

## Chapter 28 – Stratagem

During the early hours of dawn, the Sirocco witch had summoned them all in their dreams, her impartation of gravity and secrecy waking them all and putting them on edge. They had started arriving in Hamish's private study before the light broke; the urgency of Moriya's calling made it impossible for any of them to delay. As the Grey-moon began to ascend, throwing its cold light over Talia, the servants came to light the fires and, as soon as they were done, Hamish ushered them out of the rooms.

Present were: Absalom; Marcus; Idi; Katrina; Tanner; Kailin; Hamish; Cassandra; Sebastian; Myles; Leona; Voltar; and Valarie.

"How many did she call, do you think?" asked Hamish.

"We wait only for Lily and Amber," said Moriya, stepping forward and revealing herself to the group. "Ah, now that is good timing." She turned around and opened the large glass windows, where Lily and Amber both appeared and flew into the room.

"How did she get in here?" whispered Marcus to Idi. "I didn't see her come in, did you?"

"I believe she makes herself visible or invisible at will," Idi whispered back.

"Tad annoying that, don't you think?" grumbled Marcus. Moriya flicked her fingers at the windows, closing them.

"Come," she said, moving towards the desk. "There is much to discuss." She waved her hand at the desk and all of Hamish's papers, books and inkbottles picked themselves up and landed neatly on the floor on the other side of the room. She waved her hand across the table again and a huge parchment appeared, filling the entire surface. As she waved her hand over the paper, a map of Talia began to appear. Everyone gathered around the table and watched in awe as mountains, forests and cities appeared on the parchment, courtesy of an invisible brush.

"Here," she said, pointing and making an X appear on the paper, "is where the Great Battle must take place." Heads leant forward to see where she'd indicated.

The map was marked in a place halfway between Havenshire and Norvora's towers.

"From the north," said Moriya, wiggling her fingers and making miniature dwarfs appear over Tamarind, "shall come Turtledoff and seventy-five others. From the mountains…" She paused as miniature ogres appeared over the Torrean Mountains. "…Crannog-Fergal and his new family will come. From the south…" Tiny witches dressed in blue hovered over The Lakes. "…Lily shall bring the Water-clan, and from the Lowlands, Amber brings the Earth-clan." Witches in brown appeared over the Lowlands. Moriya pointed to Bluedane, and tiny ships hovered over the Silvestre Sea. "The Bluedanions will come from the west, and from here…" She pointed to an area between Rhayador and Ilfordton, and the images of men and women appeared. "…Will rise up people who have been in hiding from Norvora and his armies."

Over the castle in Havenshire, miniature knights emerged, their purple and gold armour glistening; there was no need to mention Hamish's army. Moriya looked around the table and then pointed to Norvora's three towers. A snake rose off the parchment, huge and hissing, and everyone stood back in fear.

"Fear him you should, for his evil heart has taken him to the darkest of places, from where he can never return. He spits poison from his forked tongue and transforms his men into fighting creatures, who do not question his command. You will recognise them straight away when you come face to face with them in battle, for their souls have gone and their eyes are black. Do not pity them or show mercy for they will not do the same for you."

"Surely, with so many of us standing together, we will defeat Norvora easily?" said Hamish.

"Destroying evil is never easy, and nor should you be fooled into thinking it is. It will take all your combined strength to stand a chance of defeating him," replied Moriya. "Besides, it is not just Norvora and his army." Moriya pointed to the Great Plains and goblins appeared, carrying weapons and shields. Then, as she pointed to the far west of the Torrean Mountains, demons sprang forward and darted all over the parchment.

"I thought we'd seen the last of those pesky things," muttered Marcus.

"Unfortunately not," replied Moriya.

"Why must the battle take place there?" asked Myles. "Surely it would be better to stay behind the magic wall of Havenshire that the Brothers have built?" There were a few murmurs of agreement.

"Sometimes, what appears to be a place of safety can become a prison. Trust me when I say, I have seen what follows if you take that decision. I know you must decide for yourselves because you have free choice, but I hope you understand I only point you towards a different option because I believe it will be a better outcome for you?"

"What happens if we stay in Havenshire?" asked Sebastian.

"It is not my place to tell you the future, only to guide you, if you will listen." All the illusions faded into gold dust and showered down onto the map. The Sirocco witch was already beginning to fade.

"Please, don't leave us yet," implored Leona.

"I have done all I can. May the Elements be with you." As she disappeared, the Brothers spoke out. "And also with you."

"She didn't say when we should go there," said Katrina, pointing to the north of the Lowlands.

"We have two days to get there and be ready," said Leona. No one questioned how she knew; her magic was way past what any of them could fathom.

"We will be there," said Lily, walking towards the window.

"Thank you," said Hamish. "Thank you all for being so loyal to Talia and its people." Amber nodded to the king and then followed Lily out of the window.

"We must also go, and make our people ready," said Voltar, "but I am afraid the fighters we have are few. Still, we will join you and be ready in two days' time." Voltar and Valarie then transformed into fairy size and flew out of the window.

"If no one else is going to jump out of the windows, would you mind very much if I closed them? I'm feeling a bit nauseous, watching them leave from such a great height, not to mention freezing," said Marcus. He closed the windows and came back to the table, rubbing his hands together to warm them.

"So, we have ogres coming to fight with us? Now that, indeed, is an extraordinary thing. Do you think it is true?" asked Marcus.

"I believe it may be," said Cassandra. "I met a woman called Sheryl on my way back to Havenshire. She…"

Sebastian cut in. "Sheryl? Long brown hair, talks too much?" he asked.

"That describes her pretty well. Do you know her?"

"I am suddenly filled with tremendous hope that she is in fact my wife. Tell me, please, where did you last see her?"

"I said goodbye to her at the Academy, last night."

"Your grace, may I?"

"Go, but return swiftly, for there is much to get ready." As Sebastian rushed out of the room, Hamish asked, "Anyone else leaving?" They shook their heads. "Good, because we have much to plan. Now, let's try and work out why here…" Hamish tapped the X. "…Is our best hope of winning."

By the time Sebastian reached the cobbled streets of the city, he was running and sending up silent prayers that the Sheryl at the Academy was *his* Sheryl. As he pulled himself to a stop in front of the doors, he took a moment to catch his breath and put his hands on his hips, trying to calm his rapid heartbeats. *Damn, but I'm too old for this.* He was just regaining control of his breathing when the door opened and out walked Sheryl. They faced each other for a moment, filled with shock at the unexpected reunion, both drinking in the appearance of the other. Then Sheryl flew towards him with her arms wide and he stepped forward and picked her up, swinging her round and round.

"Stop, stop. Put me down, I'm getting dizzy," Sheryl laughed.

"I've missed you, woman."

"I thought you might have found yourself someone else by now."

"Never. You are the only one for me." Sheryl started crying. "Here, what's the matter?" asked Sebastian, drawing her tight against his chest.

"When you didn't come to find me I just assumed you had found someone else," she said.

"I might not have found you, but I searched for you, Sheryl, at every chance I had to take time off. I went back to Crannog's place three times, but it was obvious no one was there. I didn't know where you had gone; I didn't know how to find you. Why didn't you come home to me?"

"I kept thinking the gateway would be finished soon, that I would get my magic back and then come home. But it's taken all this time to create it."

"So, you have your magic back?" Sebastian asked, holding her away from him so he could see her face.

She shook her head. "It's not finished, but it will be soon."

"Then why come home now?"

"Because Crannog mentioned that he couldn't guarantee I would be able to return to Talia and I just knew I couldn't go. You mean more to me than magic."

He pulled her back to his chest and wrapped his arms tightly around her. "I don't want to ever let you go again," he said, bending down and kissing the top of her hair.

"Good, because I don't want to be let go of," said Sheryl, smiling.

"Then get your things because I need to be back at the castle, like, yesterday."

"I don't have any things, Sebastian, and I have said my goodbyes to everyone already. I was actually just coming to the castle to find you."

Leaving Sheryl in the kitchens, Sebastian raced down the corridors and back to the king's rooms.

"Ah, good, you're here," said Hamish. "Leona was just about to tell us of another danger we have yet to encounter." The group had pulled up chairs around the hearth and Sebastian grabbed a stool, came over and sat down with them.

"They are half human, half dragon," said Leona, looking around at everyone. "I haven't seen them attack anything yet, but I know they are getting bigger every day and that they fly over Talia doing reconnaissance for Norvora. I've tracked them many times and they always return to his towers."

"But if you've only seen six of them, why do you think they're so dangerous?" asked Myles.

"I can feel…" Leona struggled, looking for the right description. "…Something evil emanating from them. I have also seen them shooting fire from their mouths." She shuddered. "It fills me with dread when I see their human-looking faces open their mouths, almost as big as their heads.

The flame-balls they shoot are as strong as any dragons. Their hands are like humans and I've seen them throwing spears, yet their feet are like dragon claws. They are just horrid and unnatural."

"So, as well as demons in the air, we'll also have these things you call Dragon-demons. So, how do we protect ourselves from the skies?" asked Idi.

"We need rings of archers who have some kind of covering to keep them safe. If we put them in strategic places, they may be able to keep a large area of sky clear above us," said Myles.

"What should we use for their covering?" asked Hamish.

"I have an idea," said Kailin. "In the Academy we've been experimenting with different minerals and acids. We have come across a mixture that makes wood very hard to set alight. If we make wooden domes, with cut-out slits for the archers to shoot through, and cover the dome with this new mixture we have made, then it should be fireproof."

The rest of the day was spent devising different safeguards and planning where everyone should be. When the Grey-moon began to dip behind the mountains, they were exhausted. The next day they would begin to set all their plans in motion and hoped they'd surprise Norvora by coming halfway to meet him in the open plains and rolling knolls that were the Lowlands.

## Chapter 29 – A Meal Shared

There wasn't anything more to be done to prepare everyone for the morning. Traps had been made and set, weapons oiled and cleaned, and directions given for where everyone should be.

"Is there enough food for everyone?" Idi asked.

"The Earth-clan has been cooking up a storm, I hear," replied Tanner. "I heard someone say they'd emptied their stores completely to ensure everyone was well fed this evening."

"Elements bless them," said Marcus.

"We should eat," said Katrina, looking between Idi and Absalom.

"I agree," said Absalom. "Come, I believe the Bluedanian soldiers have set up a huge tent for us in the middle of the camp."

They followed, a diverse bunch of friends, harbouring mixed emotions. The witches insisted on bringing the food to the tent, so everyone piled in and sat themselves down on the multicoloured rugs scattered on the floor. A fire pit sent up sparks of heat and a warm glow against the cold and sombre mood. Some of the Earth-clan witches served up thick vegetable soup and warm bread to everyone, and although tasty and hearty, it was eaten slowly, with most people lost in thought.

They were outnumbered by Norvora's army by five to one, and even if they managed to win the battle, many were going to lose their lives the next day.

"Let us remember that the Elements are with us," said Marcus, as the soup bowls were collected and taken away. Although Marcus had spoken, most people were looking at Idi, and he felt their expectation lying heavy on his heart. As he stared into the flames of the fire, he longed to offer them some words of comfort, but no inspiration came to him.

Suddenly, the flames jumped high and danced with erratic energy. As one, they leant backwards away from the flames, and before anyone could get to their feet, the flames began to take on the appearance of a woman. Now everyone was on their feet, pulling on their weapons.

"No need for that," said the apparition, slowly waving her hand around the tent. As she did, all the weapons instantly became too hot to hold, and were quickly let go of and dropped to the ground with yelps of surprise. The woman took a dainty step out of the fire pit and, as her feet came to touch the ground, she solidified into a beautiful, tall woman.

"Moriya," said Idi.

"Hello, Lon," she said, smiling at him. The room instantly relaxed as they realised the witch meant them no harm.

"Have you come to fight with us?" asked Absalom hopefully.

"No. I don't fight, young man. But I have come to offer the fairies something." Most heads turned to look at Valarie and Voltar.

"What would that be?" asked Voltar.

"Power."

"And what would you want in return for this power?" Voltar asked.

"You are children of the firstborn of Talia. As fairies, you've been given the ability to hide yourself away from the entanglements of humans. Yet you choose to reveal yourself and side with these people…" Moriya paused to do a slow sweep of the room with her hand. "…Even though this might endanger your own people and bring about their destruction."

"If we don't help and Norvora wins, the Sister-witches will be released and Talia will be no more," said Voltar.

"Yes, but as high fairies of Hal-Luna-Tania you know you could have gone through a gate into another world and saved all your kind." From Moriya's green-flecked eyes poured passion-filled firelight and Voltar was suddenly lost for words as he absorbed her radiance. Losia looked at him, puzzled. She had never liked him, had thought him pompous and arrogant, so this new revelation that he could have taken the fairies and run left her slightly in awe of him.

"But the blood of these people would have stained our hands and our hearts if we'd deserted them," said Valarie.

"So you sacrificed your entire race to aid them?" asked Moriya.

"No," said Voltar. "We've only given ourselves and the ones with us, who have pledged their lives to help save Talia. I left instructions for the others to go through the gate before the sun rises."

"What about the pixies?" Losia asked quietly.

"We sent word to them explaining what we were planning and giving them the opportunity to join us, either here in battle or with the exodus. So far it looks like none has joined us here."

"Actually, we came," said a voice towards the back. Everyone turned to see who had spoken.

"Elroy!" exclaimed Losia. He offered her a smile and then turned his attention back to Voltar.

"Our people have gone to be with yours, and our thanks are eternally yours," he said. "I brought with me eight warriors, the highest skilled in battle we have." Eight black-clad pixies came fluttering into view and hovered behind him. "Sheiline, our healer, also insisted on coming with us." She came fluttering forward to hover around Elroy's shoulders. "And Audrey refused to go into the new world."

Audrey, also standing in human height, placed her hand in Elroy's, squeezing it gently, and said softly, "Live or die, I stay by your side."

"How many fairies have come to be by your side, Voltar?" asked Moriya.

"Seventeen highly skilled warriors, Valarie, myself, and now it seems we have Audrey as well." He smiled at Audrey; he should have guessed she would come.

"Twenty fairies and eleven pixies," said Moriya. "I have something to propose to you all, and you must agree as one whether to accept or reject my *gift* of more power." Something in the way she said gift made it sound more like a punishment.

"Tell us plainly, witch, what it is you ask for in return," said Elroy.

"I can give you power that will increase your magic tenfold, but in exchange I'll need to take your wings and your ability to shape-shift." There was a quick gasp from several of the people present, who knew what that entailed.

"I won't be able to live if I can't fly," said Losia.

"You ask too much," said Voltar.

"Will tenfold magic be enough to win this battle tomorrow?" asked Valarie.

"It will give you more of a chance of doing so. Norvora's power has grown beyond anything we have seen before. It will take powerful magic to stop him and his army."

"Why can't the Oracles come to aid us, as they have in the past?" asked Tanner. "Surely, with them by our side, we could win this fight in moments?" A general murmur of agreement followed his question.

"The Oracles are always with you. They have already begun to orchestrate things to aid you. Yet, you need to know, the number of Oracles is low and their power diminishes. The war with the demons, which came close after the battle of Olecranon, killed a number of Oracles and, to this day, they haven't been replaced. As their numbers decrease, so does their power, which is at its greatest only when the twelve thrones are filled."

"Our magic is in our wings," said Elroy.

"And shape-shifting and flying keeps us safe," said Audrey.

"If you sacrifice your wings to me, to help save Talia, I will lodge a deeper magic into your bones. The loss of your wings will be felt in your spirit always; I will not be able to take away from you the feeling that a part of you is missing. But the magic I will give to you will be more powerful than anything else ever seen. However, you must be united, for, in exchange for this power, I must take the wings of all or none."

"I give my wings gladly, if it means I can help Talia be free of evil," declared Valarie.

Without hesitation, Losia spoke next. "Wherever my friend goes, I go, too. You may take my wings."

"And mine," said Audrey.

"Mine, too," said Sheiline. The warrior fairies and pixies also came in without hesitation, affirming their sacrifice. Now only Voltar and Elroy remained quiet, and a heavy expectation lay around them as everyone waited for their response.

"What size will we be?" asked Voltar.

"Taller than a human," Moriya answered.

"So we'll never be reunited with our families," said Elroy.

"No," Moriya answered.

"Could we win this battle without the change?" asked Voltar.

"You might, for anything is possible with the Elements by your side. However, it is the Elements that have sent me to offer this to you; I do not think they would ask this of you if it were not necessary."

"Then you can take my wings," said Voltar.

"Mine as well," said Elroy. As soon as the words come out of Elroy's mouth, a large explosion erupted around them, causing everyone to gasp in surprise and instantly duck. As the boom faded, everyone came up from their crouching position and looked at the new people who stood in their midst.

Seven feet tall, slender and amazingly beautiful, these people were only just recognisable by their facial features, the only thing of fairy and pixie to remain. Their ears, tall and pointed, stood through their hair, and their eyes (all blue) were wide and slanted to the sides. Their clothes, although remaining the same in colour, were now tight-fitting bodices and trousers, with huge leather belts that hung on their hips. Soft leather boots tied with string came over their knees, and from their shoulders hung soft wooden capes. On their backs they carried bows and quivers full of arrows. From their belts hung long, slender, decorative scabbards, which held their shiny swords.

Moriya had disappeared but her voice came floating through the tent.

"You will only be powerful if you remain united in honourable intent and, from this moment on, you shall be known as Elves."

"Who is that witch, that she can come and go as she pleases and walk in fire?" asked Voltar.

"I've heard it said that she's really an Element, the Fire Element to be exact," answered Marcus. "She appears as a witch so she can communicate with us."

"Would an Element really reveal themselves to us?" asked Katrina.

"It would explain why the Sister-witches started screaming when she came to us in Bluedane," chipped in Gallagher.

"Whoever she might be, she is the most powerful being I have ever seen," said Marcus. "But come, we should try and get some rest."

Later that night, when everyone had gone to try and grab some sleep, Valarie and Losia were still talking quietly by the fire.

"My heightened sense of smell is driving me mad," moaned Losia. "I can smell Myles's smelly socks, Tanner's body odours, and even the previously nice smell of Cassandra's lily perfume is driving me crazy."

"It is the smell of disease coming off Marcus that distresses me," replied Valarie.

"Has your hearing changed as well?" asked Losia.

"Yes, isn't it dreadful? It's going to take me a long time to sort out every sound that comes. Now, for example, I feel like the whole camp is snoring. It's torture."

"I can hear people's whispers; it's like snakes hissing in my ear. I hate these things." Losia hit her long, pointed ear, which was sticking out through her hair.

"Maybe we will get used to it," said Valarie, "if we have time."

"What do you mean by that?" asked Losia.

"I have something I need you to promise me," said Valarie.

"Anything," answered Losia.

"If I should die tomorrow, I want you to promise that you will, for all time, look after Voltar."

"You're not going to die," said Losia dismissively.

"We are unable to shape-shift or return to fairy size," said Valarie. "I fear we are larger targets now than ever before. Promise me, Losia? Voltar needs someone to love and protect him."

"I'm not sure I could ever love him, Valarie. He is arrogant and overbearing."

"Promise me," said Valarie, with pleading eyes.

"You're frightening me, Valarie. Why do you think you'll die tomorrow?"

"On the night Absalom was born, the Elements descended on Talia in the form of rainbow-coloured winds. It was magnificent. They filled the air and their beauty took my breath away."

"I remember that night."

"They told me that, when this battle came, I would have a choice to save either myself or Voltar. I knew, of course, that I would always save him."

"That's a terrible thing to have told you," said Losia, with tears in her eyes.

"Not really. I was glad. I was given a purpose for living and a reason for dying. Voltar will be the king of this new race of Elves, and he will build a magical realm for you all to live in. I will die knowing I have made the right choice." They stared at each other for a moment in the love of true friendship. "Promise me," Valarie said.

"I promise."

"Idi?" Idi turned around to see who had called him. Thomas had entered his tent and was standing in the doorway.

"Come in, Thomas. What is it?" Thomas let the door flap shut behind him and came over to Idi's makeshift camp bed.

"Earlier, when the Sirocco witch arrived, she called you Lon. I was just wondering why?"

"Here, sit down beside me," said Idi, moving along to make space for Thomas. Thomas sat on the edge of the bed.

"She called me by the name given to me by the Lady of Treffernon. To be honest, I didn't think anyone knew about it. Why do you ask?"

"The Lady of Treffernon… now I should have guessed that. The very same lady told me that a great magician called Lon would regrow my fingers for me." Thomas lifted his hand, so long ago torched by the Shee-dragon. "Will you heal me… Lon?"

Idi took Thomas's hand and wrapped his own hands around it. "I'll try," he said and closed his eyes. Immediately, Thomas felt heat flooding into his head, so much so that he wanted to pull away from it. The heat kept intensifying and Thomas began to sweat and struggle with the urge to snatch his hand away. Idi neither moved nor spoke; he just held Thomas's hand and poured his love and magic into it.

"I don't think I can take much more, lad," Thomas said, his whole body shaking with the intensity of power that was flooding his body. Idi's eyes flicked open. For a moment they were sparkling black, and then the colour faded and his own eyes returned.

"It is done," he said, letting go of Thomas's hand.

Thomas looked down at his hand and gasped at the sight of its restoration. He brought his hand up to his face and wiggled his fingers, then looked at Idi in amazement.

"You truly are the greatest magician Talia has ever had," he said, before throwing his arms around Idi and holding him tight.

## Chapter 30 – Annihilation Hill

Mist swirled in waves and covered the small hills that had been prepared for war. You could only see a short distance in front of you and the damp eeriness was putting everyone on edge. The Grey-moon would soon begin its ascent and bring some light into the freezing morning. Everyone was in place, waiting, and silence lay heavy in the air.

The ogres and the Bluedanians were yet to arrive and everyone hoped they would come with the light.

Seven archer-domes had been built by the carpenters with the aid of magic, and these formed a sort of circle around the hills. Within the circle the armies waited, weapons and ammunition piled high beside them.

Three Brothers remained in Havenshire to protect the city and the king, and to maintain the magic shield for as long as they could. The rest of the Brothers and the two witch clans had spread themselves evenly among the people.

Idi felt no fear for himself; he knew this was what he'd been born to do. However, fear for Katrina, Marcus and the others had wormed its way into his spirit. His palms were sweating and his legs felt weak. He closed his eyes and began pulling on his magic. He felt it charging through his veins, and his toes and fingers began to tingle. It brought him some reassurance as it strengthened his body, and he turned his concentration to his breathing, bringing his soul to stillness, where strength lay.

The first they knew the enemy had arrived was the swishing sound of something flying above them. Id ground his teeth. They'd been waiting hours for the demons to attack and, with the coming of dawn, everyone had begun to hope they weren't coming. Now they would be disheartened, their resolve slightly weaker.

"Light the beacons," Sebastian yelled. One by one, gigantic beacons were lit, and light flooded the Lowlands. Even though it was still misty, the soldiers were able to see enough to start firing arrows at the demons as they dived at them. From silence to chaos within seconds, with both men and demons screaming.

The Brothers climbed on top of boulders and lightning flew from their fingertips. It was timeless, feeling like both an eternity and a split second, and then the Grey-moon crept over the edge of the Torrean Mountains and the remaining demons retreated. A brief pause filled the air as they wondered what would happen next. They were to find out only too soon as Norvora's army came charging across the Lowlands on horseback.

"Wait for it," hissed Myles to his men. The horses came closer, their eyes glowing red and froth flowing from their mouths. "Wait," repeated Myles. Some of his men nervously clutched the rope, wanting more than anything to pull, but trusting their leader and biding their time.

"Now," yelled Myles. They pulled on their ropes and wooden spear traps sprung out of the ground and speared the horses. They came crashing down but the men simply jumped up and continued with the charge. The rows of riders behind the first wave simply leapt over the barriers and came rushing past the running men.

The Earth-clan took to the air and rained down magic bombs upon the approaching army. They did a good job at halting the charge as both horses and soldiers fell. Then they were joined in the air by the half-man half-dragon creatures, and the witches began to fall as they were covered in fire. The Elves came charging to the front; racing with intent and incredible speed, they leapt into the air and threw spears at the creatures. One was hit and came screaming to the ground, where men pounced on it and made sure it died.

It was impossible to see what was happening all around him, and Idi knew he needed to find Norvora, hoping his death, if he could kill him, might mean the war was over. He closed his eyes and searched in the magic-realm for Norvora's spirit. Just as he found it, there were yells from behind, and Idi knew the goblins were attacking the back ranks. He heard men screaming and wanted to help them, but knew he had to find Norvora first. He started walking, and a wind went before him, knocking everyone out of his path. Some of Norvora's men came charging towards him but simply bounced off his invisible shield.

As he went, he caught sight of Marcus, standing on one of the knolls, wielding his staff around his head and causing whirlwinds to blast the advancing goblins. He looked ahead, needing to concentrate; he could feel Norvora advancing, coming to find him.

Norvora was no longer a man; all trace of his humanity had gone. He slithered towards Idi with hate radiating from his black and green slit eyes, which lacked lids. His forked tongue shot in and out of his mouth, dripping poison. The horror of seeing a man's features in the folds of a snake's broad face nearly made Idi heave. Norvora's black and red body was larger than any tree and Idi was afraid.

They stopped a short distance away from each other; Idi began calling his magic forth, while Norvora coiled his body beneath him and began to ascend with slow, rhythmic movements.

The mist had cleared and daylight was with them. In the distance, Idi could hear the battle going on and sent a prayer to the Elements that they had done enough and would prevail. Suddenly, thunder cracked in the skies above them, and clouds raced overhead. Norvora dived on the roll of thunder, like an arrow, towards Idi, his mouth opened wide, revealing his teeth. Idi strengthened his shield and Norvora crashed against it, making it shake but not breaking it. Norvora recoiled, but before he could strike again, Idi dropped his shield and lightning flowed from his fingers. Norvora hissed in pain but flicked his tail and hit the now unguarded Idi, sending him flying through the air.

Again and again, Norvora and Idi struck at each other. Lightning and thunder hammered the skies and rain fell, drenching the earth. They were left to their private battle as the war raged around them.

Leona hated waiting, but that was what they'd asked her to do. To wait until the enemy had converged entirely within the circle, and then attack from behind. Singarti and Bleddyn stood either side of her, awaiting her instructions. No one could see them as she had covered them all with an invisibility spell. She watched as people she knew died, and cursed her promise to remain hidden for as long as possible.

She watched Voltar, Valarie and the other Elves, in awe at their speed and magical strength, and longed to be with them. Yet she waited. In the distance, she could just see Idi battling with Norvora, and she sank her spirit into the ground and pleaded to the Earth Element to help him. Absalom and Katrina battled together, sword against sword with Norvora's soulless army.

Idi was tiring; he could feel his magic ebbing slightly and knew his time was running out. It was now or never. An image of Katrina's face came to him as he leapt high into the air and came down with such speed that fire flew from his body. As he came down, he called forth a magical sword into his hand. He had learnt many things in the library in Rodanti, but he hoped this would be the most important. His love for Katrina flooded his body and flowed into his sword of fire just… as the sword sliced through Norvora and cut off his head.

Lily and her witches were in trouble. Many already lay dead, their blue dresses soaked in blood. The goblins had charged over the knoll towards them and they'd killed many of them, but then a second wave had come leapfrogging over to jump into their midst. Lily called to the falling rain and commanded it to become a living creature. The water bowed to her wishes, reaching down in ribbons and strangling the goblins. Her witches used whatever they could to kill them, but despite everything, they were losing and she knew it. They were outnumbered and there was no way they would survive.

Leona could wait no longer. She dropped the invisible spell and drew forth a silver sword. Holding it high, she yelled, "Now!"

As one, Leona and the pack of wolves went racing over the Lowlands. She went with such speed that the wolves couldn't keep up with her. She felt only one thing: rage. Her friends needed her and she would do all she could to protect them. The wolves howled as Leona reached the goblins before them, but she didn't wait. Like a blur she sliced her way through them.

Idi looked at Norvora's shrinking body in shock; he couldn't believe he'd actually managed to kill the wizard. Norvora's snakeskin fell off him in pieces and dissolved, leaving behind the broken body of an old, withered man. Idi spun round to face the battle. Would the soldiers surrender now their leader was dead? The answer to that was no. They either didn't know he was dead or didn't care, and the battle carried on regardless.

"The Sister-witches!" said Idi, and began searching the area for the orb he knew held them prisoner. Panic filled him when he couldn't find it, for surely they were keeping the soulless army going? Then, through his distraught fog, he thought he heard Katrina calling for him. Instantly, he was racing back into battle, blasting wind-bombs as he went, throwing the enemy high into the air.

Crannog-Fergal and his new family finally reached the place the Sirocco witch had told them to come to. Thara had stayed behind to watch over Timo and Daffy, and Gwawr had remained to keep humming to the door.

"This isn't good," said Crannog, as they observed the battle in front of them.

"They're outnumbered," said Celestine.

"Crannog, ladies," said Bert, nodding towards the ogres. "It's been a pleasure getting to know you, and I want you to know, if I don't make it out alive today, that I consider you my family."

"Everyone," said Bert to the Fart Platoon, "are we ready?" As one, they yelled 'yes', then, brandishing their weapons, they went charging down the knoll towards the battle.

"Human bones," said Gwynn, rubbing her stomach.

"Gwawr's going to be so upset she had to stay behind to guard the gateway when we tell her how many humans there were."

"Now, ladies, I thought we had agreed we're going to be vegetarians," said Crannog.

"Well, one last feast wouldn't hurt, would it?" said Nuala.

"Well, yes, actually it would," grumbled Crannog.

"We promise only to eat dead ones," said Agrona, winking at Crannog.

"Oh yes, definitely only dead ones, Crannog. We're not barbarians, you know," said Nuala. And then, before he could make them promise not to eat the humans, the five female ogres went stomping down the hill, causing miniature earth shudders as they went.

"Eee, I hope you know what you're doing, sending us here, Moriya," said Crannog, as he went marching down the hill behind them.

The Bluedanian army was getting close. They could hear the battle and were trotting in military files. The captain of the guard had taken control yesterday, after King Piedro had been killed in an ambush. Absalom was their king now and they went steadfastly into the Lowlands, determined to reach him.

The day was waning and dusk was falling, and still they battled on, weary with exhaustion but unable to stop, as the soulless ones and goblins continued their attack. If they couldn't pull the ranks together before it got dark, the demons would probably come and finish them off. An unspoken agreement was felt by them all, and the leaders of all the groups started pulling back into a tight circle. This meant the attackers were met with a solid wall.

Idi's spirit screamed: enough! He was searching his mind for the best way forward when Leona turned up at his side.

"Help me," she said, as she knelt down and touched the earth. Without questioning, Idi came down beside her, put his hand on her back and started channelling his magic into her. The ground began to shake and moan, and then erupted in front of them, burying hundreds of soulless ones. A couple of them were able to scramble out of the earth, but the rest were sucked into the core of the ground, never to be seen again.

"It's getting dark," he said as they stood up. "We won't be able to see who we're killing soon."

"Then make it light, Idi," she said, before turning and charging back into the battle. *Make it light? Of course, make it light!* Idi looked around for the best place to stand and decided it should be on the tallest hill. He ran through the battle, killing goblins and soulless ones as he went. As he ran past an ogre with a man hanging out of her mouth, he was relieved to see the uniform showed it was one of Norvora's men. She grinned at Idi as he ran past, her teeth tightly clenching the man. It was weird that he should feel happy to see a human in an ogre's mouth. She thumped another one on the head and squashed him to bits on the floor. Idi nodded at her and carried on running.

On top of the hill, he was a little out of the battle, but it did give him a good view of what was happening. Not only that, but Katrina and Absalom were on the next knoll and he was relieved to see they were both still standing. Idi scraped on the earth to make two impressions big enough to sink his feet in. He needed the Earth Element's help. He called to her in his spirit and She came instantly and magic raged in his body. He threw his hands up in the air and demanded that there be light.

For a moment, nothing seemed to happen, but then the Silver-moon came gliding across the skies with incredible speed. So much so that most of the fighters stopped to look into the sky. The moon came to a stop above the battle, and then, very slowly, began to descend. Now a murmur of fear spread through the battle and the goblins and soulless ones began to back away. The lower it came, the brighter it became. When it was as light as day, it stopped and hung still above them.

Bevan watched the magician call forth the Silver-moon and was in awe of his magic. He would have fled then, but from somewhere close the Sister-witches were calling him to kill Idi. There was nothing he could do; he was pledged by blood to serve them, and so he gathered his Supreme platoon to his side and left the battle. They edged into the shadows and began creeping around the outskirts of the battle, and a short time later they were close to the hill where Idi stood.

The light would keep the demons at bay, and with the arrival of the ogres things were looking up, but Marcus suddenly felt a shiver go down his spine and he looked at Idi in alarm and fear.

"They'll be coming for him," Marcus yelled, as he started running towards the hill. A few of the Elves heard him, including Voltar and Valarie, and they joined Marcus and Tanner as they raced towards the hill.

*An inconvenience, that's all,* thought Idi, as he pulled the arrow from his arm and cast it aside, not troubled by the blood that poured. He roared as he flung his arms out, lightning bolts flowing from both his palms. Anger drove him, and fear, not for himself but for *them*. His Katie and the prophesied one, fighting back-to-back on the next hilltop. He could feel Marcus getting close and was comforted that the old man wanted to be near him. Idi was tiring. Holding the moon was taking all his strength and the battle's end seemed nowhere in sight.

He roared again, the sound louder than the thousands of grunts, moans and yells going on around him. Even the knights looked at him in slight trepidation, glad he was on their side.

The magic was in control; it no longer seemed concerned with him, but wanted the moon. It soared through his body, trying to escape, so much so that little sparks kept escaping from his skin.

"Stand back," he yelled at a group of their men who were being beaten back by flying goblins. *Flying? How did they learn to jump so high?* Their leapfrog racing across the hills had enabled them to jump their makeshift barriers so easily. *Easily? Why didn't we build them higher?*

His arms moved so fast they became a blur to the normal eye, as he sent shot after shot into the goblins. Each bolt hit a mark and split a goblin in two. But it wasn't enough; there were too many of them and they kept coming, jumping, closing in. Suddenly, lightning bolts were flying through the air in all directions. People nearby ducked and swerved to get out of the way, as Kailin and Tanner joined him on the hill.

"Damn!" Another arrow hit him, this time in the leg. Trying to conserve his magic for fighting, and holding the moon in position, he pulled this one out without using his magic, the pain nearly too much. Sweat began to pour from his forehead and he staggered slightly. Instantly Matthew and John were beside him, reaching out to steady him. He knocked them away.

"I'm fine, leave me." They took just a moment to assure themselves he could stand and then turned once more to firing magic-lightning at the goblins and soulless ones.

"Demons!" yelled Valarie. Instantly, the Elves were racing around the hill, forming a circle around Idi. Their long, graceful legs sped them forward with tremendous speed. Their new magic took control of their instincts, making them fast and fearless. Arrows flew from their bows, which they hadn't even noticed they had aimed. Sparks flew from the arrowheads and every shot found a demon and extinguished it.

Leona saw the demons flying towards the two hills. She didn't know how they managed to stay in the light, but that didn't matter because they were obviously going straight towards Idi and Absalom. She raced against time itself to help them. Her elbows snapping back, her knees bent, she bolted with magic-filled power. Her long, blonde, curly hair flowed behind her. The huge wolves took a moment to wail their war cry at the sky, and the sound of their howling sent shivers down many a back. Then they were racing after her, the cry of their human mother calling to their souls as they bounded over bodies and sped to keep up with Leona. She urged them forward, for the Elements, for life and for Talia!

It became obvious to all that the battle was being drawn to Idi. He stood like a magnet on the hill and the full attention of the enemy was crashing down around him. Voltar and Valarie were shooting arrows that came from never-emptying quivers. Their arms should have been aching beyond belief by now, but instead they felt as strong as they had been at the beginning of the day. Then Valarie saw it. An arrow with a red head, flying through the air, and she knew this was the moment. She jumped the distance between herself and Voltar and, as she landed in front of him, the arrow hit her in the back. The thud of it sent her flying into Voltar and the two of them crashed to the ground.

As he rolled her over, pain soared through his body as he looked into her lifeless eyes. "Valarie," he wailed, and threw his arms around her, cradling her to his chest. Losia was by his side in an instant.

"Not now," she said to him softly. He wanted to punch her, but he knew she was right and gently laid Valarie down. Jumping up, he began racing down the hill, firing arrows from his bow like a maniac. Losia raced after him, and unbeknownst to Voltar, saved his life, over and over again.

## Chapter 31 – A Quest Complete

The hill spun, dipped and rose again, and Idi's stomach lurched, sending waves of nausea to drown him. His legs gave way first, and he crashed to the ground on his knees, registering defeat in his frail human body. He stayed kneeling, momentarily frozen, as his exhausted eyes drank in what he knew would be his last vision of her.

On the crest of the adjoining tor, Katrina and Absalom stood back-to-back, fighting yet another wave of goblins, their swords flying through the air with killer precision.

Black. Nothing now. Finished. He fell forward into silence and darkness, his face crashing into the red-streaked watery mud. Immediately, the Silver-moon began to rise, high into the sky and back into its normal position.

He was pulled from drowning in the slush of wet mud by numerous hands. They turned him over and laid him gently on a makeshift stretcher. *Go away. Leave me alone. I want to stay in the dark and the quiet.* Someone was tapping his cheeks. *Let me be.*

"Come on, my boy, open your eyes." Idi groaned. "That's it, come on, hold on to the light. It's not time to leave us yet." Idi's eyes flickered open slowly. The pain of leaving the peaceful nothing was too much and sorrow overtook him. Tears spilled down his cheeks, clearing pathways on the mud mask he now wore.

"I can't save him," Idi choked. Marcus wrapped his soft, cool hands around Idi's face, forcing him to look up. Idi knew he'd been wounded; he felt the heat more than anything else in his shoulder and left thigh. He felt the blood, which had been hot when it poured from his body, begin to turn cold as it ran down his skin. He had enough magic left in him to throw a masking spell over the pain, but he knew it wasn't enough to heal himself. One of the arrowheads must have been tipped with poison and he didn't have the strength to fight it. Soon the poison and the loss of blood would sap the life from his body.

"I let her down, I couldn't save him. I failed you all." The pain of admitted failure was far greater than his fear of the death-stalker who would be coming for him now.

Tears ran down Marcus's cheeks as he smiled softly at Idi, his chest hurting with the pain of the love he felt for him. "You haven't let anyone down. Not Oleanna, not me, not Absalom. No one."

"But I'm dying. I don't have the power to save him now."

"Look," said Marcus, cupping his arm under Idi's head to raise him slightly. "What do you see?" Idi's chin wobbled as emotion rose within his chest.

"I see children fighting without me there to protect them."

"I see the king you saved the day you picked up a baby girl in a field." Idi tore his eyes away from the battle to gaze at Marcus's sparkling blue-grey eyes. "The moment you rescued

Katrina, you saved Absalom. She is the catalyst in his life that determined the victory of good over evil. Their love for each other is what will save Talia, and as for you… you completed your quest the day you introduced them to each other."

Pain escaped the magic shield and sent a crushing stab to Idi's chest. He started coughing and bits of blood spurted from his mouth.

Marcus looked up at Damien. "Have you enough magic left to make yourself and others invisible?" he asked him.

Damien nodded. "Yes, I believe so."

"Good. James will go with you. Take him away from here and let him die in peace." Idi couldn't speak, but his eyes implored Marcus. "I promise to do all I can for them, lad," Marcus whispered as he kissed Idi on the forehead.

Damien and James lifted the poles of the stretcher and Damien instantly threw out an invisibility spell around them. They ran as quickly as they could, for although no one could see them, they were still exposed to flying arrows and stray flings of a sword. Idi closed his eyes and welcomed the quiet calm of nothing as it enveloped him once more.

They ran in magic-timing until their chests felt like they would explode, and finally came to a staggering halt near the Galayian lakes. They lowered Idi gently down on the soft grass and knelt beside him to see if he still lived. James put his hand on Idi's chest and leant forward, putting his ear near

Idi's mouth. Slowly, he sat up, his eyes watery and resigned. He folded Idi's arms over his chest and then stood and took off his cloak. He laid the cloak gently over Idi's body and, with great sadness, covered Idi's face.

"We should get back to Marcus. We can still be of some help," said Damien.

"We can't just leave him here like this," replied James.

"Why not? We are all dead now the magic is running out. There will be no one to bring our bodies to a peaceful place, so, in a way, he's lucky."

James couldn't find an answer. He knew Damien was right. This wasn't going to be a battle they would win, and the world of Talia as they knew it would be no more from this day forth. He dropped to his knees by the side of the lake and sank his head in the water to drink. Damien did the same. As they rose out of the lake, water falling from their faces, they reached for each other and embraced in a hug that meant both I love you and goodbye. Then, without words, they stood, took one last look at Idi's body, and then they were running back to their teacher and back to the battle of death.

A breeze blew through the lands, its touch soft and refreshing. James's cloak moved in the gentle gust and slid off Idi's still and cold body. Leaves dropped from the branches and floated down around him. The waters of the lake became choppy and, for the briefest of moments, the clouds parted and the Grey-moon's heat poured down into the clearing where Idi lay.

Through the gap in the clouds, Moriya came, riding her lammergeyer, its huge wings gliding them gracefully through the sky. As the bird touched the ground, the Sirocco witch slid off its back and moved elegantly across the glen towards Idi. She sank slowly to her knees and reached out with her hands to cup his face. She leant forward, as if to kiss him, her long, fiery curls cascading like a waterfall of fire. Instead of a kiss, she blew breath gently into him and then sat back and waited.

Warmth was racing towards him, although he didn't know from where it came. It was this realisation, that something approached, that chased the 'nothing' away. As the welcomed heat flooded his body, he opened his mouth and breathed.

"Wake up, Alfonso," the witch whispered over him. Idi opened his eyes to see the beautiful Moriya smiling down at him.

"Am I dead?" he asked without emotion.

"Why do you all insist on believing that death is a place where you arrive? 'Tis not that, not at all. Death is not where you arrive or what you become, it is but a journey," she answered.

"A journey to where?"

"A better place, a better you."

"I don't understand. Am I still alive?"

"Come," she said, offering him her hand. "I want to show you something." Idi accepted her hand and stood up. She hadn't answered his question and he was afraid to repeat it. He didn't feel like himself; he felt odd, like he was in a fog. He looked down at the ground, half expecting to see his body still lying there. The witch chuckled and pulled Idi behind her as she headed towards the giant bird.

She sat down sideways, crossing her ankles. "You should sit astride him so you don't fall off," she smiled. Without question or fear, Idi swung his leg over the lammergeyer. No sooner had he sat than the bird took a few swift steps forward, spread its wings and lifted them into the air.

*If I was alive now I would be afraid of falling.* Idi put his arms around the witch's waist and held on tight. She threw back her head and merry laughter fluttered in the air. It was cold and exhilarating. *What a wonderful way to get to heaven.* It didn't seem as if they had been flying very long when the bird began to dive once more. As the land below rushed to greet them, Idi became disappointed, for he had thought heaven would be in the sky.

They landed on a hill outside a small village. Moriya got off the bird and stood staring, and Idi peered hard to see what she looked at. It was a typical village. A few black-and-white timber houses in bad repair surrounded a cobbled square. A few farmhouses lay dotted around in close proximity. A tugging began in the back of his mind. *Have I been here before?*

"What do you see?" the witch asked.

Idi squinted. "Not much," he replied. "A rundown village, a poor place by the looks of it."

"Keep looking."

Idi threw her a puzzled look. "This isn't where I'm to spend eternity, is it? I know I failed everyone, but please, there must be somewhere better for me than here. Isn't there?"

"Lon, open the eyes of your spirit and look."

Idi wondered for the briefest of moments how she knew his name was Lon, but he let the thought pass as his gaze returned to the village. It was the children that did it. A small group were playing together in the village square, girls with a skipping rope and boys kicking a ball around. One of them began to cry and suddenly a pain of memory rippled through Idi's soul.

"Clodoth," he whispered, hoarse with emotion. Suddenly, memories of beatings and name-calling came crashing down on him and he sank to the ground, covering his head with his arms.

"Is this my punishment for failure? To live once more in this place, which despises me so?"

Moriya looked at him. "Are you Idi or Lon?"

The question took him by surprise. Until this very second, he wouldn't have hesitated to confirm he was Idi, but now, as his eyes went once more to the village, he knew he couldn't lie to himself. He wasn't the same lad who had left here all those years ago, belittled and downtrodden. He was Idi the magician… no, he was Lon the magician. Lon, the name given to him by the lady of the lake. The short name with no meaning. But joy was tugging at his soul, demanding to be let in. It didn't matter. It really didn't matter what his name was, because he knew *who* he was.

A very gentle smile formed on the witch's lips as she gazed at him with love. "What do you see, Lon?" she asked again.

He studied the area for a while and then said, "A place without joy, abundance or riches. A place of no hope."

"Do you think there is anything you could do, to make Clodoth a happier place?"

For the slightest of moments, a flicker of longed-for revenge danced in his mind. But just as Marcus had taught him, he took his imaginary bat and whacked the thought far from his being.

"I remember carrying buckets of water from the stream until my arms throbbed. If the well worked it would save the women and children many a laborious trip." He looked at Moriya. "Can you fix the well?" he asked.

"No, but you can."

"I've lost my magic – it's gone."

The witch tutted. "Once you believe in magic, once it dwells in you, it is there for ever. It never leaves or forsakes you."

"But on the hill it ran out. I couldn't do anything any more. That's how I got shot and why I died."

"You don't look very dead to me." Moriya's eyes twinkled.

"I'm not dead?"

"No. Like I said, there is no such thing as 'dead'."

"But I thought you had come to take me to heaven?"

"Is that what you want?"

"No. No, that's not what I want."

"What do you want?"

A multitude of thoughts flooded him, myriad different things he wanted fought in his mind for first place. He took a deep breath in through his nose and let the air out gently through his lips. The Elements would take care of Katrina; her life belonged to them. Anything he could wish for would only be fleeting, here and then gone. Nothing he wanted for himself would change the world and what it was becoming.

"I'd like to fix the well," he answered.

"Then fix it. You might have stopped believing in magic, but it never stopped believing in you."

Idi closed his eyes and searched for his light. It came bounding towards him with joy the moment he looked for it. *Hello you, my old friend. The well needs fixing.* Lightning flashed across the sky and thunder roared in the distance and Lon opened his eyes. A rumbling below the earth was first heard, and then felt, as the land shook with the power of magic.

There was a loud 'pop' and suddenly water shot from the village well, twice as high as the tallest house, before cascading down like a waterfall in slow motion. The children yelled and laughed, and started dancing in the water. Adults flooded into the square to see what had happened and joined the children jumping up and down in the water.

"Without water there is no life," the witch said. "Come, let's go and say hello." They walked down the hill together, while the lammergeyer snuggled down in a dip and remained behind. Lon had thought about returning to the village for years to punish them all with his magic. Yet now, as he walked towards his old home, the feelings of revenge had gone. Love, he realised, had dissolved his hatred.

As they were nearing the square, a tall, thin man bumped into him. "Sorry, sir," the man muttered as he rushed by.

Lon was surprised; Melvin hadn't recognised him, but he'd instantly recognised Melvin. The boy who'd tormented him the most was now a sickly-looking man. Melvin ran with a limp into the square, looking for something. As soon as he found what he was looking for, the tension fell from his shoulders and he limped awkwardly before stooping to pick up a young lad and squeezing him tight.

"Time for home," Melvin said to the lad, putting him down on the ground and taking hold of his hand. "Your ma will be awful worried that something has happened to you."

"Ah, Da, you know tis you and not Ma who be awful worried," the boy answered.

"Melvin?" Lon said as he approached. The man and lad came to a stop before them and Melvin looked at Lon with questioning eyes.

"Aye sir, that's me. What can I do you for?"

"It's me," answered Lon. No sign of recognition came from Melvin. "It's Idi, who you chased through the village too many times to count."

First bewilderment, then disbelief hit Melvin's face.

"Is that really you?" he whispered.

"Yes, tis really me. Albeit a grown-up me," said Lon, patting his stomach. Suddenly Melvin was crying. Not a few tears, but a bucketful of sobs.

"What is it?" Lon asked in concern. The little boy still holding Melvin's hand began to cry. "You're upsetting the lad," Lon urged. Melvin tried pulling himself together and wiped his runny nose on the back of his sleeve. He scrunched his eyes closed for a moment and then looked straight at Lon.

"Forgive me?"

Lon took a tiny step back in surprise.

"Please forgive me? I have pleaded with the Elements for years that they would return you here so I could beg your forgiveness. Now, here you are! I can't believe they answered my prayers!"

Lon was speechless. He had never imagined in all his years of dwelling on the past that Melvin would want to say sorry. Every last vestige of hurt dissolved and he laughed out loud as he realised that, while he had been thinking this trip was for him, in fact it was for the villagers and, it seemed, especially for Melvin, his sworn enemy. He threw his arms around Melvin and held him tight, sending waves of healing into the man. Melvin felt the heat enter his body and recognised the touch of magic, and he fell instantly onto his knees, thanking the Elements.

"Get up, Melvin," Lon said softly. Melvin got up slowly, but his knees were shaking.

"I thought you had killed yourself," Melvin said with a catch in his voice. Lon's eyes opened wide. "You never came back and everyone said there was no way you could have survived, so either the wolves ate you or you killed yourself." Lon could see Melvin was struggling with his words and felt himself fill with pity.

"I've been on a quest," Lon said. "I became a magician so I could help the future king of Talia. I would never have killed myself."

"My entire life has been plagued with nightmares of your death. I thought many a time the only thing that would stop them was if I took my own life, but then Ellen became pregnant and I knew I had to look after her, no matter how bad my night terrors."

"I'm awfully glad you didn't kill yourself, Melvin."

"You are?" Melvin answered, shocked.

"It's time for us to leave, Lon," said Moriya. Lon gave Moriya a quick look and then turned back to Melvin, his face full of compassion.

"Look after yourself, and be happy."

Melvin was choked by Lon's words; his chin wobbled terribly, making him unable to speak, so he simply gave Lon a slight nod.

Lon and Moriya began the ascent back up the hill.

"Can we go back to the battle now? I thought I was dead and not able to help, but well, now I know I'm still alive, I really, really want to go and kill those pesky goblins."

"I must return home to my desert in Salmiranda, so you must go alone."

"It's a long way," said Lon, obviously disappointed.

"It will give you time to think," Moriya said, turning and walking away from him.

"About what?"

"About the power of words," she called before she disappeared.

He stood on a hill and looked to the distance. He felt strong and healthy, so why couldn't he hit magic-timing and race back to the battle? His voice echoed through the hill and beyond as he yelled at his magic to appear. *I just cleared the well. What is wrong with me? Why can't I run?* He sat on a log and stared into the distance, trying to visualise what was happening in the battle. Had they won? Was it over already? He couldn't hear anything.

"Will somebody please help me? What am I supposed to do?" He buried his head in his hands.

"Hello, Lon." Looking up, he saw Oleanna and Draconsis walking towards him. He stood up.

"Have you come to take me back to the battle?"

"No," smiled Oleanna. "We have come to take you home." And he knew then, without further explanation, that home was Carin-dair, the palace beneath the seas. The three of them started walking together and, as they went, their feet slowly lifted them into the air and they flickered between substance and vapour.

"Have they won?" Lon asked, as they disappeared.

\*\*\*\*\*\*\*\*\*\*

Just as it seemed all hope was lost, the sound of drumming came across the Lowlands.

"Grandfather!" said Absalom and laughed. They would surely win now, for their numbers were about to be increase twofold. He swung around in a moment's quiet, grabbed Katrina, and kissed her hard.

"What's that for?" she asked with a grin.
"For still being with me," he answered, seriously.

Bevan defied the witches calling in his head and rounded up his platoons. "Retreat," he yelled repeatedly. He wanted to be gone long before the Bluedanians arrived; he'd already lost too many goblins. The soulless, however, heard only the command of the Sister-witches and, obeying without question, continued fighting.

Two of the Dragon-demons had been killed and the rest had fled, bar one, who stayed only because her wing was broken and she couldn't fly. Amber came face to face with the monster and locked visual contact with the lizard-like eyes that blinked in from the sides. Half the demon's face was covered in scales while the other part was human skin.

"What manner of vile creature are you?" Amber asked, although she didn't wait for an answer as she and three of her Earth-clan witches pulled on their magic and started firing lightning at it. The Dragon-demon opened her mouth wide, getting ready to aim fire at the women.

"Oh, no, you don't," yelled Belinda, throwing a cannonball of water through the air and into the Dragon-demon's mouth. She floundered, dropping to the ground.

Three Dragon-demons were flying high above Talia; they were young and inexperienced and wanted their lair. As their wings beat tiredly and carried them towards the Tremblin Forest, their anger suddenly flared, as hovering in the sky in front of them, on their broomsticks, were the Fire-clan. The sky became a burning furnace as flames shot across the expanse between them.

The Bluedanian army brought about the end of the war, as the very last soulless one was struck down.

The survivors looked around in horror at the death smothering the Lowlands. The only ones truly happy were the ogres, who were heading back to the mountains, pulling at least fifteen dead men each by their ankles (excluding Crannog, of course, who kept repeating that he was most unhappy with the situation and their lack of resolve, as the females talked about the delicious patta-cakes they were going to make).

"Hey, big guy!" shouted Bert, "aren't you waiting for us?" The entire Fart platoon came trotting across the plains after Crannog and the others. Crannog turned around and started laughing.

"Thought I'd got rid of the lot of you," he said. Then, when he saw Celestine's face, he quickly followed it by, "Just kidding, of course." It was a miracle they'd all survived, they were badly bruised and cut and they had to carry Hurricane, whose leg looked pretty bad, but apart from that they were good.

When the captain of the guard handed Absalom his grandfather's crown, he felt too numb by the battle to respond. There would be time later for mourning; for now they needed to check the bodies for people who might be alive and get them back to Havenshire before the cold, if not their wounds, killed them.

A great clear-up began and the dead were gathered together for burning, as there were too many of them to take home and bury. The Fire-clan arrived and Shona went to find Lily and Amber and offer them assistance. It had been a day and night of the strangest things, and the Fire-clan offering help seemed no more strange than anything else. As the pyres burnt the dead, the three clans of witches began to sing. It was in a language no one but a witch could understand, yet it was beautiful and moving. Many who had stayed strong the whole time suddenly found themselves giving in to tears and weeping for the tragedy of war.

As the Grey-moon rose once more and brought with it some light and a little warmth, they turned their backs on the blood-soaked plains and knolls and headed for home.

Victory? Well, they were still alive, but no winner's joy was theirs as they carried the scars of war home with them.

**********

They waited thirty-three days to let the people mourn, before the coronation took place. Absalom was glad they'd waited. People were smiling and waving as they made their way to the cathedral. The crowd went mad, cheering the procession as it came through the streets of Havenshire.

Hamish had died of a heart attack while the battle took place, and with Piedro also dead, Absalom was now ruler of the complete kingdoms of Talia.

Bells were ringing all over the city as he headed the parade on foot – his idea, as he wanted to be on the same level as his people, not riding in a carriage out of sight. Katrina walked proudly by his side, looking beautiful as her happiness and love for Absalom radiated from her. The Hadrian knights followed close by, and behind them walked the Brothers.

Leona was no longer with them; no one knew where she'd gone. She had been alive at the end of the battle and had helped the wounded back to Havenshire, but after that she had simply vanished and so had her wolves.

Marcus was ill, incredibly frail and bedridden, and had to remain behind at the Academy, a bunch of new magicians pestering him with questions, which, although he scolded them for it, made him incredibly happy.

Cassandra held Rubin's hand as they walked through the streets, glad, so glad, to have him back in her life. She'd been with her father at the end, holding his hand through his last breaths. For all their separation, it felt that being together at the point of death was the epitome of their relationship. When it mattered most, she was home and by his side. They took comfort in believing they would meet again in the realm of light. When the councillors had asked her when she wanted to be crowned queen, she had replied that she couldn't do it. She was tired and weary and all she wanted to do was go back to Tamarind and live happily ever after with Rubin. Her son was young and strong, and wise beyond his years, and he would be an honourable king.

Turtledoff and Martha also walked hand in hand, as they and the other dwarfs who had come to fight joined the parade down the streets.

Behind the dwarfs came the new Elves, their beauty and aloofness making them the targets of much speculation and gossip. Valarie had been given a royal funeral, and Voltar felt indebted to Absalom, who had suggested she should be with the kings and queens of Talia in the royal catacombs.

Flying overhead on their broomsticks were the Fire-clan. Children dived behind their parents as they watched the black-clad women come gliding past.

Everyone that could filed into the cathedral and, when it was packed, the massive doors were left wide open so people standing on the steps could hear the ceremony.

A short while later, when Absalom came out onto the cathedral steps, a deafening cheer went up and fireworks exploded in the air about the city. He waited for the noise to quieten down and then gave a speech that went down in the books of Shyne. He spoke of love and the purpose for living, giving thanks to the Elements for keeping them alive and giving them the chance to rebuild Talia. He stirred the people's emotions when he told how Havenshire, Bluedane, Tamarind, Rhayador and Ilfordton had all come together to defeat a common enemy and that, going forward, the cities and lands of Talia would be one.

As Katrina watched him from the side of the entrance, she was full of admiration for the man she loved. He was kind and gentle, while being wise beyond his years, and she knew he was going to make a great king. She only wished Idi and Marcus had been here to be part of the celebrations. They had tirelessly worked for years to keep Absalom safe and it didn't seem fair, somehow, that neither of them was here to celebrate.

*Papa, wherever you are, I hope you're happy. I wish with all my heart that you could know I am.*

Lon, who had been watching the ceremony in the 'Waters of Life', turned around to look at the other Oracles.

"Are you sure I can't go and have just one *little* conversation with her?" he asked, pinching his fingers to indicate a really small amount.

"Alfonso, you will wear us out with the asking. No Oracle, until they are five hundred years old, may walk and talk with people. Until you are full of grace and nothing else, you must remain here and learn, learn, learn," sighed Barush.

"Don't worry, it isn't as long as it sounds," said Yakira.

"You never told me my real name," said Lon.

"And if we had told you that your name was Alfonso, meaning ready for battle, would you have been happy?"

"Probably not."

"You were born to battle, Lon, and your destiny has only just begun," said Oleanna, as she floated out of the room.

### The End

Although, in truth, this is the beginning of Idi's journey, it is, alas, for us the end of our travels with him. I am content to know he now fully believes in himself and accepts who he is. The trials were tough, but like a diamond taken from the earth, he's been polished and now glistens, as love radiates from him. We wish you well, Lon. Be happy.

## Epilogue – Lost & Found

Seth hurt all over. He felt pain in his leg and cursed as he became conscious. *Let me die*, he moaned.

*Take us home. We'll take your pain away. Glad you'll be.*

Seth moaned again and slowly opened his eyes. At first he couldn't see, and thought he must be blind, but as he wiped his face with the back of his arm, he knocked the blood-drenched mud away and realised he could still see.

*Take us home, Seth.*

"Who are you? Where are you?" Seth pushed himself up to a sitting position and looked around. He was in a ditch on the outskirts of the battle-stained hills. Everything was still and quiet, except for the breeze that whistled all around.

*They left you for dead, they did. We'd never do that. Be our friend, Seth, we'll look after you. Take good care of you, we will.*

Seth spun around on his backside and searched all around. It was true it was dark, and shadows fell everywhere, but still he would swear he was on his own.

"Where are you?" he demanded.

*Over here. By the trees. Under the rock.*

"Under the rock? Maybe I'm dreaming?"

*Help us, boy. Help us, Seth. Help us.*

"My leg is broken, I think. I can't move it, too much pain." As soon as the word pain departed his mouth, Seth felt a heat surge through his body. He heard an almighty crack and screamed as his bones clicked back together. The pain was soon gone as the heat surged through him and filled him with a euphoric sense of wellbeing.

*Now, come and help us. That's a dear. Hurry now.* Seth scrambled to his feet, knocking mud off his body. He must have been covered from head to foot, which is why no one had found him. He raced towards the imposing firs and fell on his knees besides a square-shaped rock that looked out of place among the needle-filled earth. He lifted the stone carefully and placed it behind him, then turned to look at what lay beneath it. Mud.

*Dig, dear. Not very deep. Nearly here.*

Seth used his hands and started scraping back the earth. In the distance a wolf howled, the harmonic wave reverberating through the cold night air. Seth didn't hear the sound as he began digging in a frenzy. Nor did he see the snow that began falling, thick and fluffy, instantly covering the treetops and his head.

His nails scraped along something hard, and he slowed, going more carefully to find this treasure. And there it was, a glass orb with three wisps of black smoke swirling around inside.

*Good boy. Well done. Hurry, pick us up.*

Seth scooped his hands around the cold ball and lifted it carefully. Suddenly, a face shot forward towards him and, in a start, he nearly dropped the orb. The face was instantly recognisable as being hate-filled and, having second thoughts, Seth went to lower the orb back into the ground.

*Don't you dare. You stupid boy. We can kill you.* Pain shot through Seth's forehead and he dropped the orb and clung to his head. Just as quickly as it started, the pain was gone.

*Silly boy. We don't want to hurt you. Now, come on, pick us up.* Seth gingerly reached down for the glass orb and picked it up, trying not to look into it.

*Now then, boy. We must go home. Back to Havenshire.*

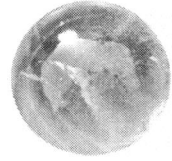

Book four of the 'Born to Be' series is called
**Katrina and the Unicorn Hunt**
Publication date yet to be announced

For book updates, join me
on Facebook
https://www.facebook.com/t.n.traynor
Or Twitter
https://twitter.com/tracy_traynor
Or Webpage
www.tntraynor.co.uk

**Acknowledgements & Thanks**
Clare Price for her fantastic book cover
www.clareorchard.co.uk
Karol Griffiths for manuscript guidance
www.karolgriffiths.com
Anne Stokes for the sketch of Leona, Singarti & Bleddlyn
http://www.annestokes.com
Dan Fionte for the sketch of the walled garden

Printed in Poland
by Amazon Fulfillment
Poland Sp. z o.o., Wrocław